THE
TREACHEROUS
WIFE

Other Books by Saundra

SAUNDRA

THE TREACHEROUS WIFE

DAFINA

kensingtonbooks.com

Content Warning: drug use, murder, violence

All Kensington titles, imprints, and distributed lines are available at special quantity discounts for bulk purchases for sales promotion, premiums, fund-raising, and educational or institutional use.

Special book excerpts or customized printings can also be created to fit specific needs. For details, write or phone the office of the Kensington Sales Manager: Kensington Publishing Corp., 900 Third Avenue, New York, NY 10022. Attn. Sales Department. Phone: 1-800-221-2647.

DAFINA and the Dafina logo Reg US Pat. & TM Off.

ISBN: 978-1-4967-5226-0
First Trade Paperback Printing: February 2025

ISBN: 978-1-4967-5227-7 (e-book)

10 9 8 7 6 5 4 3 2 1

Printed in the United States of America

THE TREACHEROUS WIFE

Chapter 1

Tabitha, 1996

"*Agghhhhh!*"

I screeched so loudly that my throat felt like it was on fire. My head fell back away from my shoulders and the rest of my body felt as if it was going limp. The sharp, knifelike stabbing pains that were slashing my abdomen apart and ripping their way to my pelvis jolted me back to my reality. *Agghhh . . . I can't . . . I think I'm dying.* I panted in huffs. Despite being so weak, I raised my feet from the stirrups. Desperately wanting to get out of them, I then tried to lift myself from the spot, but my butt was just too rooted in.

"No . . . no, don't do that." Dr. Adams raised his head from under the sheet where he had been commanding my pushes for the past five minutes. "And you are not dying, but I need you to breathe easy, then put all the pressure you can gather on your bottom and push, push hard."

I knew he was only doing what was best for me and the baby, but he really didn't understand what he was asking. "But . . . I can't . . . I'm so tired," I cried out. My entire body was feeling overwhelmed, and this intense flash of heat was coming over me. I could feel the perspiration on my face. Another sharp pain attacked me. My head flew back again, and my mouth opened wide, but this time I did not scream. "Ummm . . . ummm." I grunted with force and my whole body shook, and I was sure I heard my pelvis bone crack.

"That's it. I see the head. It's there. Right within my hand's reach. Come on, one more time . . . push." Dr. Adams's tone was calm.

With my body still rebelling against the excruciating pain, I breathed in deeply and shut my eyes so tight that I could feel the rim of my eyelids burn. "Ummmm." Suddenly, I felt a slippery gushing force burst from me, followed by a faint, then high yelping of a baby—my baby. Exhausted, my body fell backward onto the pillow. The light above me seemed to shine so brightly. As my body swooned, a sudden feeling of surreality came over me. I had just given birth. "Is he okay?" flowed from my lips just above a whisper. Carefully and slowly, I lifted myself up with my elbows.

"Can I see him?" I said, this time with a stronger voice. The young white nurse smiled down at the bundle she held wrapped in a green and blue blanket. She reached out her arms gently and handed him to me. One look at the yellowish baby with large, deep, inherited light hazel eyes and I was in love.

"He's perfect," I mouthed to Dale, his father, who was hovering over me.

Tears fell from Dale's big, hazel eyes. He had snuggled close to me. Mikka, the name we had chosen for our son, poured from his lips with love. He leaned over and kissed my forehead.

Home from the hospital, I didn't waste any time getting back into the swing of things. For me, that was making the almighty dollar. I never let anything get in the way of wealth-building. It was an essential part of my life. Even though I attended college at the University of Michigan on a full-ride scholarship that included room and board, I had decided to live off campus with my new boyfriend, Dale, now the father of my baby. Dale was not in college. He rented a small apartment not too far from the university because he did a lot of business with the rich students. That's how we met. One day he was on campus making a play and we bumped into each other by accident. We've been inseparable ever since.

Dale had his usual hustle, a D-Boy, as he liked to be called. As his lady and a natural-born thinker, I moved in with him. When it came to enhancing his drug empire, I helped him where I could. The apartment was small but comfortable. I was sitting at the kitchen table measuring and sacking up weed when I heard the front door open and shut. Quickly, I closed the last baggie I was working on and stepped around the small wall that separated the kitchen from the living room.

"Hey, babe," Dale said as soon as he laid eyes on me. He walked straight up to me and wrapped his free arm around me. The other hand was holding a small duffel bag.

I missed you all day, I mouthed to him, my lips grazing against his neck. I had been home with Mikka for almost a month now. We had gotten settled into a daily routine. Dale hustled during the day while I slept, watched Mikka, and sacked up the product. Between the two of us, we were running a smooth and profitable operation.

"I missed you too, but I brought you something for your trouble," he teased before handing me the duffel bag. "Is he asleep?" he asked about Mikka.

"You know it. Come on." I led the way to the bedroom. I knew he couldn't wait to lay his eyes on Mikka. Since we'd brought him home, Dale was a proud and doting father. Immediately after coming through the door whenever he went out, Dale would go looking for him. We both stood over him sleeping soundly in his crib. After gawking at our sweet boy for a few minutes, we headed back into the living room and sat down in front of the television.

"I just finished sacking up for the day," I said to Dale while pulling back the zipper of the duffel bag. The smell of sweaty hands and worn-out paper filled my nostrils. The money always gave me the sense of dirty hands touching it, and I hated that feeling. As nasty as the thought was, my love for money outweighed that, so I gulped down the dirty smell and went on. "Babe, we have got to find a bigger place. I don't like weed being so close to Mikka. The scent could get into his skin." I knew I was probably exaggerating a little, but I knew he would understand what I meant.

"I'm already on it. Been doing some digging around this past week while I was out hustling. I have a few places lined up tomorrow for you to look at. I got y'all, babe. I'm going to take good care of you two. That's a promise," Dale assured me, and I knew he meant every word. That was one of the reasons I'd loved Dale since the first time we met. He always put me first. When I told him I was pregnant he made sure I knew that me and the baby were his number one priority. He didn't miss one doctor's appointment.

"But look, I have to go back out to re-up tonight. I'm going to need that re-up stash," he said.

"No doubt. What time do you have to go out for re-up?" I asked. This was the part I didn't much care for. Him having to leave when he had just come in. But it was the life of hustler, so I had to suck it up. This was what I had signed up for.

He twisted his gold watch around his wrist so that it would face up. "Couple hours."

"Cool. I'm going to get this counted and locked away. Then I'll grab the re-up stash. It's all rubber banded and ready to go," I assured him.

"Good. I just don't like keeping that much cash here with you and Mikka here. It's just too risky."

"I know."

He had been telling me to go get another safe deposit box for the past year, but for some reason or another I was always too busy. He was right in saying it was too risky, keeping re-up cash in the house. I understood that more now that Mikka was here, so I made it my business to handle it. It's funny how when you have a child you put things into perspective quickly.

"Aye, while you count the cash, I'ma grab me a sandwich. I'm hungry as hell. Been hustling so hard today I haven't ate shit. All I had is a stick of gum. Stomach grumbling like a mutha."

"Babe, I keep telling you to eat during the day. You know with the baby and all, I ain't cooked shit. I also ate another dry-ass sandwich. One of us got to eat something good, and since you out and about, it might as well be you." We both chuckled. "Well, let me count this money. I need to try to get some sleep before Mikka wakes up to be fed."

I poured the money onto the coffee table just as the house phone rang. I dashed from the couch to grab the cordless phone from its cradle hanging on the kitchen wall. The last thing I wanted was the ringing phone to wake up Mikka. Dale hated the house phone, so he rarely answered it. He was bent over in the fridge, gathering up what he needed to make his sandwich. Like I said, he hated the phone and would gladly let it ring all damn day long.

"Hello," I greeted without looking at the caller ID. My mind was still questioning if Mikka had been awakened. I didn't hear any crying, so I assumed we were saved for now.

"Hey, sweetheart," my aunt Margie said on the other end. I could hear the love in her tone.

Dale walked over to me and whispered, "I'm going to check on Mikka."

I nodded at him. "How are you, Aunt Margie?"

"I'm fine. I am just wondering when you gonna bring that baby down to Inkster. It's been a month now," she reminded me. I knew she was getting antsy to see him.

"I know. I know. I promise to bring him in about two weeks. I was waiting for him to get his shots first. Got to make sure he's safe when he's out in the world," I explained. My aunt Margie had raised me since I was twelve years old. She was the only blood family I'd ever known. When I was a baby I somehow ended up in foster care. Aunt Margie was my biological mother's sister. According to her, she had no idea I existed until I was eleven. Not long after she found out about me, Aunt Margie started the process to get custody of me, and from that point on, she raised me. I lived with her in the small Michigan town named Inkster until I left for college.

"But how have you been? I haven't spoken to you since last week," I said.

I silently counted the money as I continued to listen to Aunt Margie. I was on a mission, and Dale had somewhere to be.

The sun shining through the window stirred me awake, and then I heard a cry from Mikka that caused me to sit straight up in bed. My hair scarf, which had been tied securely around my head, had worked its way off and was now buried somewhere beneath the sheets. I ran my right hand through my long, straight, thick hair. I glanced to my right and noticed Dale was not in bed next to me.

"*Agh! Agh!*" Mikka wailed out again.

"Aww, sweetie." I got to my feet and reached down into his crib for him. One look at the smile on my face and he quieted down. "Good morning, my love," I cooed at him. He stirred his little lips, licked them, and smiled. It pulled at my heartstrings, knowing he loved me back.

I went into the kitchen to prepare his bottle. I glanced around the living room and there was still no sight of Dale, which seemed strange because the bathroom door was wide open. That told me he wasn't held up in there. Testing the bottle on my hand and satisfied with the temperature, I picked up Mikka from the crib and cradled him in my arms. Then I sat down for the feeding. After sucking up a full bottle and a good burp, he was satisfied. Laying him back down, my mind drifted back to Dale. *Where the hell was he?*

Had he left this morning without saying anything or leaving a note?. That was unlikely because he always woke me if I was still asleep and he had to go. He never left the house without telling me. Walking over to the nightstand next to the bed, I grabbed my two-way pager. No messages were there; there were no numbers listed.

I picked up the phone and dialed his pager number with the hope that he'd call me back quickly. I then took a peek at Mikka. Since he had already fallen back to sleep, I decided it was a good time to take my shower. Anxious to hear back from Dale, I showered faster than usual, dried off, and put on Dale's oversize Oakland A's baseball jersey. Back in the living room, I picked up the phone and dialed *69, just in case in I had missed his call. With no luck there, I checked my pager again, but there were still no missed pages.

Growing more concerned by the minute, I turned on

the coffee pot to let it brew. Then I sat down at the table for a minute with my head cupped in my hands. *Where was Dale?* The coffeepot buzzed. Opening the cabinet, I grabbed a mug and filled it with coffee. My stomach started to twist in knots. "The car wash," I suddenly said out loud. That was where Dale had told me he was going to re-up. I had to go there to find him. Back in our bedroom, I opened the closet, snatched a pair of my Girbaud jeans off a hanger, and slid them on since they were the closest thing to me. Then I made my way over to Mikka. Not wanting to disturb his sleep, I picked him up gently and we headed out the door.

My jaw dropped to my feet as I pulled up to the car wash on Michigan Avenue. There was a crowd of people gathered around, flashing police lights, cops everywhere, and men in suits who I knew right away were detectives. I put the car in Park and carefully removed Mikka from his car seat. I wasn't sure why, but my feet felt as if they had turned to stone as I approached the crowd. I could hear the police as they urged the crowd to step back. My breath caught in my throat, and I felt completely horrified at the sight of Dale's black 1990 Chevrolet Camaro IROC. I stood frozen there for a minute until I was able to summon the courage to take another step forward.

"Ma'am, ma'am, I need you to step back," I heard a voice over my shoulder say. At first, I didn't realize the policeman speaking to me had touched my shoulder. It wasn't until I gazed up at him and saw his hand resting there that I snapped to attention.

"That's my boyfriend's car. Has something terrible happened?" I asked the police officer. I turned my focus back toward the car just as the two detectives took a step backward and I saw my nightmare come true. "Dale." His name rolled off my tongue in a whisper as if it were a secret.

Suddenly, I heard screams, and my legs buckled beneath

me. The strength in my arms disappeared. Someone yelled, "Get the baby!" Those sudden screams had come from me. As I fell to my knees, one of the detectives reached me in time to grab hold of Mikka. The unknown cop who had tried to stop me from moving forward now tried to pick me up off the ground as the other detective did his best to comfort me. I was sick with grief as I broke free and ran toward Dale's lifeless body. He was covered in blood, his body riddled with bullet holes. He was gone. A piece of me died that day with him.

Three Weeks Later

I still couldn't believe we had buried Dale a week and a half ago. It was just too surreal. I couldn't eat or sleep. Every time I closed my eyes, I saw his face and kept hearing his voice asking me to help him. It was a nightmare that I had to wake up from. My fear was I would never sleep again. The worst part was I'd still have to live with the fact that he was brutally murdered, and the Detroit police would probably never find out who was responsible. The fact that he was a drug dealer increased the chances they wouldn't take his homicide seriously. The one thing I knew for sure was, had I known who pulled the trigger, I would do the same to them if given the chance. The big question was, who? Who exactly was the Connect?

While I did help with counting the cash, inventorying the product, and strategizing his plays, I never really knew his clients or who his Connect was. I was just a behind-the-scenes kind of girl. In my mind I knew it was either his Connect or a client who had betrayed him. Or it could've also been a secret enemy who came disguised in the form of a so-called friend. Snakes like that were always lurking around in Dale's line of work. Just because he was found where he was and said he was scheduled to re-up really meant nothing. The cops found no money or dope lying around. Truth be told, it could have been anybody. The game was built like that. This was a dog-eat-dog world we lived in.

"Tabbi . . . Tabbi . . ." The sound of my name being called interrupted my running thoughts.

"Yes, Aunt Margie." Once again, I was so deep in my thoughts that Aunt Margie had to call my name repeatedly before I gave her my attention. This had been happening since being back in Inkster. I arrived a week ago with Mikka. I stayed in Detroit long enough to bury Dale, but after that I knew I had to get out of there right away. I really needed to be around family, and Aunt Margie was the only one I had in my life now besides Mikka.

"Dinner is ready. You really need to try to eat something. You skipped breakfast and lunch," she said to me.

Concern was etched on every inch of Aunt Margie's face. I hated to make her worry about me, but I had no appetite. The hole where my food should have passed through had a knot there that would not seem to move. Although I knew it wasn't a real knot, just my grief eating away at me, I didn't know how to push it aside. I was afraid that anything that tried to get past it would only end up choking me.

Instead of saying just that to Aunt Margie, I forced a weak smile. "I'll try," I said. And I really would try, but I doubted I would succeed. Pushing myself toward the edge of the sofa with the intention to stand, I said, "I need to check on Mikka."

Aunt Margie waved me back down into my seat. "No, he is fine. I have fed, burped, and changed him. Now the king sleeps," she teased, and I could only smile.

"Thank you. I really appreciate it."

"No need for that. You know I will always be here for the both of you." Aunt Margie sat down next to me and patted my knee. Everything about her was love; it had been that way since I was twelve. Her comfort just made me want to cry even more. I had missed her so much when I was away at school in Detroit. Between taking full-time classes, spending time with Dale, and helping him with his hustle, I was always so busy. I hardly ever made it down to Inkster to visit with her. For that I also felt guilty because growing up, Aunt Margie had always put me first. Once she got custody of me she never allowed anything to come before me.

"I'm so sorry, Auntie, that I haven't been coming out to see you the way I should."

"Baby, I told you to stop apologizing about that. I understand you are busy with school. No need for that, okay?" she replied.

I nodded in agreement, but I still felt bad. I knew I had been selfish, putting other things like making money before her. In the future I would make it my mission to do better.

"Now, what is your next move?" she asked.

I hadn't thought about it much but one thing I knew for sure was I had to get back to school. That was the one reason I ever went to Detroit in the first place, and that still was my goal. Hustling was Dale's thing, and while I did love the fast money, a good education had always and still was my number one goal in life. Even more now that I had Mikka to raise.

"Well, I have to get back to school. I can't drop the ball on that . . . no matter what." I sighed, feeling overwhelmed, but I was adamant in my determination.

Aunt Margie nodded in agreement, and a hint of a smile said she was proud of me. College was also her number one goal for me. She had preached a good education to me since the first day I entered her home and I had bought it lock, stock, and barrel. I agreed with her then and now. It was the one thing no one could take away from you.

She reached for my right hand. "You go on back to school and leave Mikka with me. I'll take good care of him," she assured me while squeezing my hand.

"Aunt Margie, I can't ask you to do that; you just retired. It's your time for you. Besides, you already raised me. You did your job. I know you are being nice and I'm grateful. But no, I can't let you do that." I wouldn't even consider asking her to give up her life to raise my son. How selfish of me would that be?

"Girl, I tell you, you are still stubborn." She chuckled. "From the time I brought you into this house, you were stubborn and hell-bent on being in charge of me. And that hasn't changed. Now you listen to me. I raised you because I loved you from the moment I was told you existed. Can you believe that? Before I ever laid eyes on you. Sure did." She nodded at me with a huge grin. "And I love that baby in there. As long as I exist, I'm going to do what is necessary to make sure y'all have what you need. So, you pack up your little bags and head back to school. Me and Mikka, well . . . we gone be okay. And when you walk across that stage for graduation we will be in the crowd. Because that is what family does. Now I don't want to hear nothing else about it. Ya hear?"

A flood of tears ran down my face. Between me crying over Dale and Aunt Margie, my heart was bursting with love. I would simply never stop crying. Two days later, I hugged Aunt Margie and held poor Mikka for a long time before kissing him goodbye. Bound and determined to be successful, I pointed my 1993 red Ford Mustang toward Detroit Michigan But something in me had changed, and I wasn't sure it was for the good.

Chapter 2

Tabitha, 2010

"Thanks for tuning in this morning. I'm your host, Tabitha Knight. This morning we're reporting on a homicide . . ."

I glanced at the teleprompter as it spilled the news and gave the camera my best posture and nothing but face. I was a natural. After watching Norah O'Donnell on repeat for years I felt like a pro. The people agreed; I was the top host at WBTV and had my own segment called *Truth with Tabitha Knight,* for which I won several awards in the state and one nationally. I was at the top of my game and everyone who tuned in knew it.

After graduating from DMU with a degree in communications and a minor in journalism, I had multiple offers to pick from. I chose Arizona and hit the road and I haven't slowed down since. Achieving success was my ultimate goal, and I was riding the wave. With my shift over, I checked in with Felicia, the executive producer of my segment, grabbed my notes for our upcoming show, and then hit the streets.

The sun, humidity, and plain smell of the heat choked

me as soon as I exited the door, but after being in Arizona for more than ten years, I was dealing with it. Don't get me wrong, being the Midwestern girl that I am at heart, I still wasn't totally used to dealing with it. It's not that I missed the cold because I dearly hated it. But I had to admit that the cold flowed through my lungs better. Sliding with poise into my all-black Porsche, I hit the interstate and drove at top speed until I veered off my exit. Breaking down the speed, I pulled up to Ride Luxury, the car lot owned by my husband of eight years, Calvin Knight.

I met Calvin two years after arriving in Arizona, while I was out reporting on a story about a shooting that happened next door to one of the first car lots he owned. Calvin came over and asked if we would be filming his spot for the segment. According to him, it was a free promotional opportunity. After laughing at his comical suggestion, he sparked up a conversation in which I engaged. I thought, *Why not?* He was tall, strikingly handsome, and funny. Plus, I was bored, and soon I learned that he was a small-time businessman. I knew without him telling me that he was a hustler. That appealed to me because I grew up in Michigan, where everybody hustled. I had dated a hustler before, and even became a part of his hustle. In short, I knew a hustler when I met one. When the time came I showed Calvin Knight how to take his nickel-and-dime hustle into the big leagues. Now, thanks to me, he was connected in the game, and because of that, he owned a luxury car lot and the sky was the limit. And now I was wifey.

"Hey, love," Calvin greeted me as soon as I walked into his office. He stood up immediately and walked around his custom-made mahogany desk. I was in his arms in no time flat. I loved his tall stature as much as I had the father of my son, Dale's. I loved tall men. Calvin was six foot five, with nice, wavy hair that he wore in a flat fade cut. He had a chocolate-colored skin tone, dazzling white teeth, and a muscular build. Calvin was definitely fine. He wore mostly casual clothes and always smelled so good. He kissed me before I could respond.

"Are you ready?" were the first words out of my mouth as soon as my lips were free. I was so excited. We were on our way to the airport to pick up Mikka, who was coming in from Inkster. I had waited so long for this day and finally he was coming to live with me after all these years. When I graduated from college and decided to take a job in Arizona, Aunt Margie thought it was best that I get set up first and then bring him here later. By the time I got myself set up, I was so busy but managed to find childcare. Aunt Margie thought it wouldn't be a good idea to bring Mikka out here and put him in day care when she stayed home and could care for him personally. So, we agreed he should stay a little longer with her. That turned into years, and before we knew it, time had flown by. But today he was coming for good, and I couldn't be happier.

"Yes, I am. We can take my truck. Let me grab my keys and we can head out," Calvin said.

"Oh, baby, I'm so happy and nervous all at the same time." I was fidgety and could not stop smiling.

"Why nervous?" Calvin located his key and looked over at me wearing a curious smile.

"Well, what if he's not happy here? He's fourteen now, a growing boy and no longer a baby. He has his routine set up. He's leaving his friends and Aunt Margie, who he's very attached to. I don't know, I worry about his happiness. Maybe I'm being selfish taking him now."

Calvin stepped back around his desk and pulled me into his broad chest. I loved it there. He smelled so good, and I felt safe in his arms—always. "Everything is going to be fine, love. Mikka wants to be here. He's said so many times to me. Remember, he wants to come here. He'll find new friends. Besides, he has us here. He loves you the same as he loves Aunt Margie."

I closed my eyes and pictured him as a baby. I saw myself on that delivery table, remembering the way he looked at me the very first time. I smiled. "Yep, I'm just being silly. Thanks, baby." I wrapped my arms around his waist, tight. After Dale I thought I'd never love again, but Calvin had woven me into this web. And I did love him intensely.

"Besides, he's already asked about taking his permit test for his driver's license. Once I buy him that new 2011 Dodge Challenger off the showroom floor, he'll never want to leave," Calvin reassured me.

"Oh, so your plans are to continue to spoil him. He's already that, remember," I replied.

"Not spoiled; he's privileged. There's a difference. Now let's ride, before he gets pissed off that we left him at the airport longer than he wants to be. Of course I will be blaming our tardiness all on you."

"Oh, blaming me, huh." I playfully nudged his shoulder. "You are such a suck up," I teased further.

When we got to the airport I looked around the baggage claim area. It had been a year since I had seen Mikka in person. I'd been so busy trying to keep my segment number one. And while setting things in motion for my newest adventure, I hadn't had the time.

"I don't see him anywhere. Do you?" I asked Calvin, my head still spinning in the airport in search of my son. Calvin was busy doing the same.

"That's him over there." Calvin pointed with his right hand toward the light-skinned, tall young man pulling a Gucci suitcase off the conveyor belt, then reaching for another.

"Mikka," I called out his name, and he turned to me. I could not believe how tall he'd gotten since the last time I saw him, twelve short months prior. He smiled at me, and I saw Dale's exact twin but with a hint of me in the background. He was a combination of us both. I raced up to him and wrapped my arms around him. "I swear, you have grown five inches taller." I was sure he was about six foot and only fourteen years old. "Stop growing already." I hugged him tight until he cried out.

"I can't breathe, Ma." He laughed, towering over me.

Tears were running down my face so fast I could feel my makeup melting. Reluctantly, I released him. He had no idea how much I missed him when we were apart. Calvin went in for a hug too. They had grown so close over the years. I loved their bond. Looking at him, I suddenly felt a mountain of guilt. Why had I allowed so much time to go by without bringing him to live with me? I felt sick with regret. I had moved to Arizona and built my career. I also met and married Calvin and was too busy to raise my own son. As much as I hated to admit it, I wouldn't be running for mother of the year anytime soon. I wiped my tears. I had no other choice but to suck it up. Somehow, I would find a way to make up for my absence in his life.

"Is this all of your luggage? I told you not to bring anything. Shopping spree, huh? Whole new city means a whole new wardrobe," I reminded him.

"Yeah, sounds great to me. But you know Aunt Margie does not believe in wasting things. She would never just let me leave all this stuff behind. My room is still packed with brand-new things that still have tags on them."

I could hear Aunt Margie on the phone. *Tabbi, you spend too much money on Mikka. He's one kid. You have to stop spoiling him like you do. All of these things he left behind. He is growing like a weed and won't be able to fit into half these clothes when he visits.* She had gone on and on. "I know, she called." I chuckled. Calvin wheeled one of the Gucci suitcases and Mikka the other as we exited the airport.

Back at the house, Mikka was wowed by his new home. It had only been twelve months since we had seen him last, but five since he had been to Arizona for a visit. For the past five years I had been making my way out to Michigan to see him. From there we'd all go to Disneyland, Disney World, and Hawaii. We'd even taken him to Jamaica. Now we resided in Scottsdale, in a five-bedroom, six-bathroom, ten-thousand-square-foot home. It was our little mansion. High up in Silverleaf, with views of the Upper Canyon, we had long passed the Jeffersons.

"This house is dope, none of my homeys would believe it. I gotta send pictures." Mikka bounced down from his king-size bed. His room was huge, with a closet so big he could fit his entire bed inside of it and still have room left over. "I'm going to be on cloud nine up in here. I can just live in this room forever. It's like having my own apartment. Yep, that's it. This is an apartment, not a room." He grinned from ear to ear.

"That it is," I agreed as I looked around the room. Growing up in foster care, I could never have imagined living in a house like this. But I worked hard and hustled harder, and this was the fruit of that labor. "I'm glad you like it, and yes, you can stay here until you are well past sixty." I laughed and then sat down next to him.

"Stay here until I'm sixty." He laughed. "Where is my wife going to live?"

My jaw dropped and my mouth flew wide open. "Your wife? What wife? Boy, you are only fourteen and already you are thinking about getting married?"

"No, I ain't thinking about getting married." He grinned. "I don't even have a girlfriend yet. I probably will soon, though. And I'm sure by the time I'm sixty I will have a wife. We can't live here with you."

We both laughed. It was reasons like this why I was glad my son was here to stay for good. We could have good laughs together over silly stuff all the time, and the life lessons we would be sure to go through together.

"Mikka, I'm really glad to have you here now. I already have you signed up for school It's a private one that is close by." Instantly, I noticed the unease on his face. "Why the look? What's up?"

"I was really hoping to get a shot at public school here. You know I really hated private school in Michigan."

I was well aware of how he felt about private school. But I felt it was for the best. I was not slacking off when it came to his education. "I know. But you know how I feel about your education."

"Yeah, you want me to be like preppy, but I'm too street-smart for that. Living with Aunt Margie around the way and going to that private school, I learned them both. But I adapted more to street life because all of my real friends lived in our neighborhood."

Hearing him say this to me out loud made a rush of guilt come over me. I had tried more than once to move Aunt Margie to the suburbs, but she had flat-out refused to sell her home. So, I had to put Mikka in a private school so that he could get the education I wanted him to have and be exposed to a different type of environment until I could bring him to Arizona. But maybe I had been selfish, putting myself first. Had I failed my son?

"Things are going to work out either way. You are here now." I scooted over closer and hugged him.

It was nearly an hour's drive from the news station, but I had come right after shooting my segment. I pulled into the parking space of an old, abandoned warehouse on the outskirts of town. The scenery was nice to look at. There was a lot of green grass and thick trees. You could always hear the sound of birds chirping and sometimes crickets singing in the evenings, which was comforting. The building itself didn't look bad on the outside structure-wise, but the roof could stand to be replaced. The inside could also use a bit of touchup paint, and the concrete floors were a bit rough in my opinion. But it had several different rooms that we could use for meetings, shipment, and the occasional torture if someone was disloyal. The concrete floor was sometimes used as part weapon during a torture session, which is why Calvin refused to cover it. I pulled in and parked close to the entry door and climbed out. Two of Calvin's henchmen were guarding the outside door.

"Babe, sorry I'm a little late. Shooting ran over a bit." I found Calvin sitting at a table in the room we normally met in.

Calvin stood up. "It's okay. I was able to get a few calls in." He kissed me and pulled out a chair for me.

I put my keys and Kate Spade purse down on the table. "Well, I see, the meeting is in order." I got straight to it. I still had other obligations I had to make for the day. I hated to put him on a time frame, but he understood my drive.

"The territory is ready to go. I had Pete and Rocko clear up three major spots on the Upper East Side that are going to be hot spots for business," Calvin explained.

"What about that competition trying to come out of Oakland?" I asked.

"Taken care of. We can move in tomorrow, if need be, for testing. My thought was to send Pete in at the beginning of next week. But my concern is the re-up and supplying it adequately. We've got to come out the gate swinging. Our clientele got to know we supplied up and open for twenty-four-hour business with no delay."

I looked at him with full confidence. When it came to strategizing, I didn't play. I approached the game the same way I approached my career. I was a lioness ready to eat all prey. I was going to the top no matter what. "Handled. Go ahead and send Pete in for the test next week. There will be extra product in the shipment that is coming in. We will split the kilos down, which will supply the new territory during the test. There will be no delay. Trust me."

"I can always count on you." Calvin winked at me. "But one more thing. I have to go out to LA to meet up with Diablo. He's going to be there on business. I would like you to come with me," Calvin said.

Diablo was Calvin's Connect from Spain. They had been working together for the past five years. Diablo was cool and things had been solid, but I really didn't like meeting with him. I preferred to stay behind the scenes as much as possible. My goals were such that they required me to pull out of the limelight. I had to distance myself as much as possible, which we did a good job at. But Calvin counted on me a lot and felt secure in his decisions about having me at his side.

"Aw, babe, I don't know if I can make it . . . I have a lot coming up and . . ." I started to say.

"Look, I know you have a lot going on, but this meeting is very important to our business. I really need you in sight." Calvin's sense of urgency was clear in his tone, which implied he really needed me. The word *No* was really on the edge of my tongue, but I had to remember my obligation to our empire. And to be honest, I did want it all, and so far, I had been at 100 percent in making sure I got it.

"Okay, okay . . ." I gave in. "I'll be by your side, but you got this no matter what. This empire grew in a short period of time. And you now have two successful businesses." I always wanted him to see his potential. Sometimes I think he really doubted himself without me. True, I had come in with my knowledge and skill and pushed things to the next level. But his muscle behind my brain power was essential.

Calvin was quick to agree. "Yes, that is true, and you have been a huge part of that. In fact, it is because of you that I have been this successful in the car business. So successful we're going to open the third dealership . . ."

"Aye, aye." Rocko interrupted us with his presence. Rocko was Calvin's right-hand man and best friend since they were young kids. They were more like brothers than anything. They were loyal to each other at all costs, and I respected their bond. They had secrets they would take to the grave. Talking about them in any courtroom would get them both the electric chair.

"Well, I guess that means my time is up. Male bonding time in order," I teased.

"Aww, come on, Tabbi. You know you always included in this male bonding time," Rocko said. At six foot two, with jet-black skin, a bald head, sparkling white teeth, and the physique of a body builder, Rocko's appearance certainly fit his name.

"Mayday! Mayday!" Pete stepped in the room next, chanting. He was only about five foot seven and had caramel-colored skin. He had a low-cut fade hairstyle and there was a long, razorlike cut down the side of his face. To me, he looked more like a pastor than a street thug. But the fact was, he was no pastor and not to be played with.

"Aw shit, this is really too deep for me," I said, standing up. "Both of y'all in one room. I just can't handle that," I teased some more. Rocko and Pete always have a good time. Both were jokers but were no joke on the streets. They were a real flex and commanded a lot of respect. Rocko was like a deadly sniper and Pete wouldn't think twice about cutting out your throat, literally.

"All I want to know is can I move in on my Oklahoma thief's territory?" Pete asked.

"You sure can. It belongs to you come next week," I answered, smiling.

"And I'm behind my man with the scope," Rocko added. He was ready to close down any interference from any range.

Calvin egged them on. "Let's make the waves."

"I'll follow up with the preliminary, but I'll let y'all meeting commence. I'm out."

They were about to have their meeting with the crew runners. Rocko and Pete normally showed up first so Calvin could catch them up, then the rest of the crew would show up. I never met with any of the crew members. I was a known public figure and had to keep a low profile. Most crew members knew who Calvin was married to, but none knew of my involvement, or that I was the true brains behind the operation.

Two Months Later

"Before I sign off today, I would like to say something to all the listeners who have supported me as an anchor and have made *Truth with Tabitha Knight* successful. I want you all to know that I appreciate you and will be forever grateful to all who have tuned in consistently for to watch. But this will be my last time reporting or recording the show for a while. I have put in my application to run for mayor of our great city and with the support of my husband and nephew, I will be moving forward."

I had to fight back the tears as my eyes diverted from the camera and off to my right, where Calvin and Mikka stood. They had come into the studio for support while I was making one of the biggest announcements of my life. While I was ecstatic to report my new venture, I felt horrible announcing to the public that Mikka was my nephew.

Mikka's face wore a smile, but I wondered what he was

feeling in his heart. He truly was a good sport. I had shared with him previously that when I first moved to Arizona and started my career, I did not tell people I had a son because I was afraid that would prevent me from getting a job. In the nineties, single mothers were feared in the corporate world for not being able to hold a full-time job and take care of a child at the same time. A single mother was like the plague. So, at the time I thought it best not to mention that I was a mother. With Mikka being with Aunt Margie, it made the lie easier to tell. However, as time went on and I became successful, things had changed in the way a single mother was viewed. Then, because of my profession, I was ashamed to tell people that I had not raised my own son. Years later and now that I was running for political office, if I decided to tell people the truth, I'd be considered to be a liar. I'd lose my credibility, which I needed to be elected as mayor. People would know that I had intentionally deceived them throughout my entire career, which might have caused them to start digging into my past. If that were to happen, they would find out about Dale, and that he was a drug dealer who was likely murdered because of it. And they would surely use that against me.

So, I had sat Mikka down and explained to him as best as I could that I needed to tell people that he was Calvin's deceased sister's son. Mikka agreed and supported me, but that did not make me feel any better. I felt like shit because of it. But what other choice did I have? As a mother, I felt this must be devasting for him. But I knew I was meant to be mayor of this town, so I couldn't allow one small lie to stop me from achieving greatness. Me becoming mayor was just one more step in my dream of getting to the top. And I was well on my way. Nothing was going to stop me.

Chapter 3

Detective King, 2014

"Come on, man . . . stop the bullshit!"

I slammed the palm of my right hand down on the hardwood table. I was sitting across from Rafford Penny, who went by the street name Price. Price was a known dealer on the streets of Maricopa County, and he was now being accused of murder. The interrogation had been going on for almost four hours. It was time to get some answers or shut it down.

"Look, I told y'all that coke ain't mine. And a nigga ain't never fucked with no meth." He was adamant and didn't blink. But I wasn't letting up.

"Coke and meth . . . that's the least of your worries." I shook my head and gave him a look that said *pathetic*, then I let out a deep chuckle. "Murder one will be the charge. And more than one body. Rest assured." I smiled, then leaned back in my seat. I wanted him to see that I had all night. I knew he was tired of the back and forth—the repeat.

"King, you can't put no murders on me. I ain't killed shit," he hissed.

Picking up the file in front of me, I flung it across the room with so much force the papers inside didn't scatter as they should have. I stood up fast, pushing the table forward and towered over it coming face-to-face with Price. "I'm done with this . . . Forbes, start the process; lock his ass up with the rest of the murderers." I stood back up and adjusted my tie, preparing to leave.

"Okay, okay, wait a minute! Now let's all calm down." Detective Forbes, my partner for the past seven years, stepped in. It was his turn to play good cop. "Price, my partner here is just a little emotional, but let's try to go over this again. We good, Detective?" He played the part that was supposed to show I was calm now. Forbes stood up, walked over toward the corner of the room, bent over, and picked up the file. "Price, we have you on wiretaps," he informed him.

"And you sold to an undercover." I jumped right back in, my tone full of aggression. I was on his ass and wasn't about to give him any breathing room. "And we have a witness on one of your murder charges. We got you cold." My tone was hostile on purpose. I had no sympathy for scum like Price and I wanted him to know it. "It's time to talk or your new home will be one of two places, Red Rock or Arizona State Prison, for life. You've never been locked up, so you're going to be fresh as they come. The boys in the yard will thank me personally for you." I chuckled to taunt him.

Price's eyes had been cast downward, but his head rose on cue at my last words. His eyes darted from me to Forbes. He huffed with anger and shoved out his chest defiantly. "How do I know what's on your so-called taps? You could be lying . . . hell, we all know that's what y'all do. All cops are fuckin' liars. Worse than a nigga like me."

"Man, it's your ass behind the eight ball. What are you

gonna do? And there will be no deals unless you give us names." I wanted to be clear on that.

This time he looked down at his hands, now balled into fists. I knew he was no fool. Price had family still in the game, and he knew if he told us anything it might incriminate them. Whether it be by the courts or the streets. But he wasn't the prison type. I could smell the fear.

"No deal, Detective." Price gazed at me with a small smirk spread on his lips.

He wanted to one-up me. Show me I didn't break him. But he also wanted me to continue to beg in case I was desperate enough to make a deal. But I was not. I stood up. "They'll get you booked and suited" were my final words before exiting the room with Forbes trailing behind me.

After leaving we walked two doors down to the camera room. As soon as I shut the door behind me, Detective Forbes laughed out loud. "*The boys in the yard will thank you personally.* Man . . . that shit took me out when you said it." He couldn't stop laughing.

"Hope he takes heed to that warning." I folded my arms and watched him on the camera. His hands no longer balled into fists, Price scooted back in his chair, held his head back, and ran both of his hands across his bald head. "I think he's going to fold. He worried about that murder charge. He can't see how we can deal that one. And he's not ready to trust us."

"Yeah, you ready to call the DA just in case." Forbes finally was able to control his laughs.

"Let's wait until . . ." A knock on the door interrupted us. Detective Saul pushed the door open and leaned in.

"Forbes, you still going to the range tomorrow evening?"

My cell phone started to ring, so I excused myself and started for my office. I answered just in time before missing the call. "Hey, sweetheart." I shut my office door and sat down.

"Hey, I just thought I'd call and congratulate you on your big night."

The sound of her voice and hearing how proud she was of me made me smile. "Thank you," I said.

"Are you nervous?"

"Nah, but I do loathe being the center of attention," I admitted. Being a detective, I was out front and center all the time, seeking out strangers, talking to them, and speaking to the press. So, one would think I was used to crowds, but I was quite the opposite.

"Hee, hee, hee." She laughed on the other end. "Come on, it's me you're talking to. You don't have to be modest. I think you soak up being crowned," she teased me, and I joined in her laughter. "Well, I have to go, but I just wanted to call before . . . You know it's times like this I wish I could be there by your side." The energy in her tone had shifted downward. The reality of her words and their truth brushed guilt all over me.

A tap on my door grabbed my attention. Forbes pushed the door open. "King," he said my name before opening the door all the way and seeing I was still on the phone.

"Sweetheart, hold on."

"Sorry for interrupting. He's ready." I knew he was speaking of Price. As predicted, he was ready to fold. Being behind the eight ball normally brought even the loyalists to their knees, ready to snitch.

I nodded at Forbes. "Sorry for that." I apologized for putting her on hold. The silence on the other end was worse. "Listen, things will . . ."

She grunted to get my attention. "Hey, it's fine, but I have to go."

"Gia," I said quickly, but she had already hung up, not giving me any time to explain or reason. I sighed. I had to figure it out. But for now, I had to go speak with a murdering, drug-dealing snitch so that I could get home to my beloved wife.

Finally home, I raced straight up the stairs to the bedroom. I opened the bedroom door, and my beautiful wife of ten years, Joyce, stepped out of the bathroom looking like a Cover Girl model. Joyce was still everything any man could dream of having in a woman: tall, milk chocolate skin, and curvy in all the right places. I looked at her like a fat kid looks at a slice of delicious cake. Seeing her dressed in only her bra and panties, I wasted no time pulling her into my arms. Her skin felt baby soft and she smelled so good.

"I see you have been waiting on me." I kissed her gently on her full lips. They were as soft as a fluffy pillow. I squeezed her tighter. "You are just what I crave." My lips landed on the nape of her neck, and I buried myself there for a minute.

"Mmm! Babe," she moaned, putting her hand behind my head and pulling me down for another kiss. After she'd had her fill she released me. "Okay, enough of that or we're going to be late." She broke away from my embrace. We both giggled. "I need you to jump into the shower and get dressed, top speed. We will not be classified as being on CPT this night." I chuckled at her joke of us showing up on Colored People Time, an expression Black folks use for being late. "No, sir, Mr. King, not on the night you are being honored."

Tonight was the night I would be receiving awards and being put on the spot so people could say I'm worthy. Then they expected me to make a speech to say thanks to them because they thought I was worthy. I hated making speeches. I had been dreading it for weeks and I still had no idea what I was going to say. Joyce had encouraged me to write it down and study it. That had never happened. And now I had run out of time. However, I was optimistic it would work out.

"That's right, I am the man tonight," I teased with sarcasm.

"Babe, to me you are the man every night." She doubled back and rubbed my chest.

"This is true," I quipped back with a smirk.

"Oh, that ego; go and dress. We are not doing that tonight either." She playfully pushed me. I really had to get a move on. I had planned to get home a bit earlier so that I could relax for a minute before getting dressed, but obviously that did not happen. The interrogation with Price had gone on much longer than expected, but the results were well worth it. No one would argue it was what I did best. And no less the reason I was on my way to being honored for my brilliant detective work.

Chapter 4

Detective King

After maneuvering through heavy traffic, we finally arrived at the venue where the ceremony was being held. I pulled up to the valet, climbed out of the car, and quickly moved around to Joyce's side to open the door for her. As usual, she looked stunning in her sky-blue, one-shoulder midi dress. It really complemented her long neckline. She smiled at me as she wrapped her arm around my elbow.

"Mr. King," she said and winked at me.

"Let's do this, Wifey." I winked back.

We slowly made our way inside, stopping every now and then to speak to colleagues who were there with a family or a friend. A live band was playing light jazz so as not to disturb the greetings everyone was making. The mood was very classy and elegant.

"Well, if it isn't the beautiful Mrs. King," Chief Rogers appeared from behind us.

Joyce turned on her heel toward him wearing her welcoming smile. "Chief Rogers, how are you?" She leaned in for a side hug. "Leslie, how are you?" Joyce greeted Leslie Rogers, the chief's wife, as she approached.

"Hi, how are you, Joyce?" Leslie leaned in for a light hug. "How are you, Ronald?" She then leaned into me with a side hug.

"I'm doing well. And you?"

"As good as a girl can be under the stressful circumstances when one decides to pack up and move." She waved off, looking at Joyce.

"Move?" Joyce's eyebrows raised. She was a real estate agent. She worked at one of the top agencies in Maricopa. Her face appeared on billboards and bus stop seating units. You name it, her lovely face was everywhere. She was making her mark, and Leslie no doubt was well aware of that.

"Yes, we are finally ready. Will you please put our home on the market?" Leslie grinned. According to Joyce, Leslie had been taunting herself for months with the decision to sell and the frustration of repurchasing. Joyce was constantly advising her on the current market, and I guess this had proved to be the turning point.

"Say no more, I'm on it." They were talking as we continued to make our way to our table, where we all would be sitting. I pulled out Joyce's chair and she sat facing Leslie, who by now was also sitting.

The food courses started flowing and we all made small talk. I didn't have much of an appetite. I'd become so nervous about my speech, obsessing about the fact that all eyes would be glued to me while I spoke. I sensed that Joyce could feel my apprehension building, her eyes telling me over and over again that it would be okay. The chief got up and left the table about forty-five minutes before my name would be called. He had to deliver the opening speech because it was his precinct that was being celebrated.

The way his speech was winding down made it evident I was about to be called up, "Tonight, we show appreciation and honor to a man who has served this city and been selfless in his contribution to the state of Arizona. Detective Ronald King has been at the First Precinct for fourteen years. He has been our top homicide detective for several years and was also the first to be appointed as the lead narcotics agent with eighty percent of solved and closed cases. King, please come up and accept this award for outstanding service, leadership, and being a compassionate servant leader."

The clapping and cheers boosted my confidence as I made my way to the podium. I had not practiced a speech, and with each step I took I regretted more and more not having prepared beforehand what I was going to say. But now it was too late, I didn't have one, so I was going to have to wing it. Chief Rogers held out his right hand for a handshake while gripping the round crystal plaque. With grins that stretched out to our cheekbones, we shook hands. He placed a beautiful, engraved plaque in my hand. "Go ahead, say something," he said to me, loud enough that only I could hear because people were still clapping.

"Thank you . . . thank you." I continued to smile as the clapping still ensued. My eyes fell on Joyce, who was shedding tears like I'd just won a million dollars. I could see it written all over her lovely face that she was proud of me. "Thank you all so much," I said again as the clapping tapered off into silence. It was now my turn to speak.

"I know it might sound weird, but as many people as I talk to in this city, whether it be a suspect, a family member, or a witness, public speaking rattles my nerves. So much so that I have dreaded this speech since being told I was going to be honored here tonight. But here it goes. Doing this job comes with its challenges, concerns, and disappointments, but the outcomes that make this city safer, whether it's catching a murderer, solving a case, or pulling a deadly drug off the street that might harm someone, are worth it. But cleaning these mean streets is no one-man job. That is why I must thank all those who have assisted me in any way. Whether it was passing me a message, or bagging evidence, it all lines up in the main event—solving the case. I want to thank my partner, Detective Forbes. Forbes is dedicated and has been relentless in backing me up and running down leads in some of the deepest, darkest holes you can possibly imagine. I must say this award really belongs to the both of us." I used both hands to pick up the award and thrust it in Forbes's direction. "Forbes, I would be honored if you would please come up and accept this award with me." Forbes grinned and then started to make his way toward the podium. Everyone clapped as I placed the award in his hands. He mouthed, *Thank you* to me.

"Last but never least . . . I would like to thank my beautiful, patient wife Joyce." I eyed her with so much love I thought I might cry. But I pressed my manhood button to prevent me from doing so. I laughed inside at the silly thought I'd just had. "As all of you know, success starts at home. Joyce, my sweet, I want to thank you for being dedicated to my job. The countless hours I spend being a servant leader for my people take me away from you. And never once has she ever complained. So, thank you for allowing me to be absent and always encouraging me." I could feel the flash of the few cameras that snapped my pictures. I held my smile but sighed inwardly from the huge relief that that part was over with. Now I could drink, eat, and relax.

I sat at the kitchen table scrolling through the pictures that were sent to me from the award ceremony. As nervous as I had been while giving the speech, I was surprised at how calm I appeared in the pictures. My favorite so far was the one with Forbes and me, both holding the award at the same time. The part of the speech where I touched on him being there was absolutely spot-on. The brother had been a loyal partner like no other. I was grateful to have him watching my back and sharing the same passion as I did on the job. I tapped forward on my cell phone and then scrolled until I reached Gia's name in my contact list and hit Send.

"Morninggg," Joyce sang as she rounded the kitchen corner.

Her voice over my shoulder caught me off guard. I clicked out of my text and laid my phone face down on the table. "Good morning, babe," I barely managed to say before turning around to see she was face-to-face with me, her soft lips on mine.

"How is your coffee?" She bounced over to the refrigerator, full of energy.

"Good. It's competing with this slight hangover from those Cuervo shots the chief challenged me to. I'm thinking that having lost would have served me better this morning." I rubbed my forehead, as if that might ease the throbbing pain. "But with the assistance of the two Extra-Strength Excedrin pills I took, I think I'll be fully recovered in about ten more minutes." I continued sipping from my coffee mug and praying my wishful thinking didn't disappoint me.

Joyce chuckled out loud as she shut the refrigerator door. Then she turned toward the cabinet and grabbed a glass. She had told me not to do it, but my competitive drive wouldn't let me give in. "I knew it, and as your dear wife, I tried to share my good wisdom with you." She opened the Tropicana carton and started pouring it into the glass. "You know, the chief can go all night. You might as well have let him win. I would have thought that after all these gatherings, you would've learned by now. But nope, my husband is the Pied Piper," Joyce teased.

I grunted in pain. "Yeah, I guess you are right." I rubbed my forehead again and reached for my phone.

"Did you get the pictures from last night?" Joyce asked me.

"Yeah, I was just scrolling through them. Did you get them also, or I can send them to you?" I offered.

"No, I have them. Leslie sent me some, plus the ones I took. I tried to snap a thousand. I'm so proud of you, babe. You delivered the perfect speech and didn't even break a sweat or choke up," she teased me, knowing how nervous I had been. But like the loving, supportive wife that she was, Joyce had assured me a thousand times that I would do fine. She had that much confidence in me.

"Hahhh! I see you got jokes," I said.

Joyce smiled as she pulled a banana from the bunch lying on our island counter.

She sat down at the table, sipped her orange juice, and then started to peel her banana. "Are you going into the station this morning?"

"Yeah, I'm about to head back up and jump into the shower. This pounding, life-sucking headache is starting to fade now. I'm back." I picked up my coffee mug and finished off the now-warm contents that were inside. "I was thinking that I would like to take you to dinner around eight tonight."

"That sounds great, babe. I'll be too tired to cook with this busy day I have ahead of me." Just then, a message pinged her phone. She picked it up and read it. "I have a few houses to show throughout the day. Then I'm meeting with Leslie Rogers about putting their house on the market. After that I'll head home around six thirty. At least that's the plan,"

"Sounds good enough for me." I stood up to put my cup inside the dishwasher. I had to get a move on or I would never get out of the house. If I didn't arrive at the station in an hour or so, Forbes would probably start tracking me down like a bounty hunter.

Joyce came over to put her cup in the dishwasher as well. "Ah, I have to get going. Time is money."

"Well, you have a good day." I leaned over and kissed her goodbye.

Two hours and a bunch of traffic later, I was at the station sitting at my desk, looking through a file. My cell phone went crazy, alerting me of incoming texts that I opened.

Gia: *Thanks for the pic. Sorry for hanging up on you.*

King: *You never have to apologize, you're always forgiven.*

Gia: *Enjoy your day.* ♥

King: ♥

"Hey." Forbes appeared in my open doorway.

"What's up?" I looked up from my computer screen. I was checking the database for a follow-up on some fingerprints I had sent off to the lab.

"Got a lead on that Dunbar case. There's a witness who is willing to talk to us if we can get there within the hour," he announced.

I glanced at the time on my phone screen. "Lunch rush will start soon. So let's ride now." There was no more to be said. I never hesitated when it came to talking to a witness. They could change their mind no sooner than they spoke the words they were willing to talk. I slid into my suit jacket and we were out.

I looked at my watch for the third time as I sat down on the couch in the den to have a light drink. It was now after seven o'clock. I had been home for an hour, showered, dressed, and Joyce wasn't home yet. I was certain she'd said she would be home by six thirty. I pulled out my cell phone and dialed her number, but it just rang a bunch of times before sending me to voicemail. I didn't leave a message because I knew she would probably call me back.

Normally, it was her calling me because I was running behind, so I decided it was her turn to keep me waiting. I knew that more than likely she was catching up with a client. I reached for the remote control. I figured that while I waited for her, I might as well catch up with the latest basketball game.

My eyes popped open and roamed about the room before I sat up. The sun had disappeared and darkness was now outside the windows. I picked up my cell phone to see the time. *Ten o'clock*, I mouthed to myself. "Joyce," I called out as I stood up. Had she come home and not woken me? Sometimes she came in and even if we had plans she'd let me sleep. I hated when she did that, but she always fussed that I didn't get enough rest. And so she refused to bother me when I did. My stomach rumbled. I was starving because I had skipped lunch. As usual I was too busy working during the day to grab a bite to eat. Out in the hallway, I called out to Joyce again but was met with silence. I noticed the house had darkened and there were no lights on. I hit the hallway light switch, and a sudden burst of brightness filled the air.

It was clear that Joyce was still not home. I dialed her cell. Again, no answer. This was no longer normal. My stomach stirred with nerves, and I felt a hint of a sickening feeling overcome me. Joyce was hardly ever late, but now it was almost four hours past the time she had assured me she'd be home. And she had not even called my phone, which was extremly unusual. I paused and started to think. She had said her last appointment was with Leslie. Then it occurred to me that I should call the chief so he could check with Leslie. I was scrolling through my phone for the chief's number when the doorbell started to sing.

I made big strides toward the door and then I opened it with force. Upon seeing Chief Rogers and Forbes standing in front of me, I became confused, but I waved that off immediately.

"Chief, I was just about to call you," I said.

There was a a look of horror written all over his face, and Forbes's head was hanging on his shoulders, his eyes refusing to meet mine.

The next words that came out of the chief's mouth broke me down to my knees. Later, I was told that I had fallen forward and collapsed. Joyce, my beloved wife, was found shot. She had been murdered.

Chapter 5

Tabitha, 2016

"Whew."

The small crowd that attended the ribbon-cutting ceremony chanted after the owner snipped the ribbon. It was so hot out, I felt as if my wig was slipping. I really wasn't in a clapping mood, but I braved it for the people. With the biggest and warmest smile I could muster up, I gave an Oscar-winning performance.

Now that I had been elected mayor, I was doing my civic duty as a public official. I was now a pro as these five years had flown by since the first time I was voted into office. Nowadays elections were a piece of cake for me. Running for my spot was as easy as reading from a well-written script. I had the people in the palm of my hand, and they hung onto my every word, as if their lives depended on it. Today, I was here to speak at the opening of a much-needed free clinic on the low-income side of Buckeye.

"Today, we all witness a step in the right direction for our community. Everyone deserves the right to have prompt and accessible health care regardless of their zip code or income level. This clinic will be the gateway to the start of healing for all who seek medical attention, regardless if they are covered under health insurance or have none, when they step through these doors. Let this be the first of many to come." My smile was modest when I stepped away so the owner could take the mic.

Afterward people in attendance and other community leaders stepped up to shake my hand. As usual, between the *hellos* and *thank yous*, I received dozens of invites to attend other events. My trusted assistant, Rhonda, who was standing close by, took their business cards for later contact. Right on cue, I assumed my usual pose wearing a big smile and took pictures with the owner and developers of the project. Mikka and Charles stood close by, watching everything and everyone. Mikka had grown up and was now head of my security detail, and he went pretty much everywhere I did.

"Again, I want to thank you, Mayor, for coming out and being a part of this project. We will be sure to invite you to the next opening. As you've said, let this be the first of many to come," Mike Depree said. He was the owner of the clinic and a known philanthropist in our city. He had made his money playing the stock market during the early nineties. Rumor had it that he was a billionaire. I didn't have any solid proof of his actual net worth, but he also was part owner of two hospitals in the Los Angeles area, so I didn't doubt it for a minute.

"You're welcome, Mike. Thanks for investing in our communities." I shook his hand one last time as Mikka approached.

Rhonda approached me at the same time. "I'm going back to the office to scan the documents for the governor's office. The deadline is drawing near," she announced.

"Okay, and that's great. We don't want to miss the deadline. Be sure to copy me and the finance department on the emails," I reminded her.

She nodded her head as I spoke. "I'm on it," she confirmed. With that, she ducked around a few people who had gathered near me and made her exit.

Mikka stood at my left shoulder; he was within earshot, so he could whisper to me, and he did. "It's about time we bounce," he informed me.

I had to give it to Mikka. He was good at yanking me out of a crowd, keeping me mindful of my time. And I thanked him for it, especially when I ran into a person who was a bit too chatty or long-winded. Most times, people would approach me with their own personal issues, expecting me to respond to their demands on the spot.

"Charles will walk with us to the car." I kept a smile painted on my face but nodded that I understood. I shook the last two hands that were outstretched to me, then fell into place behind Mikka. Charles followed close behind me.

My personal driver, Jessie, was already outside the vehicle waiting for us. He opened the door to the SUV as we approached. Jessie was Calvin's first cousin. He had worked for Calvin for a long time as one of his mechanics, which, according to Calvin, was his dream job. But an injured back had crushed that dream, because he could no longer bend and maneuver the way the job required. Now he drove me around when needed, and I paid him well to keep his mouth shut and drive.

"Have you confirmed the delivery for tonight. We can't afford for it to be held up like the last time," I said, point-blank.

"Yes, Trey is going to meet me in an hour so we can secure the delivery. The cash has already been stacked and everyone is ready for re-up in the morning," Mikka responded.

I nodded my head in approval. "Okay, no screwups, Son. I'm trusting that. Now I want to make sure you are at this event tonight. No exception." Mikka's eyes were glued to the outside as we drove down the interstate and headed for my house.

"Mikka," I called his name. I needed his undivided attention. His head shot in my direction. "Would you stop staring out the damn window? We have been over this a thousand times. I need you to be on point tonight. This is vital for our future. There's a new chess piece being put on the board, and it must be played the right way. I have everything riding on it."

"Ma, I got you. Please stop worrying. I'm going to get the drop secured, then get back home to get dressed and straight to the venue. I will not let you down," he assured me.

"Thanks, Son." I smiled at him. I knew I could count on him. Since Calvin was murdered two years prior, it was me and Mikka against the world. Without my son, I don't know how I could've gone on with the business and still remained mayor.

After Mikka arrived in Arizona at the age of fourteen, I was so adamant that he continue to receive the best education that we could possibly give him. And he had. He graduated with honors and was valedictorian of his high school. We couldn't have been prouder of him. But even in high school, Mikka had made it clear that he didn't plan on going to college. He was more interested in being a part of the family business. And he wasn't talking about the car business. Mikka wanted to hustle. I had objected, but Calvin made me see reality for what it was. At first I was reluctant, but eventually, with my blessing, he taught him the game. Now I continued where Calvin had left off.

The SUV came to a complete stop. Mikka and I wrapped up our conversation just as Jessie pulled my door open. I thanked him as I climbed out and headed inside. In my massive bedroom, I showered, touched up my makeup, then slid into my ivory-colored sleeveless faux wraparound minidress. Modeling it in the mirror, I slid my hands down my perfectly formed hips. At thirty-eight years old, I still had it going on. Even though I was the mayor and kept a crazy busy schedule, I still ran a tight ship when it came to prioritizing my work, my hustle, and my body. Tired or not, I still managed to work out four times a week and I ate healthy most of the time. Some would say I was blessed with good genes. And I would probably just agree. I proudly stood five feet eight inches tall with a slender build and curves in all the right places. I was considered a great catch and constantly received offers from men to go out on dates. But I politely turned them down. I had other plans, and tonight was the start of reeling in a big fish. And with my wits, gift of gab, and this body, I would reel it in—hook line, and sinker. I gave myself one last glance in the mirror, a big wink followed by a smile, and was out.

Chapter 6

Detective King

BOOM! BOOM! BOOM!

My fist pounded the steel with so much force I could feel the pressure of it crack my knuckles. "Maricopa County Sheriff! Open up, we have a search warrant."

I paused, but only for a brief second. *BOOM! BOOM! BOOM!* My fist attacked for the second but final time. My team of narcotics agents surrounded the house, front and back. A tip-off had assured me that Lunzo was inside, and we intended to put cuffs on him. All escape routes from the house were covered; there would be no sneaking out. We had been investigating him for over a year and it was time he talked to us.

I eased back from the door and signaled to David, one of my top agents, that I was about to make entry, meaning it was showtime. With extreme force, my army-style boots went up and landed on the dead bolt. The white steel door came off the hinges just as it was designed to do. We descended upon the house like the cavalry with guns drawn.

Fully suited with my bulletproof vest on, I moved down the hallway with a ready SWAT team. In plain sight sitting on the couch, bold as shit, Lunzo sat as if he had not heard us just take his door down like the thunder.

"GET DOWN! GET DOWN! ON THE FLOOR!" my voice boomed.

Lunzo raised his hands in the air. Other officers could be heard yelling the same thing I was. The female who had also been sitting on the couch rose up and assumed the position. Her eyes bounced around, but I didn't see fear in them.

Keeping their guns trained on the suspects, two agents came from the back of the house with two males and a female, all in cuffs. I noticed a baby sitting in a swing, asleep despite all the commotion. Suddenly, she woke up, saw the strangers, and burst into a crying fit.

"Is anyone else in the house?" Forbes asked. Task force members started to pat down the males.

"Ain't nobody up in here." Lunzo raised his head, but he didn't look at me.

"Agghhh . . . agghhh," the baby continued to wail.

"Let me get my baby," the girl on the floor next to Lunzo cried out. Her request was denied.

We had previous knowledge that a baby might be inside based on surveillance, so we had come prepared. We brought along Rita Corner from Child Protective Services to assist if indeed a child was in the home. I turned to Forbes and signaled him to bring Rita inside. She was outside waiting.

"Y'all need to let me see that damn warrant." Lunzo sounded agitated.

I pulled the warrant out of my back pocket and tossed it on the floor in front of him. "Fuck that fake-ass paper," he seethed.

I decided to ignore him as I leaned down and snatched him up. The handcuffs locked on his wrist and I tightened them, to teach him to watch his damn tone.

Forbes led Rita into the room. Then he reached down and helped the female up off the floor so he could secure the cuffs on her. "Please, please, don't take my baby away," she pleaded, her eyes fixed on me. "I'm all she has." Tears ran down her face.

Suddenly a tussle started with the female who had been brought up from the basement. "Get these damn cuffs the fuck off me. I ain't done shit!" She twisted and jerked her body, trying to free herself from the grip of the agent who had handcuffed her.

I stepped over to her and calmly said, "Ma'am, you need to calm down before you're charged with assaulting and endangering an officer."

"What you talkin' about? I ain't assault him. I just want these cuffs off." The woman stopped struggling and huffed as if she were tired.

"They will come off once we get down to the station," I told her.

She released a loud grunt, but then she chilled.

"Lock them up in a holding cell for the night," I instructed the guard. We had just made it back to the station and unloaded the arrestees. The ride back to the station was longer than anticipated. A semi-truck had turned over on the interstate.

"Give 'em time to sweat over what's going to happen," Forbes added.

Forbes and I jumped on the elevator and headed upstairs to his office. As soon as we were inside, I started taking off my bulletproof vest. "In the meantime, I'm going home to relax. I'll be back early in the morning," I announced, feeling free from the vest. I hated it whenever I was in one. I always felt like I was on fire.

Forbes, now taking off his bulletproof vest, turned sideways to face me. "Home? You're not going to the gala tonight?" His right eyebrow was raised.

"The gala?" I set the vest on the desk in front of me. "Hell no! I'm not going to that. Brother, I need some sleep. I was up all night questioning Bruce McGill in that murder case. Sleep—and I mean a good night's sleep—is my goal tonight." I sighed and sat down in the chair that was in front of Forbes's desk.

"King, you do realize you had an invite from the governor's office and that request came through the mayor," Forbes was quick to point out.

"I'm not special. You and I both know all public officials got an invite." Hopefully this reminder would minimize the next words of encouragement that I knew he might try to throw at me.

"No, actually only some public officials were invited. Not everyone. C'mon, this is a chance to attend the gala. It's a big deal, my brother."

I was too tired, and having fun really wasn't on my agenda. Taking a long shower and having a strong drink was all I wanted. I couldn't think of a more perfect way to wind down and think about Joyce until I drifted off to sleep. "You just have fun and tell me all about it later. I'm really just burned out," I told Forbes.

"I get it. But lately it seems as though you're always burned out. You need a fun night out. Ever since Joyce . . ."

The sound of her name instantly gripped at my heart. I thought of Joyce and dreamed of her constantly. My head dropped as visions of her smiling ran through my mind. I never spoke her name in front of others. Everyone knew it was a sensitive matter for me, so they tried their best to avoid speaking of her in my presence. I could see the regret on Forbes's face as soon as her name came out of his mouth, but he had already messed up. Chief Rogers had kept me far away from the case, but he'd promised they would keep me posted if anything turned up in the investigation. It was still an active murder case, but not one shred of evidence had been found. What perplexed me all the time was if it had been a robbery, why wasn't there at least one fingerprint left at the scene? Everything at the scene of the crime screamed robbery. I raised my head because I had a pretty good idea what Forbes was about to say.

Forbes sighed deeply. He knew perfectly well that he had to finish what he had started to say. "Listen, all I want to say is she wouldn't want you getting all swallowed up by this job. She would want you to laugh sometimes. I haven't seen you do that since . . . well, I haven't seen it. It's been two years."

Tears stung my eyelids and I could feel the sockets overflowing quickly. I had been crying regularly for two years now. I did my best to sniff back the tears in front of my partner.

"Two years, huh?" I gave a weak attempt at a laugh.

Forbes just nodded his head in agreement. Then he said, "Now go home and pull out one of them old-ass nineties' starched suits you've been saving for a rainy day. Come on out so you can mingle with other adults."

I couldn't help but smirk at him for calling out my outdated suits. Forbes was five years younger than me, so he liked to call me old.

"My suits are not from the nineties; at least I don't think they are," I protested.

We both busted out with a chuckle. Forbes was right in saying it had been two years since I'd had a real laugh, not to mention breathing in some fresh air. Since Joyce's murder, every day was solemn and a reason to be busy with work. No one but Forbes had dared tell me I needed to start living again, though. But I just wasn't ready to listen to him. "Look, I appreciate you, man. You've always been a good friend to me. And I needed to hear that. But I'm good for now," I said to him.

I could see the disappointment on Forbes's face. But then he perked up with a smile. "All right, suit yourself. But this brother is going to party." He snapped his fingers. "Oh, and I'm gonna have all the free drinks they'll give me. Don't sleep too hard; I might need a designated driver when I'm done."

"You a trip. Good night," I replied right before exiting his office. I laughed for the second time, and it really felt good.

Chapter 7

Tabitha/Detective King

The gala I was attending tonight was held every year by the governor in honor of one or multiple organizations that have made a sizable contribution or impression on the city and/or state. The recommendations normally came from the elected mayor as well as other city officials such as councilmen, state senate members, and a few others. This year was exceptionally important. I had made it a point to make the 1st Precinct Police Station the pick to be given a sincere thanks for the hard work it was doing to reduce crime in our city. My role as the mayor suited many causes, but benefiting myself was first and foremost. Tonight was going to be the start of me pulling off one of my biggest hustles.

"Tabitha Knight, how are you?" Governor Rhett Mercier approached me with his hand extended out in greeting. He had been in office for the past three years. I wouldn't say that I was particularly impressed with anything he did. But so far, he had stayed out of my way and supported my ideas or agendas.

"Governor." I took a hold of his hand, dished up a good smile, and pretended to give a fuck.

"It's always a pleasure to see you. I must thank you for all that you do for this city. The drive and commitment you show is simply amazing. Your efforts in making this city safe for everyone have been immense, and I can assure you it has not gone unnoticed," he made it a point to say.

I would have laughed in his face if doing so wouldn't compromise my political career. Since it would have, I thought it best to save that gut buster for when I got home. Instead of doing what I really wanted to do, I stretched my cheeks back again for another fake smile. "Thank you so much! The people and this city are my number one concern."

"Homicide in our city has been decreasing the past two years. This year alone it's down sixty percent. And I have heard so many good things about the First Precinct. I really hope they are in attendance tonight."

"Governor, I can assure you that anybody who is a part of this good work was invited tonight," I made clear.

Several photographers approached in just the nick of time to free me from this alone-time the governor had forced upon me. I silently thanked them as they all requested pictures at the same time. The governor and I both had grown so accustomed to taking pictures that it was second nature for us to fall into our usual poses and keep smiling frame after frame of flashing lights.

Governor Mercier leaned into me while the flashes continued, his camera-ready smile never wavering. "Remember, tonight is a night for relaxation. Be sure not to work too hard and enjoy." His assistant approached, and he finally told the group of photographers, "Thanks." That was his way of telling them that he'd had enough. They all caught the hint and retreated.

* * *

Before stepping all the way into the large extravagant room, I paused for a second because it had been so long since I'd been to a function like this. The last event I had attended like this was the honor celebration held for me and a few other coworkers. Joyce had been by my side. One look inside brought back the vivid memory of her speaking with the chief's wife while looking so beautiful.

"Excuse me," a soft voice that seemed to come from behind pulled me away from my reminiscing.

"Sorry." I immediately stepped aside as an unknown female stepped around me to enter.

I proceeded inside. The first thing I did was take a glass of wine off the silver tray a waiter had extended out to me. I thought having a drink might relax me and force me to be more open to enjoying the moment. Forbes had made some good points, especially the one about Joyce not wanting me to be completely swallowed up by my work. Throughout our marriage, she had consistently encouraged me to enjoy life outside of the office, and she did everything in her power to make sure I did that. The very last thing I wanted to do was dishonor her wishes by being selfish and using her loss as an excuse to check out on my life. So despite being extremely tired and preferring to have stayed home, I decided to honor her instead. I had to start somewhere.

Another voice from behind caused me turn on my heels. This time I recognized Forbes's voice right away. "I see you made it. I thought for a minute you might actually follow through with that crazy idea of not coming."

I sucked my teeth and grinned with a nod. "Yep, I guess I do listen to you some of the time," I joked.

"Wait, is that you, King? I thought you weren't coming?" Chief Rogers seemed genuinely surprised by my presence as he approached us with a drink in hand. I was convinced based on the extra excitement and the perked-up tone in his voice he had already laid back a few. His right hand slapped my shoulder.

"Yep, I had considered it. But once I got home, I said, *What the hell?* so here I am."

The chief raised his glass to his mouth and took a big drink, clearing it. "Good, because what you don't want to miss out on is getting your ass kissed by the governor, free drinks, food, and some fine women," he said.

I cut my eyes at the chief. Forbes and I burst out laughing at the same time. This type of talk when he was out and full of liquor was normal. It was well known that Chief Rogers was a ladies' man even though he was married, but no one pried.

"Thanks for that sentiment, Chief," I added just as an unknown person started to pull him away. The chief told them to hold on just a second as he caught up to the closest waiter to grab another drink.

"Man, you already know he's wet as rain. I've been here for thirty minutes watching him work," Forbes said. We both laughed again and shook our heads in unison. "But you know he is right about one thing, though."

"What's that?" I asked right away. I could never make any sense of the chief's drunken shenanigans.

"Look around you, my brother. There are some fine, and I do mean very fine women in here tonight." Forbes's eyes roamed the room. I decided to do a quick glance as well.

"Stop." I grinned. "I'll settle for the governor kissing my ass and the free drinks. Oh . . . and the food." I chuckled and placed my empty glass on the collecting waiter's tray that was passing us by.

"Man . . . stop being such a square. You better rub yourself a little booty tonight." We both laughed again. It felt good to be doing so much laughing. I knew he was trying to jump-start me back to life. "But speaking of food, I think it's time for us to take our seats for the long-awaited speech and dinner," Forbes suggested.

I looked ahead of us, where all the decorated dinner tables were set. I knew the placeholder cards on the table had everyone's name written on them that would be seated there. "Damn, we have to look for our names. I hate events like this." I sighed in frustration. We both took off in a slow walk. Everyone else seemed to have the same thoughts as us as people were making their way to the tables. We glanced at the cards as we continued along.

"I doubt we are going to be seated at the same table. You know they always try to separate friends and coworkers," Forbes declared.

"It'll be just my luck if I'm sitting next to the governor." The thought really annoyed me. I knew what those types were like, looking for validation about themselves from those they thought they were better than. To get it, they were willing to talk your ears off. "I would really like to eat my free dinner in peace," I complained.

Forbes followed up. "Better you than me." We separated to find our tables.

Right at the front of the room, close to the stage, I found where I was supposed to be sitting. I sighed with relief because I was tired of walking around. An unknown man and woman were already seated. They spoke to me right away as I pulled out my chair and sat down. Two other people sat down right after me. The only seat left was the one right next to mine. I dared to look at the name on the placeholder card in front of me, fearing it might be reserved for Governor Mercier. Thankfully, it was not.

I reluctantly looked up, and right across from me I saw Forbes. To my surprise, there was the governor, sitting at his table. I breathed a huge sigh of relief and an inward smile followed. I picked up my phone to text Forbes.

Me: *Damn, bro* . . . I added two laughing emojis for good measure.

Forbes: *Bullshit* . . . he typed, with an angry emoji.

The speaker stepped onto the stage. I went to my notifications and turned off my ringer and vibrating sounds. I reached for my glass of iced-cold water and took a sip as I saw the chair next to me being pulled out.

"Good evening," everyone around me said at the exact same time. I didn't want to appear rude, so I swallowed immediately and looked over to say hello to the person who had just joined our table. I was surprised to see a face that I'd often seen on television for one reason or another. It was none other than Tabitha Brown, aka Tabitha Knight, our mayor.

I wasn't starstruck by her, but for some reason "Hi" slipped from my lips slowly.

"Hi." Her lips moved, and I saw a perfect set of white teeth. The screen on my phone lit up. It was a text from Forbes.

Forbes: *DAMMM BRO!* followed by a laughing emoji.

I looked over at Forbes and gave him a slight smile.

With both hands behind my head, I lay in bed staring up at the ceiling, replaying the night over and over. The gala turned out to be better than I had expected. Forbes had been right that it was exactly what I needed. Meeting Governor Mercier had turned out not to be so bad after all. He thanked me for my contribution to the city's reduced crime and homicide issues. And not once had he tried to sell me on his agenda for the city. That much I could appreciate. Now, meeting the mayor had been much more interesting. From the time she sat down in the chair next to me, I thought my dinner was in fact ruined, but I smiled at her despite it.

Soon, it became clear that everyone at the table knew her and had a great deal of respect for her. Once the speech and dinner were over with, everyone mingled. She made it a point to make the rounds and introduce herself formally to all of the detectives in attendance—me included. We struck up a conversation in which she informed me that she was aware of the 1st Precinct and its contributions to cracking down on crime, namely homicides and drugs. I was actually impressed by how much she appreciated what was being done.

I made it clear to her that while we had done a lot, there was so much more that needed to be done. I explained that drug distribution was on the rise and homicides would only increase because of that. I told her in a matter-of-fact way that getting drugs off the streets of Maricopa County was my number one priority to tackle. Our conversation had gone on for a long time, but it definitely ended way too soon. Her views on stopping drug traffic were parallel to my own. She told me she was amazed at my precinct's passion for our community. She suggested that her office and the 1st Precinct should work together on putting together a two-year plan. I gave her my card and told her I would love to sit down and talk to her again about it.

The sound of my cell phone receiving a text interrupted my thoughts. I briefly closed my eyes and said a quick prayer that Forbes was not texting me an address to a crime scene. Normally, that was followed up with a call. Sitting up, I reached for my cell phone.

GIA: *I know it's late. I just wanted to say goodnight.* A heart emoji followed.

KING: *Good night.* I tapped two heart emojis.

I gazed at the time on my cell phone. It was two a.m. I started feeling an overwhelming heavy body feeling, which meant it was time for sleep. I yawned and reached over to turn off the light on my nightstand. No sooner than my head hit the pillow I felt myself slowly drifting into a peaceful slumber when a notification sounded on my phone.

Annoyed, I grunted. "Please, just let me sleep," I protested out loud to myself. I ran my right hand down my face, hoping to wake myself up. I reached for the phone and touched the screen. The number was unknown. I decided I was not reading a text sent by an unknown. It was probably one of those scam texts. I clicked off the screen and put the phone beside me. Then I scooted back under the covers, hoping that sleep would overtake me. My consciousness started to run with unpleasant thoughts. What if Gia needed me and she had to call from an unknown number? Only someone who really needed me would text this late. I sat up, grabbed the phone, and then clicked on the unknown number.

Unknown: *It was a pleasure meeting you Det. King, Sweet Dreams TK.*

Confused, my eyes scanned the text over and over. I had never seen that number before, but that in itself wasn't strange. People text the wrong number all the time. What was strange was that this text addressed me by title and name, which definitely meant it was for me.

"TK." I said it aloud to help myself, confirming the initials. There was no way what I was thinking could be true. The text had come from our mayor, Tabitha Knight. I eased back onto my pillow, and that smile when she had first said hello to me appeared.

Chapter 8

Tabitha, 2018

It was still hard for me to believe that Calvin had been gone for four years. After Dale was murdered, I thought I'd never truly love anyone else. While I must admit that my love for Calvin never reached the intensity of what I felt for Dale, it was still special. Calvin's most endearing quality to me was the fact that he loved my son. From the moment he met Mikka, he treated him like he was his own, and he never veered from that road. From that he went on to earn my love, and there was really only one other way to do that, and it was showing me his loyalty. Growing up in foster homes had ruined my trust in people; I only knew love when my aunt Margie took me in. By then I was a twelve-year-old girl and there were some parts of me that had been ruined when it came to trust. But Calvin had managed to squeeze it out of me when I thought Dale had taken the very last drop.

So, when I got the call that he was murdered, I went completely numb. I can still remember the call from Rocko like it had just happened yesterday.

Tabbi, shit went left . . . niggas tried to rob us. They

were like ten deep. No one was supposed to be at the meeting but the bosses. But that snake-ass nigga had henchman coming out the works. They hit Pete and got him in the chest... and they got Calvin... he's gone. FUCK!" he had roared from the other end.

I can also remember being in so much shock, I wanted to scream, but I couldn't. Instead, I just froze. I had been sitting down on the couch watching a movie with Mikka. I stood up with the intention of taking a step, but when I got on my feet I couldn't move. It was like being stuck in cement. I recall squeezing the phone so tight in my hand that my circulation felt like it stopped. Mikka noticed, and he realized right away something was wrong. Somehow, he pried the phone from my hand and assisted me in sitting back down on the couch. He spoke with Rocko, and he filled him in on the situation.

I didn't speak for almost twenty-four hours. Mikka called Aunt Margie and she hopped on a plane. With her here, I finally decided to go identify the body, and a week later we buried him. Pete didn't die, but he ended up in intensive care for nearly a month. After that he was able to recover. Two more of Calvin's henchmen were murdered that night as well. But Rocko, along with the other henchman Calvin had taken that night were able to get the product and our money, all of which he delivered to me.

Lamar James had escaped that night. He was the savage who had dared cross us. Calvin had been dealing with Lamar for over five years. Lamar lived in Vegas and had a mass territory out there. Calvin was his plug because he had a major Connect with Diablo. Lamar had grown jealous and thought he'd take Calvin out, rob him, and at the same time become Diablo's main connection. But his army had not won the battle. Two months after the death sentence he'd given Calvin, I put two bullets in him, with Rocko and Pete watching my back. Not even two weeks after that, Rocko was murdered by an ex-girlfriend. Then Pete got caught slipping with a kilo and a gun and was sentenced to eight years in prison. Shit had just gone haywire out of nowhere.

Time flew by quickly, and I continued with our family business. What Calvin and I had built I would let no man destroy. This thing was bigger than us; Mikka stood strong by my side the whole time. For him, I would continue to build what was now his legacy by ensuring the empire grew stronger and more secure than ever. And I was willing to do that by any means necessary. About two years before Calvin was murdered, the city had toughened its grip on catching murderers and putting drug dealers away. Around 2014, we came to the realization that there were some desperate steps that needed to be taken to weaken some of our potential problems. We had to protect the business by taking the goats' eyes off the prize and place their focus elsewhere. I personally had been more than willing to do that.

Of course, we all knew that every now and then some goats bounced back, and once again shit got real. Because I was a girl from Michigan, I was always up for a challenge. I would do whatever was necessary to secure my son's dynasty. I meant that literally, and tomorrow was going to be the day it would all fall into place. Tomorrow, I was going to marry for the second time. But this time around it wasn't going to be with a hustler. Instead, I had set my sights on someone who was well known for hunting down hustlers and putting them away for a long time. Tomorrow I would be marrying Detective Ronald King.

We had decided to tie the knot at Andaz Scottsdale Resort & Bungalows, a huge resort known to attract the who's who for extravagant weddings. The grounds were absolutely beautiful, and I made sure we spared no expense. Although I was on a particular mission, that didn't stop me from being a girl who could appreciate the beauty of a good party. The venue had several areas to choose from for the ceremony. We went with the Albers lawn, which was about 14,000 square feet. It had a sprawling area of three connecting lawns that had excellent views of Camelback Mountain. Between both of us, we had about a hundred guests coming. I had chosen such a large square footage just to ensure guests attending another wedding couldn't get a free peek at the mayor getting married. Privacy was a must.

"I'm just so happy for you, Tabitha. I prayed hard that you would be able to find love again. And here I am, about to witness you getting married for true love." Aunt Margie's eyes were full of tears. The light makeup that she had applied earlier in the day was ruined from the tears that had already fallen. We were at the wedding venue, preparing for the big day.

"Thanks, Auntie, that really means a lot. I'm just glad I had another reason to get you out here. It's so hard to get you out here. I dang near have to lose a kidney for you to come." We were sitting on the venue patio outside our rooms, where we would spend the night.

"Lose a kidney?" Aunt Margie burst into laughter, and I joined in. She sniffed back tears. "Chile, I swear, you tickle me. Baby, you know I would come all the time, but your aunt just hates planes. I get on them when necessary. But I do love you and Mikka and worry about y'all all the time."

"We know, but I don't want you to worry. We are fine. And now we have King," I wanted to assure her.

"I never told you this, but after Calvin died, I thought with your busy schedule as the mayor of this city that you would throw love away. I know how dedicated you are when it comes to your career."

I sipped from the champagne glass that I had been nursing in my hand. "I almost did, but Ronald King had all the reasons I needed for me to change my mind about tying the knot again." And that much I knew to be the truth. I added, "He's a special kind of guy. Some might say one-of-a-kind."

"He is a nice guy, always respectful. He seems really honest, understanding, and sincere." Then Aunt Margie dropped her head, and I knew she was about to say something disagreeable. When I was coming up she was always easy on me when it came to discipline because she figured me being in foster care all those years had been enough punishment for me. If something needed to be said for my own good, she would tell me. I waited as her eyes returned to meet mine. "I never tried to question your parenting when it comes to Mikka. Because if I don't know nothing else, I know you love him, and that all you do is for him. And I know you have your reasons as mayor for not telling everyone he is your son. Calvin knew you had a child and he accepted Mikka, even loved him as his own. Everything he did proved that. Now, as I said, I think Ronald is understanding, and sincere. He appears to be caring, and I believe anything or anyone you love, he will as well. Even accept. With that being said, I think you should tell him about Mikka being your son."

I had suspected something serious to come out of her mouth but not that. I gripped the flute in my hand so tightly, I thought it might crack. I truly was shocked and caught off guard by that request. Why she would even be thinking of me revealing such a secret to my soon-to-be detective husband was beyond me. Had she not been my aunt Margie, I would have yelled many obscenities at her until she ran from the room. But I had never disrespected her and I was not about to start now. My lips twisted on the sides into a half smile, and I gave her a reassuring look. It was all I could do to compose my growing rage at the thought of what she had dared to say.

"Aunt Margie, King . . ." I called him King because I preferred it over that weak-ass name Ronald. I continued on, "I do believe that he is understanding, but this thing . . . this thing with Mikka being my son will always be our secret. No one—and I do mean no one—can ever know outside of this family. And by this family, I do mean Mikka, myself, and you." I had to be clear. "My mayoral campaign was based on the premise that I am a woman with no children. I can't just come clean now. Not even to him, the man I'm going to marry. I ran for political office as a *big fat liar!*" I shook my head in disgust. "The man, no matter how understanding he might be, will think I'm a scam. He will undoubtedly question, if I lied about that, what else have I lied about? No . . . this *must* . . . remain a secret," I was adamant in saying.

Aunt Margie didn't waste any time in responding. "I must say that I don't agree with you, but I'm going to trust your judgment because I trust you. And I always want you to feel like and know that you have my support. There's not a day that goes by that I don't thank God for bringing you into my life and I'm so proud of you. I always have been. But I just want you to promise me one thing: promise me that you will continue to make Mikka first in your life. I do understand that he is a grown man now, but I raised him. I know he wants your love and acceptance most of all . . . the boy cherishes you."

Her words had touched me deeply because if anyone knew Mikka it was her, and I knew she was speaking the mere facts. I used to beat myself up all the time, wondering if he thought I was not a good mother because I had not raised him. Her words had given me some relief. Tears began to fall freely from my eyes. I tried to sniff and snort them back, but I couldn't.

"And I ado . . . ado . . . adore him." My words broke up, I could barely get them out. I was so emotional. "He's my heart and joy." My chest shook, and as I cried, Aunt Margie reached over and we hugged. We were both sniffing back tears from the heart. A knock at the door pulled us apart.

"You expecting anyone?" Aunt Margie asked. I shook my head no. "Guess we'd better head on back inside. It's getting late and you must take care to get plenty of rest for your special day. You certainly don't want any bags underneath those eyes." We both laughed. After hearing the knock again, we rose to our feet. I grabbed the bottle of Dom Pérignon and trailed behind Aunt Margie inside.

I didn't realize how good the Dom had me feeling until I stood up and nearly stumbled. I wasn't drunk, but I was feeling tipsy. And I liked it. Inside, I sat down on the chaise lounge. Aunt Margie skidded out around the corner to the door. I refilled my flute and kicked my feet up. I noticed Aunt Margie as she made a beeline from around the corner, her eyes a bit bulged.

My eyebrows instinctively stood in an upward motion with a question mark. "Is everything okay?" I assumed something was up that was unusual. Her dramatic corner turn had suggested that.

"It's Ronald at the door asking to see you," she whispered.

I sat up straight. I certainly wasn't expecting him to be at the door. He had been married before, so I knew he was well aware of the basic rules. "For what? He knows he can't see me." That was the second strike on someone trying to piss me off the night before the wedding.

"I reminded him, but he still insisted. Just crack the

door, but stand behind it so he can't see you," Aunt Margie suggested.

Reluctantly, I dragged myself from the chaise, wondering why he had to bother me. All I wanted to do was drink my Dom Pérignon and catch a buzz. Instead, here I had Aunt Margie trying to ruin my lies because of this thing called understanding, and King interrupting my peace for who knows what. I rolled my eyes as I pulled the door slightly ajar.

"Tabbi . . ." he said when the door opened. I wanted to say, *Fool, who else could it be?*

"Yes, it's me, but you have to go. We're not supposed to see each other. I shouldn't have to tell you this because you already know it. Why are you not at your bachelor party? You've been looking forward to this for weeks now," I reminded him.

"Yeah, I was there. I kinda snuck out," he admitted.

"Why? What could be that important? I thought this was like a man's rite of passage before marriage."

He chuckled. "Nah, it's not that deep for me. Trust me, it's overrated. But listen, we really need to talk."

"Talk?" My eyebrows raised in confusion. He sounded serious. Maybe he already knew about Mikka. Aunt Margie probably had told him out of sincerity. I quickly dismissed that because I knew she would never do that. "About what?" I asked. "Can't it wait? We are getting married in less than twenty hours. We should be focused on getting enough sleep so that we are not zombies at our own wedding."

"I know . . . but please, just a few minutes. I promise I'll make it quick."

Aunt Margie standing behind me tapped my shoulders. I turned to face her while still holding the door ajar to hide myself. She whispered so softy I had to read her lips. "Telephone." She raised her hand to her ear and made a phone suggestion, like we were playing Pictionary.

I sighed and said, "Okay, we can talk, but over the phone."

"Good, I'll take that. Thanks, baby." I could hear the appreciation in his voice. Now I wondered what the hell was this last-minute discussion about. Did I have cause for worry?

Chapter 9

Detective King

Never in a million years would I have thought I'd find love with Tabitha Knight, the mayor of Maricopa. After our brief encounter at the gala and she reached out to me via text, nothing between us was ever the same. One date turned into over fifty. We fell for each other seemingly overnight. No two people could have connected the way we did. After the many conversations we had, she schooled me on the loss of her husband, and I shared the death of Joyce. After she told me that she'd consider getting married again, I knew I had to propose before she got away. I was that sure she was the woman for me.

I knew she was curious as to why I showed up out of the blue at her door, demanding that we speak. After she agreed only to speak via phone, I raced back to my room so that I could have some privacy to make the call.

"Hello," Tabitha's sweet voice came through the phone.

"Hey, babe, I'm sorry I popped up on you," I apologized, and my tone was sincere. I really had not planned to show up. But I had to speak with her before we said our vows.

"King, is everything okay?" she asked. She sounded more worried than curious. I had not meant to worry her.

I gave a light chuckle. "Yes, babe, everything is fine."

"Your bachelor party must really have been boring." I knew she was teasing. "Is it really already over?"

"It's not quite over, but I left the fun to the guys. Trust me, the party is in good hands," I assured her.

"Wait, you left your bachelor party early to talk with your soon-to-be bride? This can't be good. Either you are really nervous or attempting to reconsider your proposal. Are you trying to jilt me at the altar, Mr. King?" she teased.

Her sense of humor was one of the things I loved about her. She always made me laugh. One of the things that attracted me to her when we first met was that she was down-to-earth and humble. She didn't have one entitled attitude bone in her body. "Jilt you?" I laughed out loud. "Nah, Ms. Knight. You will be Mrs. King come sunrise tomorrow. You ain't getting rid of me." And on that she could stake her career. I was one happy, grateful, and lucky man.

"Ditto, Mr. King." She gave a girlish laugh.

Just talking to her shifted my whole mindset as I pictured her soft lips on mine. I could only imagine her in my arms, the way her body curved into mine. I shook my head to get rid of those thoughts. I was off track. I cleared my throat. "The reason I wanted to talk is, we need to discuss where we are going to live after we return from our honeymoon." I could not believe we hadn't discussed this already, but we both were so busy with work and planning the wedding, it just had never come up. Suddenly this morning, it hit me like a ton of bricks. This was going to be a major part of our marriage and it couldn't wait until after the nuptials.

"I thought that was already settled. We will live in my house." Her tone was nonchalant and matter-of-fact.

"You can put up your house for sale if that's what you decide to do. Or you can always keep it as a third house. I have the cabin, which will belong to both of us." Her response was not a huge shock to me but honestly not what I wanted to hear.

"Well, I figured that was kind of your wish for us to live in your home, but I have to be honest . . . I really don't feel comfortable living there. Tabbi, it's nothing short of a mansion." Now was the time for me to be honest about why I did not wish to live in her house, her lavish home. I didn't admit it to myself, but maybe it was half the reason I had blocked out having this conversation with her before. "Listen, everyone knows that on my salary I can't afford that house. I don't want people to think that I can't take care of my wife, because I can." I knew what I was saying sounded petty and childish, but I couldn't help myself.

She burst out laughing. My mouth flew open with shock. I couldn't believe she was laughing at me. I'd said nothing that was a joke or funny. "King, babe, don't be ridiculous. No one will think you can't take care of me. You make six figures annually; you are hardly poor."

Hearing her say that brought me back to reality. She was right; I wasn't poor. Maybe I was being ridiculous. But the fact was that even on my salary, I would not be able to afford the house she lived in.

"So, now that this has been cleared up, there's no reason we shouldn't live in my house. Besides, no one will be wondering about our income. Everyone knows that Calvin was rich from the car businesses he owned throughout Arizona, which I inherited as his widow, not to mention all the money he left me. All the nosy people you speak of are aware of this. No one will judge you. It would be pointless to do so."

Everything she said made perfect sense. I was being silly, but her speech didn't make me feel any better. It proved my point. The rich marry the less fortunate. Compared to her wealth, I was considered poor, but she was not willing to entertain that. "I know, but . . ."

She wasted no time in cutting me off. "There are no buts. We will live in that big-ass house and be cozy and happy. And it is not my house any longer. It's our home," she pointed out.

Her tone was full of love and sincerity. Besides that, I knew how stubborn she could be. She had the gift of political gab. What she said went. It would be her way or the highway. She didn't give a damn about other people's views. I could either give in now or right after the honeymoon, when she would really put her foot down to get her way.

I sighed, then relented. "Okay, we will live there."

Chapter 10

Tabitha

I could not believe King had asked me where we'd live after our honeymoon. He must have been out of his damn mind if he thought I'd even consider living in that mediocre house of his. Don't get me wrong: The place is nice. It's a nice four-bedroom, three-bathroom home in the suburbs worth about six hundred thousand dollars. It isn't anything to sneeze at. But let's just keep it real. I live in Silver Leaf in an eight-million-dollar home. There's no way I could go back to being modest. It wasn't up for discussion; that conversation was dead in the water. For his own good, he agreed to move into my home because, if need be, I would have his little cottage burned down to the ground for some encouragement.

"How was your nap, sleepyhead?" King whispered in my ear. We were lying in bed after having gotten in in the early evening to play around. Afterward, we had both fallen asleep. He had me wrapped in his arms as if I might escape. It was two weeks since we had gotten back from our honeymoon, and just yesterday, I made a big announcement to the residents of Maricopa County. Not only did it shock them, but I am certain Governor Rhett Mercier was quite taken aback to learn that I was putting in my bid for governor in the upcoming election.

"Good, Mr. King." I squirmed in his arms with a light stretch, trying to free myself from his death grip. I was not successful. "Be honest, babe, how do you think I did yesterday?" I had replayed the speech I gave over and over in my head from the night before. It was way more intense than when I ran for mayor.

"You did well. You articulate every word eloquently, you speak well. I could never be as confident a public speaker as you are. Anytime I ever had to do it, I was a ball of nerves," King replied.

"Really? . . . Hmm. I never think about being nervous. I guess that comes from having been a television news anchor in my former life. I was transmitted into the homes of millions of people every night when the news came on. Guess that gave me confidence." I grinned just thinking about it.

It seemed like a million years had gone by since I had been on news. I remember the first time I'd gone on to report the news live. I didn't think about my nerves; all I did was hope the current anchor who had been out ill didn't get well anytime soon, because I didn't want it to be the last time I reported. "However, I do sometimes wonder if my hair is out of place or if my posture is exact," I admitted to my new husband.

King nibbled on my ear. I squirmed with laughter. "I can assure you, based on the speeches I've seen you give, you look perfect. I'm sure CNN still regrets that they didn't snatch you up when you were still anchoring."

I wiggled myself free of his hold and turned to face him. "Aww, babe, thank you." I kissed him deeply on the lips.

He suddenly pushed himself up in bed. "I've got an idea. Why don't you give me a live performance right now?" He peeled back the covers, leaving me trembling from the cold.

"Babe . . . I'm naked, it's cold in here, and there is no platform," I whined and reached for my Ralph Lauren blanket, which he was still holding hostage. He pulled it back more out of my arm's reach.

"You have everything my eyes need." His eyes glided up and down my entire body with lust. "And there's your platform." He pointed to the empty space in our huge bedroom.

I smiled so hard it turned into a giggle, and I too was now filled with lust as I fled the bed. I strutted my stuff as I modeled to the center of the floor to be sure he got a good look at my goods.

"Baby, baby, baby, just like that," King chanted. I turned to face him, and his eyes were glued to me. He licked his lips at the sight of my supple breasts, my nipples hard. I smiled seductively, then balled up my fist to pretend I was holding a microphone.

"People of Arizona, I am dedicated to you and will be honored to serve as your newly elected governor. And I will do anything . . . and I do mean anything . . ." I seductively licked my lips, "you ask of me."

King grinned. "Well, Governor, you have my vote, if only you will jump back into this bed and straddle me with pressure and grind into my saddle."

"At your service. And I see you are at full attention." I raced back to the bed and climbed directly on top of him with my hips pointed up, and I mounted him. "Damn, Detective King," I moaned out of pleasure. He placed his right hand behind my head, pulled me in, and kissed me deeply. I grinded deeper, riding him like he was a stallion.

I nearly paused at the initial ringing of his work cell phone. But I refused to let that break my stride. I continued to ride him eagerly, unwilling to stop. The phone stopped ringing and I slowed my pace but kept a steady rhythm.

"Shit," I said out loud as the annoying ringing chimed again. Like a stick shift breaking down the clutch, I slowed down again, but this time it was clear my slow mission was to come to a halt.

Both of King's hands gripped my sides tighter and tighter. "No, no, babe, please don't stop," he begged me.

I sighed. "Not with that thing screaming at us." I referred to the phone. I had now come to a complete stop.

"Uggh," he grunted with frustration as he reached for the phone, me still on top of him. "What's up, Forbes?"

I knew it was that damn partner of his. I just looked at him as he shook his head up and down, taking in the information that was being fed to him. He ended the call and let out an aggressive sigh. "Well, duty calls." He lifted his head slightly and smacked it back down on the pillow.

I slowly climbed off, lay on my back, and gazed up at the high ceiling. "So, this is the life of a detective's wife."

"Babe, I am so sorry." He leaned down and kissed me on the lips. Then tickled my nose.

"Stop it." I laughed and brushed his hand away. I was ticklish and he knew it.

"Will you please wait up for me?" he asked.

"Wait up for you? Hmmm. Let me see . . . why would I do that?" I teased him.

" 'Cause you love me."

"Sir, that can't be a reason for me skimping on my beauty rest. To keep this tight skin, I must get a full night's rest." I sat up and chuckled. He grabbed me, lay me back down, and kissed me.

"Please," he begged. "Besides, nothing could interfere with that natural beauty you possess."

"So, are you trying to bribe me with your detective moves?" I accused him.

He begged again. "Bribe, you never . . . aww, come on, please."

"I guess. But after I make my official bid for governor, I'm going to need you around."

"And I'm going to be right here." He jumped out of bed and headed for the bathroom.

I knew his role as a homicide and narcotics detective was a busy one, so it came as no surprise for him to be called out in the middle of our evening romp, and now it was late. But Detective King was now married to me, and changes were sure to come. It was like they say, keep your loved ones close and your enemies even closer.

Chapter 11

Detective King

I loved my career as a detective. It was my life, and nothing challenged me more or left me with a feeling of greater fulfillment. I truly felt I was a servant leader for Maricopa County. But it was times like the one I was just enjoying that I had to admit it was an inconvenience. I could have thrown the phone across the room when I saw Forbes's name light up on the screen. I could predict what the call was about. But it was the sacrifice that was made for a bigger cause, and I never regretted that. I arrived at the scene of the murder, which, sadly, was familiar territory. There were two men on the ground: an unknown black guy and, to my surprise, the other body was that of LG, aka Long Gangster. I had recently been trying to bring him in to question him about Lunzo.

Lunzo's and LG's beef was known in the streets. It had escalated when Lunzo returned back out on the streets. I had arrested and locked him up two years prior. Lunzo had done a short stint in prison because I had conspired with the DA to be sure that happened. He was worth more to me on the streets than in jail because he was linked to someone who I really wanted to take down. A prime catch, to be exact, known as Boss B.

I shook my head in disappointment as I stood over LG. I had not been able to get to him in time. "A call came in to 911 that shots were being fired. Five minutes later, another call came in that someone was shot and was not responding," Forbes filled me in.

I sucked my teeth. As usual, a million questions were looming in my mind. "Did anyone see anything?" That was the obvious first question to be asked. That question was always a longshot, but we hopeful detectives asked anyway.

Detective Forbes chuckled. "Pfft, yeah right." He was being sarcastic.

Police were moving around, keeping back the crowd that had started to build before I got there. The harder the police pushed them back, the harder they seemed to charge to get closer. Everybody wanted to see the body, but no one wanted to give up any helpful information. You could hear people asking who it was and others saying who they thought it was. Some shouted obscenities because the cops wouldn't let them get closer. They claimed it was their neighborhood, so they deserved answers. I leaned down to examine the body position more closely. Forbes stepped back to speak to the medical examiner who had arrived on the scene. I noticed LG had two gunshot wounds. The medical examiner, now next to me, confirmed that. The unknown guy had one gunshot wound to the center of his skull. The bodies were lying opposite each other.

I stood back up. Forbes was beside me now, writing on his notepad. "That's a casing," I pointed out. It was lying next to LG.'s right leg.

"You can go ahead with the photos of the bodies,"

Forbes directed the female photographer. "Be sure to get alongside curbs and those bushes also," he pointed out.

"Forbes, the morgue will be here in about half an hour. Let's spread out and knock on some doors before it gets too late," I suggested. But even I knew it was already too late. It was superdark out. Residents mostly wanted us to get out of their neighborhood, not hang too long snooping around, which is what they considered us to be doing. Unfortunately, we had a job to do, and I would make sure it was done. "I'll take this right side of the street, you take the other," I said to Forbes.

Forbes nodded his head in agreement. We split up along with a few other uniformed officers. This was where the job really got interesting. There were close to fifty people standing around outside watching the action. Several individuals were standing on their porches, but everyone's answer would more than likely be they didn't see anything. Some would deliver that answer calmly, while others would have an attitude and slam their doors in our faces. A few would simply not answer. They would lounge on their couches and listen to us knock. But this was the job.

Knocking on doors produced all the results I had projected, and we were back at the station with no leads and no witness to question. This was my first time back at the station since I went on vacation to get married. Even though I was officially back on duty two days ago, I had not been to the station. It felt good to be back at my desk. This was my element, my place of comfort. But at the moment, I would've much preferred to be home in bed with my beautiful and sexy wife. Instead, I was on a new case tangled with murder, drugs, and no solid suspect.

"By the way, welcome back from your honeymoon. On behalf of the department, we thought we'd bring you back properly. And what better way than a double homicide." Forbes chuckled.

"Thanks, I couldn't ask for a better homecoming. You guys know how to represent in style." I joined in on the humor. We approached our responsibility as detectives and officers with seriousness daily. But we also tried to keep it fun. Without a few laughs we would all go crazy with all the things we saw, full of unhappy moments. "Check this out, though. This shit got Lunzo written all over it." I leaned forward and rested my elbows on my desk, then rubbed my forehead.

"Yep, I toyed with that in my head already, and it's leaking back to your boy Boss B," Forbes said.

"For sure. They can't seem to keep quiet for shit. They shit loud and clear. They make sure we know which way to go."

"No doubt," Forbes agreed. He nodded his head at the same time.

"Oh, and I don't think we gotta worry about Lunzo much longer after this. LG's crew will get him off the street. That much we can count on."

I knew the results of LG's death and it would be gunplay. I also suspected that the unknown and LG were shooting at each other, but I had to wait for proof of that. Assumptions were never good in law enforcement, so I didn't poke around with them. Evidence in the form of proof and facts were my recipe for solving cases. "Well, we have to wait on ballistics to get more solid proof on the shooting."

"Well, well, if it ain't Detective Ronald King." Chief Rogers appeared in my office doorway with a grin plastered on his face. "Welcome back."

"Thanks, Chief, and what a welcome y'all have laid out for me." I was sarcastic on purpose. I laughed, and so did he.

"Hey, you know we will never be accused of not knowing how to throw a party." He moved in closer and stood next to my desk. "What'd you guys find at the scene? I'm sure there was a shitload of evidence laying around." It was his turn to be sarcastic.

"Hah!" Forbes hooted.

"Yeah." I smirked with a gruff laugh.

"Well, there are no witnesses to the actual shooting. So there are no leads. I'm in the process of putting in an order for possible camera footage that may be in the city area radars." Forbes filled him in on our actions.

I added, "I put in a call to the gang unit to try to identify the unknown male at the scene. I'm also running the lineup to see if we can identify him through pictures until the coroner gets back with the fingerprints. Right now, we are in our favorite place, the waiting game."

The chief smirked and shook his head with a satisfied nod. "All right, I'm headed out for the night." He turned to leave. "I almost forgot." He snapped his fingers as he turned back around. "King, congrats on the wife announcing she will bid for governor."

"Thanks, Chief."

"I guess you'll be leaving us soon, possibly becoming famous and all. We'll have to go to the big screen to catch a glimpse of you," he joked.

"Aye, that's what I told him the other day," Forbes said. He had called me the day he heard the announcement. He'd sworn I was *on my way up the ladder and leaving the small people behind.* That's how he had put it.

"Hah, hah, you two got jokes. Nah, protecting and serving, that's my life. Scout's honor." I saluted them. I had no plans of leaving the department anytime soon. I had too many homicides to solve and just as many drug operations to shut down. If anyone were to ask me, I was too fresh in the game to walk away.

The chief chuckled again. "Wait, you protect and serve; why don't I feel safe?" He continued to joke around. We burst into laughter; the chief waved as he exited.

Before Forbes and I could call it a night, we still had to wait on fingerprints, ballistics, and a list of other things, all of which could have waited until tomorrow. Besides, I was in a hurry to get home to Tabitha. The thought of climbing into bed next to my beautiful wife made me push the gas pedal harder. I arrived home just in time to catch her awake, and we finished what we started earlier.

Chapter 12

Tabitha

My bid for governor was official and my head was 110 percent in the game. But I still had duties as mayor that had to be fulfilled, and in the public's view, I had to show the people those duties were still important. The same votes I had received as mayor I intended to get and much more at election time for governor. So tonight I was attending a school board meeting at a low-income high school. The school's faculty was interested in starting a full technology-based curriculum for the incoming freshmen. However, besides money, they needed to show full cooperation from the elected officials and surrounding communities. This would help parents know that the program was serious and creditable.

"We are pleased to announce that with the help of the mayor, who is in attendance tonight, all of the money has been raised," Lois Gray, the principal of the school, announced.

I had helped advertise the fundraiser in an attempt to get more attention, and it had helped. "That is awesome news," I praised. "And we are pleased to see the project come together. The community is excited about this new opportunity that will provide the students with a more technical education that will better prepare them for college. How is enrollment going?"

I felt like some of the attendees who I assumed were parents were giving me the side-eye. I had to appear abreast of the situation. But I was a bit removed because just a few months ago, I thought the money and the support from some of the other board members might fall through. Truth be told, I had turned my attention toward finishing up projects as mayor that I knew were a go and preparing for my governor bid.

A board member named Rose spoke up. "Well, the waiting list has reached capacity, so we can't take any more applicants."

A hand went up in the audience. Lois gave the yellow-skin-toned, beefy-shouldered woman the okay to speak. "When do y'all plan to pull from that waiting list for enrollment? This school year is almost out, and the new freshmen will be starting soon. I need to know where my daughter is going." Her tone was matter-of-fact.

"Yeah, our kids have been asking," another yellow-skinned lady with a birthmark on her cheek spoke up without asking for permission.

"Listen, we are in the process of pulling from that list now. Everyone just needs to make sure their address is updated if it has changed since they did their application," Rose answered. I could see the expression on her face, which read, *Don't try me.*

Another hand went up from a tall dark-skinned man in the crowd. Lois gave him the go-ahead. "This is for the mayor. Is your run for governor going to interfere with your duties as mayor? 'Cause I have been calling your office about the fact that they want to let me apply for the program. My daughter needs this technology class because she wants to go to college." His energy was aggressive, his voice getting louder as he went on.

Lois waved her hand as if to stop him. "Sir . . . the mayor has nothing to do with the waiting list. And as we said, it's full, but . . ."

"We know it's full, but some of us need to know how we can apply. The mayor should be able to answer this type of question," another seemingly upset Hispanic-looking female joined in.

It was clear they wanted to hear from me. "Sir and ma'am, to answer your question . . . yes, I am still mayor at the moment. Furthermore, I am actively performing my duties as your mayor. Now, this technology program is designed to prepare students for college, and it is our greatest wish to serve as many students as possible. So please see Mrs. Lois Gray after this for information on future applications."

I would have said more, but my phone lit up. It was Mikka, so I decided to wrap up my speech. I wanted to be done anyway; the energy wasn't right. There was always some asshole trying to put me on blast, but as a politician, I was used to that. So, I remained professional and let my words do the talking. And in this case, I hoped my answers told him and that mouthy bitch to kiss my ass. Lois picked up where I left off, answering a few more questions and concerns about the program. Then she wrapped up the meeting, which I really appreciated.

I stood up and even shook a few hands for good measure. Even the man who tried to blast me by insinuating that I couldn't do my job as mayor and put in my bid for governor at the same time snuck in for a handshake. He was lucky I had no choice but to be on my best behavior. Determined to make an exit, I ducked and squeezed my way out of the room with my assistant Rhonda, Mikka, and Charles trailing closely behind me to ensure my safety.

Charles made sure Rhonda got to her vehicle and I rode away with Mikka.

I rolled my eyes as I thought about the man and the woman who were worried about my run for governor. "I tell you, sometimes I get sick of these people, aka citizens or whatever they want to call themselves. They get on my damn nerves with all their stupid-ass questions. Then they have the damn nerve to try to ask for a handshake or slide in beside me for a picture."

Mikka laughed straightaway. He knew exactly what I was talking about. "But Ma, you the mayor," he said, full of sarcasm. I wasn't in the mood for his humor, though. I cut him a side-eye look that said, *Knock it off*.

"Anywho, never mind the riffraff." I changed the subject; we had more important things to discuss. "What's the word on the shooting the other night?"

Mikka peered into the rearview mirror and then the side mirror before switching lanes. "That shit got Lunzo ass all over it. So, you know the word came down from Boss B. And the streets are saying that he just got back from Spain a couple of days ago. Says he got that work. What if he met with Rio while he was out there?" Mikka shot me a quick glance, then focused back on the road. I caught the concern on his face.

This was not news to me; I had caught word of this earlier in the day. The streets were boasting, but I didn't believe it. I was confident in the fact that Boss B, like most men, had an ego. Boss B never knew of my involvement; Calvin had made sure of that. That didn't change the fact that Calvin had someone out here who was a major threat to him, and he took pleasure in trying to beat the game. He enjoyed it so much; I knew he would never tell anyone on his team straight out that he worried about the competition. "Nah, that didn't happen. We would know if it had. Boss B would have made sure of it." That much I knew.

Mikka frowned, then he shook his head with disgust. "Them niggas make the game look like a joke. Their messy way of handling business is now fucking with our money. Police have been riding some of our territory heavily. Trey was on it, though, keeping the crew in line."

I nodded with gratitude; Trey was Mikka's right-hand man. Trey was Rocko's nephew, and just like Rocko, he understood what loyalty meant. Trey and Mikka weren't much different. They had been hanging out since Mikka came to Arizona to live. Rocko aka Terrance and Calvin had both helped raise Trey and taught him the game. Trey was good at silencing problems and details. He was an asset to our crew and like family.

"But three of our main territories' crew leaders have reported heavy police presence like a motherfucka since them niggas was murk'd," Mikka went on to explain.

I understood exactly what Mikka was getting at. Anyone responsible for bringing heat down on our empire had consequences to pay. LG's and Lunzo's shit was bad for business because when tracking down one crime organization they came for all. And that was a no-no . . .

"In exactly two days . . . Lunzo takes a long nap." My decision on that was final.

Mikka nodded his head. He knew exactly what I meant, and his smirk said he was eager to oblige. "Done," he assured me. "I got to go by the cash store tonight," he added. The cash store was any one of three laundromats we used to clean money. Mikka was in charge of making sure all of the money that went in was accounted for.

"How is the cleaning going?" I asked.

"Good. But once we expand, I can tell you now we are going to need at least two more stores here. And two in the other cities we expand into."

"I figured that. You can start shopping for the two needed here and we will sort the details later. I will have the budget done in about two more weeks for the outer city stores."

"No doubt." He turned into my gated community. I was almost home and glad. I was exhausted and done with the hot Arizona heat for the day.

"In two days I will be shooting a commercial for an advertisement for the governor's campaign. Make sure you have Charles there with you on security detail," I instructed.

"I got you. You know Rhonda already put that on my schedule. She ain't gone let me forget." He threw the SUV in Park. I told him good night, and then I gladly went inside.

Once inside, my mindset was destination bedroom. On the way, King popped out of the den with a glass of wine in his hand.

"Sweetheart." He smiled right before kissing me on the lips. "How was your day?"

I wanted to say, *None of your damn business*, but instead, I sighed, held my head back, and cracked my neck. "I'm beat like a run-down Chevy Oldsmobile," I joked. I was dead serious, though. Long days had become a way of life for me. Usually, I stared them down with no problem. Other times, I was over it and wanted to say, *Fuck it*.

"I'm so sorry to hear that. Can I pour you a glass of wine?" King asked.

"Please. As a matter-of-fact, fuck the glass, bring me the bottle. I need it all. I'm going to take a long shower first."

"You do that. I'll be up in a minute with that bottle and a chilled flute." He leaned over and kissed me on the lips again.

"Mmm." I pretended to savor the taste of his lips. "Thank you, babe." I walked toward the stairs, a hot shower calling my name. I felt gritty from the muggy heat and the shaking of strangers' hands all day.

"Tabitha." King said my name. I turned to face him. He wore a huge grin. "My wife, a servant leader for the people."

Pride was strong in his voice. I pressed my lips into thin lines and forced a fake smile. I wanted to say, *Nigga, please,* but instead, I said, "Yes, darling, anything for my people."

I could barely hold my composure. I wanted to scream with laughter, so I turned quickly and headed for my room. I rolled my eyes so hard, my eyelids burned. The nosy-ass people he was referring to were a pain in my ass. If I could do anything for them, it was to give them the advice to fuck off.

Chapter 13

Detective King

"Good morning, babe."

Tabitha walked into the kitchen bearing a huge smile. I had been up for a few hours and even went for a run. Some mornings I got up and worked out in our home gym, even though I still held my membership at the YMCA, where I had been a member for as long as I could remember. Joyce and I used to work out there together when she was still alive. She was more of a workoutaholic than I ever was. Sometimes when she went to the gym with me, I'd have to beg for mercy to get her to let me leave. After she was gone I got into the habit of taking a lot of five-mile run instead of hitting the gym. There were too many memories of us there. Since moving in with Tabitha, I used the home gym instead of going out. This morning I craved a run, with the early morning calmness and the fresh air, so I did. Now I was sitting at the table, looking over the fresh file of the shooting death of LG and the unknown guy who had been identified as Keith Harris aka KK, which stood for Killer K. Just as we thought, KK was a shooter who was known to affiliate with Lunzo.

"Good morning, beautiful," I serenaded my wife. She blushed and pulled open the refrigerator.

"What'd you have for breakfast?" she asked while retrieving the cream cheese from the fridge and shutting the refrigerator door.

"Nothing special, just a slice of toast and some coffee. I wasn't really hungry this morning. I thought about scrambling an egg or two but changed my mind." My eyes scanned the file as I double-checked the information that was in it. I had to be sure we didn't miss anything from the report that we'd put together.

She popped a bagel in the toaster. "What are you looking at? Another big case?" I was just about to reply to Tabitha's question, but the news and the mention of the murders grabbed my attention. Tabitha's eyes also went toward the television on the wall.

This morning, we have the names of the victims in the double homicide of two African American males that occurred a week ago today. The victims were identified as twenty-six-year-old Brian Lewis, also known as LG, and thirty-one-year-old Keith Harris, also known as KK. Police are asking if you have any information to call Crime Stoppers.

I pointed at the television. "That's it right there, babe. My new case that I need to crack. It's going to be messy."

I could hear Tabitha suck her teeth. "They are killing one another with no remorse and probably over some petty shit." She waved in a dismissive manner as she peeked over as her bagel popped up in the toaster.

"Nah, this is bigger than that, but yes, senseless all the same. Gotta get this drug trafficking under control in this city."

"Well, baby, we have increased the budget, or at least

we've done so as much as we can. This way departments can crack down on all the crime across the city, especially those that are drug-related," she stressed.

I watched her move about the kitchen in such a careless manner. I loved her more and more each day. She really worked tirelessly to see that things were better, or at least everyone had a chance to try. "I know, and that means a great deal to the people at the department and not just our precinct but across the city. We discuss available resources and shortages as we try to fight this crime. But I'm determined to shut down this drug shit, even if I got to squeeze the entire state," I ranted just as I gazed at Tabitha, who was wearing a grin. She was enjoying my speech.

"They got you all fired up. But not too much, because you, sir, are going to be wife to the governor of this state." She winked at me and then bit into her bagel.

I could only smile. Her confidence was unmatched. She had been claiming her spot from the day she decided to run for office no matter what. There wasn't a doubt in her mind that she would be governor. Everything about her was a boss move—and I loved it. She was also right when she said I was fired up. I was sick and tired of young men and women dying because they thought they only had one or two choices in life—crime or drugs. While I had already received awards and been told that things were much better since I came on the scene as a homicide detective and lead narcotics agent, I just wasn't buying it. I knew things were far from being better, and I had a lot more to do. I wasn't going to settle for a few arrests and a small percentage of the death toll going down. No, my goal was still to get crime and drugs off the streets for good, while continuing to support agencies such as the Boys & Girls Clubs, Big Brothers and Big Sisters, reform programs for convicted felons, and any positive voice and action that showed them other choices existed. But to do that, we had to catch the big fish. And I was going to continue to be relentless in my search.

"But babe, when I become governor, I'm going to need all of your support. You really need to think about retiring," Tabitha said to me.

Now this was different. Surely she was joking, or trying to get my reassurance that she did have my support. That much I could assure her undoubtedly. "Babe, retirement? No, not that. But I promise to give you all of me." I stood up and quickly moved in behind her and wrapped my arms around her waist. My lips gently landed on the back of her neck. "I promise," I whispered in her ear, then tasted her neck again. She shuddered with the pleasure.

"No fair, Mr. King. You can't try to cloud my mind with these types of antics," she protested.

This time my lips moved to the nape of her neck. She ground her bottom against my pelvis and slowly turned to face me. Our lips met and we feasted on each other. I opened the silk robe she was wearing and felt pleasantly surprised to see she wasn't wearing anything underneath. I whispered in her ear, "The housekeeper isn't due for two hours."

She wrapped her right leg around me. "Come here." Her hands pulled my head down and I winced with pleasure as her lips and tongue massaged my ear.

If I didn't have her soon, I would go crazy. I lifted her up onto the kitchen island. "You're in trouble now," I warned as she arched her back and begged me to give her more.

Chapter 14

Tabitha

It was nine o'clock in the morning and traffic had been ridiculous, but we finally pulled into the airport and drove onto the tarmac, where Mikka, Trey, and I would be boarding a private jet. We had to make a quick trip to LA to meet up with Mateo on some very important business. I had to cancel two engagements, but it had been the only time Mateo could meet, so I sacrificed my mayoral duties in order to tend to my secret empire. As I said, no other business was more important than my own. Mateo was someone who could open doors. He had been Calvin's Connect before he linked him to Diablo, whom Mateo was closely affiliated with. The best thing of all was that Mateo had the ear of Rio Zarrio—and that was gold.

Pilot Jim Watts was known for transporting celebrities. He owned a small private jet company, but he only flew certain clients, and I was one of them. He had flown Calvin for years. He was dependable and he kept his mouth shut. Jim greeted us, and one of his two flight attendants met us at the staircase of the luxury jet. Once inside, we buckled up and prepared for takeoff. A bottle of bubbly was already out and ready to be poured. Jet life was always unbelievably worth it. They catered to you from the time you sat down in the luxury seats until the time you stepped off.

Once in the air, the second flight attendant brought us a light snack, as requested. They were trying to feed us shrimp cocktails, sushi—you name it, they had it. It was lunchtime, so I was hungry, but I only had a few olives. I didn't want to meet with Mateo on a full stomach or smelling like the sea.

"So, since we haven't had a chance to discuss it, what's the plan once we arrive?" Mikka asked. Trey glared at me for the answer as well. Their curiosity was clear.

I popped another salty olive into my mouth, chewed, then swallowed.

"I just want to be clear," he added.

I sighed and then looked out the window at the clouds for a minute. I turned back to give them both my attention since they were eating me up with their stares. "Well, the plan is simple. I will offer him both of your two pinkie fingers."

Mikka batted his eyes quickly, then lowered his head as he gazed at both of his hands. "You got jokes." His head rose back onto his shoulders. I burst into laughter. And Trey's voice boomed into laughter behind mine. Trey's cheeks were stiff as he continued to laugh.

Mikka shook his head and grinned at me. I loved to tease him. "Basically, there is no plan," I dropped. "It's pure ambition," I said matter-of-factly. I paused to let that sink in. I knew he would need to process where I was going with this.

His eyes told me he was catching up to what I was trying to convey. "It's simple. We go in there. We assure him of what we can do for him to make this happen for us." I looked them both in the eye individually. "We have no more time to waste with expansion. The foundation has been laid. It's time to move on it. The first step is Rio. He's the key to the rise of the empire. But we are the key to making that successful. So, the meeting with Mateo is whatever it takes." I eased back in my seat and watched the clouds grow and fade as we flew through them.

We arrived at one of Mateo's many houses, this one out in Bel Air. The house was huge; it had to be the size of a football field. The doorman let us inside. Then two of his henchmen escorted us to him.

"Tabitha, the Queen of Arizona." Mateo greeted me with enthusiasm as he always did. Mateo was attractive, tall, with tan-colored skin and a nice build. He had straight teeth that he showed off every time he smiled. He was Hispanic, with nice wavy hair.

"Hi Mateo," I returned.

"It's been a minute since you graced my city. You can't be taking this long to visit us."

"Listen, I love LA, but I had to give it a break. This city seems to pull the party animal out of me. And I'm not in that life anymore. I try to avoid the club scene," I said, smiling.

"We try to understand how it works for senior citizens," he joked.

"Senior citizens?" I repeated with surprise. "I know you ain't going there, do I detect a gray hair." I teased. "Mateo, you are funny." I was tickled with this humor, which he loved to entertain me with whenever I allowed him to.

"Mikka, my guy. I must thank you again for the last ordeal you handled for me," Mateo said, looking at my son, his tone was full of appreciation.

Mikka had come out to help secure some of the territories when Mateo was having some employee malfunctions. Mikka had no doubt made his presence known when he was in the city. And things were quickly back on track and running in Mateo's favor. Mateo had made it clear that he was grateful.

"Hey, anytime. The work broadened my résumé. I was glad to do it." Mikka and Mateo laughed.

"No doubt, no doubt," Mateo agreed. His gaze then fell back to me. "Tabitha, take a walk with me. I must show you the garden," he requested. We were in his massive backyard, which appeared to have come straight out of a high-end landscaping magazine. Trey and Mikka hung back, as well as Mateo's henchman. We fell into a comfortable stroll.

We had done enough preliminary talk; it was time to get down to the business that could potentially pay off for me in a big way. "Listen, you know I'm out here for a reason. So, I won't beat around the bush. It's time for me to get the Spain Connect." I was forward. I wasn't playing around. Time was money.

Mateo chuckled because he knew me to be direct. I was the same way when Calvin was alive, and I had not changed. "Okay . . ." he finally said. "I've been knowing you for a long time . . . and I want you to know that I think you are ready for Spain. That's why I'm going to speak for you."

I wanted to throw my arms around his neck and yell, *Thanks!* But for one, that wasn't the kind of person I am, and second of all, I was not done. He had to know. "Mikka is ready too. Calvin and I both groomed him. I'm going to be stepping aside and allowing his growth. We are wrapping up a few loose ends and opening new doors. Spain is a must and Mikka must be out front. I need to know, what can I do?" I left it open on the table. He knew my question was not a bluff. I was a woman of my word and a match for any man.

"You just leave it all to me. I got you." Mateo's tone

was certain. "Calvin was loyal all the years we were connected. Never once did I have to second-guess him. And I know you were the power behind his moves. Which made him blow up." He chuckled. "He told me so himself. Not that I couldn't see it. I always knew it was you."

I thought about what he had just said. And it served as an affirmation that you should always be on your game because you never know who's watching.

Mateo stopped walking and I followed suit. "You go back to Arizona and focus on your governor seat. You'll hear from me."

I had no other words, so I nodded with understanding.

"Now that the business is done, when are you going to make me the happiest man alive and a bigamist when you marry me?" Mateo asked. We both burst out laughing.

"Mateo, really." I waved him off for being silly. Mateo had always made it known that he was attracted to me. He had even told Calvin that he had a crush on me, but it was all innocent. Mateo had a beautiful wife who he had been married to for twenty years and they were in love. He adored her. But he just couldn't keep himself from flirting with me.

"You're right, I'd better knock it off. Calvin told me if he died before me, he would haunt me." He grinned.

"And he meant it," I teased.

"Shit, well, at least let me get you all lunch before you leave. A feast has been prepared in anticipation of your visit today."

The mention of food made me think of the chef Mateo employed, a guy named Petri who was very well-known for cooking for millionaires all over the country. Petri would be in LA one day, Atlanta the next, then back up to New York like clockwork. He was no joke. I had never used him personally, but I had tasted his cuisine, and it was smack-fingers good. Honestly, since I'd gotten off the plane, I had not thought of food, only this meeting. But now my stomach was growling, so he didn't have to say much to convince me to stay. "Yes, please. I skipped breakfast."

"My pleasure, and during lunch, you can tell me more about this new detective husband of yours. You know, the one you jilted me for," he joked.

"Hah, special missions." We laughed again as we headed back up to the mansion. The day was nice and breezy. It felt great sitting outside. Mikka and Trey were invited to eat with us. The food was magnificent. Petri prepared dishes in ways I could not describe. The mustard greens were fancy as hell, but they were so good. They had the taste of being cooked down South. The man truly had skills in the kitchen. I could understand why people paid so much to have him cook in their homes. I would definitely be flying him out to Arizona on a private jet to cook for me. The man's seasoned greens said that to me loud and clear.

Chapter 15

Detective King

"Good morning, Detective King." Reese, one of our front desk officers, stuck her head in my office door. I sometimes left it open when I wasn't busy. I hated repeating *Come in!* when people knocked. It was so redundant.

"Morning, Officer Reese."

"Detective Gordon just asked me to drop this file off to you. He had to leave early. He also asked me to apologize to you."

"No need for all that, but thanks." I took the file into my extended hand. Detective Gordon was working on a murder case that he needed my insight on. My caseload was heavy, but a lot of the other detectives came to me when they felt they might be overlooking something.

I opened the file just as Tabitha's name lit up on my cell phone. "Hey, beautiful," I cooed into the phone. I loved hearing from her. She didn't get to call much during the day because of her grueling schedule. I was faced with the same challenge, but when we could call, we did.

"Hey, handsome," she played along, and I loved it.

"So, you miss me already?" I teased. The phone was smashed into the side of my face.

"Who wouldn't miss a tall, strong, chocolate delight like you? Just hearing your voice, I have to squeeze my thighs tight," she flirted.

"Girl, you better quit before I have to leave work and slide through them juicy thighs of yours." We both chuckled.

"King, you make me misbehave too often." She continued to laugh. "No, for real babe, I was calling to see if you were still going to make it later for the commercial shoot . . . that's today, remember?"

Even if I had forgotten, I'd been married before, so I was smart enough not to say so.

"Oh yes, yes. I will be there," I assured her. I could overhear someone talking to her.

She answered them, "Yes, in just a sec." Then, "Babe . . . I have to go, but I will see you soon." She rushed me off the phone. Before I could answer, she had ended the call. She was just so busy being the mayor. I could only imagine what being the governor of Arizona was going to mean for her. But no matter what, I would support her all the way.

Again, I opened the file that Detective Gordon had delivered to me, but this time my office phone started to buzz. I answered.

"Detective King, there is a Miss Moore here at the front desk to see you about her son's murder case," Reese spat off to me. My mind only wondered for a second and I knew who she was speaking of.

The chief had ordered me into his office about two weeks ago and handed me the file. The case was three years old and was now considered to be a cold one. I was informed that the mother was consistent in checking up on the case. As of yet, no one had been able to give her any answers. I was now obligated to try to do that.

"If you would, Officer Reese, take her down to interview room three and I'll speak with her there." I put the phone on the hook. At the file cabinet, I looked through my cases and fished out the file.

"Miss Moore, hi, I'm Detective King," I said as soon as I entered the room. Instantly, I could see the frustration in every crook of her face, which read pain more than anything else.

"I already know who you are." She gave me a weak smile. I pulled out a chair to sit down. I was prepared to take any flack she had about the department. I would listen, because after three years she deserved to be heard. "I have researched you and I know that you rank in the top ten homicide detectives in this state. Now my son has been forgotten by the system. He's seen as only a number . . . but he was my only child. My baby." Tears filled her eyes and her lips started to tremble, but I could see she was trying to be strong. "I won't let him be forgotten." She sucked back her grief and sat up straight in her chair, but one tear escaped her right eye.

"Miss Moore, first let me apologize for your loss. I can assure you it has never been the department's intention to forget any victim. I promise you that I have been given this case, which I take very seriously, and am dedicated to bringing the suspect or suspects to justice."

Another tear escaped her eye as she sniffed back the hurt and pain. She gave me a nod that she understood. I opened the file that I had brought with me. "I have been reviewing the file and I see that there were no eyewitnesses. And seemingly no motive. I know you were interviewed three years ago when this happened, but can you tell me what happened the last time you saw or spoke with your son?"

Miss Moore set her purse on the table, then rubbed her hands flat across the table. She sighed. "Well, just like I told the detectives back then, nothing was different about his demeanor that day. He had just started a new job. You know, Sam had just started his career as an engineer. He called that morning and said he would stop by the house to see me that coming Friday. Nothing was out of the ordinary." Her head dropped and she fidgeted with her hands.

"Then his cousin, my nephew James, called me looking for him. James said that he and Sam were supposed to meet the night before to hang out, but Sam never showed. And that he couldn't reach him and had been by his house but got no answer. That in itself was unlike Sam. He was a man of his word, so I knew something might be up. Before I could call Sam myself, Detective Rehner was at my front door saying Sam had been murdered. Then he asked me if Sam was into drugs or ever in a gang. Can you believe that?"

Her tone and body language said that Detective Rehner had offended her with that question.

"Well, I told him no . . . Sam was never into any of that kind of stuff. He was smart, he stayed in his books when he was in school and was now a career man." Her words were matter-of-fact. She was now comfortable remembering him as he was.

"Everything was falling into place for him. The only other thing he desired was to be a good father to his daughter and to provide for her." Her eyes squinted, and anger was apparent. "Except for the baby's mother. Ugh . . ." she grunted. "That girl and her selfish choices." The words had to seep through her now tightened lips. She shook her head in disappointment.

"So, this baby mother, did she and Sam get along? Were they together?" I asked.

"No. I won't lie. She had been an okay girl when she was in school. She was smart just like Sam, but . . . she hung around the wrong crowd. And I knew that was a problem. Sam thought he could change her, but then she dropped out of school. Things were a mess after that. I told him to let her go and he did, but then she called up saying she was pregnant. Sam of course was happy and wanted to be there for his child. I mean, what was he to do?" Miss Moore shrugged her shoulders.

"By the time the baby came she had a new boyfriend who was into a different lifestyle, and she had moved in with him." She sighed, looked away then back at me, and went on. "Sam told her he didn't want his child there in that house. That he'd get custody if he had to."

"Did he? Did he ever go down and file for custody?" I questioned.

"Nooo . . ." She twisted up her lips. "She agreed to get her own place. Sam was happy again because they were getting along. As I said, he was loving his new job . . . he was happy."

"Exactly what type of crowd was the baby mother into?"

"It was dealing, and I know that for a fact. Two weeks after Sam was found she was arrested with that boyfriend, and my grandbaby was put into foster care. She called me up to get the baby because she thought she was going to prison. But they locked that boyfriend up instead. Anyways," she huffed and twisted her lips, "she got herself together now, I guess. But I barely see my grandbaby anymore."

It was time I asked for the baby mother's name. I noticed Miss Moore had not voluntarily given it to me during our conversation. "Can I get her name and contact information?" I pulled out my pen and a notepad that I had brought with me. "I need to speak with her. Maybe she remembers something that might be important to this investigation."

Miss Moore crossed her arms and huffed again. "You can try, but that girl . . ." Then she rambled off her name and last known address. After confirming I wrote the information down correctly, I thanked her for coming in. And told her I'd be in touch.

Back at my desk, I typed in the name *Melissa Logan*. My jaw dropped open with surprise and I was a bit stunned at the familiar face staring back at me. I was surprised the name hadn't rung a bell. I had arrested her years ago and the baby had gone to foster care. I would never forget the young woman pleading with me to give back her baby.

I slid off my chair and rushed out of my office down to Forbes's office. His door was open. He looked up at me and asked, "How'd things go with Miss Moore? Officer Reese told me you were in room three with her."

I sat down in front of him. "You'll never guess who her son, our victim's baby mother is. Melissa Logan. Lunzo's girlfriend. Remember, we arrested her and the baby was taken into foster care?"

Forbes's eyebrows lifted. "Hell yeah," he boomed.

Seeing that he was with me, I shook my head. "Now get this shit. Sam, our victim, was on her about the baby being around her drug dealer boyfriend aka Lunzo's lifestyle. We need to talk to her."

"Damn right we do." Forbes was now on the edge of his seat. "You got an address?"

I smirked. "Let's ride."

Chapter 16

Tabitha

"No. As governor, I promise I will do . . ." I glared into the mirror in my dressing room as I rehearsed my lines for the commercial. I liked to see my facial expressions so that I could control them when I made the actual speech. All of it would be rehearsed: my words, my posture, my facial expressions, and every emotion.

I used the mirror to look over my shoulder as my dressing room opened. Rhonda, my assistant, entered. "We start in five minutes," she announced. The makeup artist was on her heels. She stepped around her and started touching my already flawless face.

"Rhonda, is King out there?"

"Not yet."

The makeup artist smiled and assured me I was ready. I stood up, gave myself one last glance-over, and approved myself. The black Veronica Beard two-piece suit looked exceptional on me. I winked at myself.

"I'm ready," I announced as I strutted toward the door. Rhonda was on my heels as a good assistant should be.

"How are you feeling about the speech? Are you feeling

comfortable?" Rhonda asked as we stopped before approaching the commercial crew.

I turned to face her. "*Comfortable* is not my goal. But *believable* will do," I shared. What the people believed was truly all that mattered. Some might say I had the gift of gab, so I was ready to start the show.

Rhonda was used to me saying such things and she gave me a weak smile. "Right," she said.

I almost laughed at her sometimes. She was so innocent, it was funny. And she knew not to ever cross me. She didn't know of my dealings in the crime or the game. When she had come to work for me, I quickly discovered she was being brutally beaten by her then-boyfriend. He had gotten into our office one morning after she had broken up with him and beat her until she passed out. I was so pissed. I had warned the nigga previously to never step foot in my office again and he'd disobeyed my wishes. So his days were numbered.

Unaware of my plans for him, she begged me to help her. Maybe she thought I could have him locked up. Either way, I granted her wish. Since then, she'd never seen him again. And not once had she ever asked me about him.

"All right, crew, let's start the shoot." Phillip, the head production guy, summoned his crew. "Mayor, please step up here." He gestured me toward the stage-like platform they had prepared just for me.

I stepped up and could see Mikka and Charles standing close by. Rhonda, the production crew, and the makeup artist were the only people in the room. We got started and ran through at least six takes before getting the perfect one. I was glad when we wrapped up. Rhonda and I went back to my dressing room as we talked while preparing to leave.

Knock, knock. We both turned in the direction of the door in time to see King entering late. Mikka came in behind him. I was annoyed as hell with King, but I wasn't in the mood to show it so I kept my cool.

"Ah, I see you made it." My tone was calm. *"As they say, better late than never."* I was cool, but I would not get rid of the sarcasm. He had earned that.

He leaned over and kissed me on the cheek. I continued to pack my briefcase, piling the papers that I had been looking over back inside it. "Babe, I am so sorry. I received a huge lead that I had to follow up on." He apologized, which annoyed me even more. Apologizing was a pussy move, in my view. I ignored him as I looked around him to speak to Mikka and Rhonda.

"Since we are done here, you two can head out. Rhonda, let's follow up tomorrow about the debate questions."

"Okay. Remember, I have an appointment in the morning," she reminded me.

I nodded.

Mikka stepped closer to me. "I'm going to walk you out. Charles left already."

"No, you can go ahead, I'm fine. King is here. He's got me."

Mikka still seemed reluctant to leave me. For a minute, I thought he was going to protest some more, but he left. I was tired and ready to go home. I told King what to grab and we headed out.

The drawing room was my destination upon entering the house. Inside, I raided the bar and poured a shot of Don Julio into a glass. I downed it and waited for its effect. I could feel it and it rejuvenated me. King walked into the room, and I nearly rolled my eyes at the sight of him. I was not in the mood.

He started apologizing right away. "I am really sorry; I know you are upset."

I just wanted to enjoy my tequila and relax. So I ignored him and sipped some of my shot. I could feel his eyes on me.

"I promise, I had every intention of being there on time," he insisted.

Since he was insisting on being in my damn ear, I decided to oblige him. "Intention is not action, King. Doing is. Or did they not teach you that in cop school? If not, sign up and go back." I waved him off.

"Babe, I would never stand you up without good cause."

I popped my neck to look at him. "So, there is good reason to stand me up. Do tell." I decided to be sarcastic since he was annoying me with his mere presence.

"Sorry, that's not what I meant. You know that's not what I meant." He had some nerve, trying to flip it on me.

"No, I don't know what you meant. I generally think people mean exactly what they say. Don't you agree?"

"No, listen, I would never intentionally stand you up. But I was handed this cold case, a murder victim. And the mother happened to stop in to check on the progress of the case today. She didn't have an appointment, but the case has been lagging for so long, and now it has landed on my lap. Long story short, after meeting up with her today, I ended up with a lead that I really needed to follow up on. It couldn't wait. Plus, traffic was bananas, and the time slipped away from me."

"King, I know your work is important to you. I get it, I really do. But I need you with me on this run for governor. I know you think this is easy for me because I already hold a political office, but it's not. If anything, it makes things worse because of the expectations. So, as my husband, I need you now more than ever that the bid is in and the campaigning has started. That means I need you every step of the way . . ."

"Okay, fair enough . . . What do you need from me exactly?"

"What I need is for you to retire from the force. And before you say no, just understand that I must have your full support to achieve my dream." Now that it was all out I lifted my shot glass and emptied it.

"Retire." King repeated the one word like I had said *death*. And his face looked the part. He gazed at me; his facial expression said confused.

Maybe he thought I was not sure in my statement. Maybe he thought he'd heard me wrong. I reiterated for the slow detective aka husband of mine. But I had to fake it until I made it. Therefore, I had to make it sound as passionate as possible. "My political career is my life and I have sacrificed so much to realize it. And am willing to sacrifice even more." He still looked dumb, and before I told him how stupid he looked, I decided to excuse myself.

"Listen, I've had a long day. I'm going to take a hot shower and relax," I announced, reaching for a glass and a bottle of wine.

Chapter 17

Detective King

Two days had gone by and I still was in a fog about Tabitha's request. Retire. Me. For the second day I had come into the office, sat at my desk, and done next to nothing. This really had me stumped. The seriousness of her request blindsided me. Retirement was something I never even thought of. Before we were married, she had shared with me her career path and yes, her sacrifice. But I had never considered the pressures she might have on her political climb along with the demands of my own career. Joyce and I did not have that problem. Our careers never clashed.

I toyed with the fidget spinner on my desk. It helped me relax so that I could organize my thoughts. One thing I was sure of was that I loved my wife and she loved me. Suddenly, I knew this would work out. I wouldn't have to leave my career and I would 100 percent be the support she needed. I would not allow anything to get in the way of that.

I pictured her beautiful grin and her confidence as she stood in front of crowds, telling people how she genuinely cared for them. My heart smiled. The sudden ring of my office phone caused me to jolt a little in my seat. I pulled it out of its cradle and fumbled with it in my hands.

"Detective King," I answered. I listened as Chief Rogers told me a body had just washed up in the Arizona River and it was my case. "Got it, Chief." I hung up the phone and dialed Forbes. He told me Rehner had just called, saying he got a tip on the body and thought he'd get the case. But I confirmed that it was indeed our case. I told him to meet me there. I grabbed my suit jacket and raced out the door.

The coroner had already arrived by the time I got to the scene. I walked down the riverbank to join him. The crime scene team was already out, waiting around to take orders on getting pictures. I could smell the body before I was even close.

"King," Forbes called out from behind me.

"This one's got to be a few weeks old." I rubbed my nose to reference the smell. It was horrible. I had to breathe in deeply to keep it from spilling over from my stomach.

"I knew this might be the case, so I threw up before I got here," he joked. The smell was so horrible I couldn't even laugh at his joke.

"Dave, what we got here?" I asked. Dave was the coroner working on this case. I had worked with him on over twenty homicide cases. He was organized and detailed.

Dave shifted his eyeglasses on his nose and whipped the sweat off his forehead with a handkerchief. He reminded me of how hot it really was, the same reason I had left my suit jacket in my car. He sighed as he examined the body a bit more. "Well, as you can see, the body is badly decomposed. It's been under the water for about two weeks. That's going to be the cause of all this skin slippage, as you can see." He pointed out a few places where the skin was either hanging or missing, the thigh area and a bit of the rib cage area as well.

The body was naked, and the decomposition had set to the point that it was unidentifiable by looks. The face was unrecognizable. It was clear that some water animal had taken a couple of bites of whoever the unlucky person was. "We can assume the clothes were removed to tamper with identifying the body," I concluded.

"Geniuses," Forbes joked.

"Right." I waved the crime scene analyst on the scene over. She was talking to an officer in uniform. "You can go ahead and take the fingerprints. Can we get a rush on those?" I asked.

"Sure. I just spoke with Dave, and he told me of the decomposition, which means it might be a missing person. I'll get them to you asap," she answered. Forbes, myself, and a few others poked around for evidence before leaving the scene.

"We need to pull the missing persons list for all males in the past thirty days." Forbes and I had just entered my office. I sat down in front of my computer. Forbes sat in one of the two empty chairs in front of my desk.

Suddenly, I burst into laughter as I thought about our visit to Melissa Logan's a few nights before. She had told us that she didn't know where Lunzo was. According to her, he was either missing or with another bitch. We had asked her when the last time was she'd seen or spoken with Sam. We also questioned her about where Lunzo was around the time Sam was murdered.

Forbes gave me a concerned look. "What's so damn funny?"

"I was thinking about what Melissa Logan said about Lunzo being missing or out with a bitch." I chuckled again. "Maybe that's him."

Forbes's head went back as he roared with laughter. "Man, you're crazy."

I hunched my shoulders and grinned. We were detectives, it never hurt to speculate, even if only for fun. I continued to fish the database for missing males.

"But for real, we need to bring her in for more questioning," Forbes stated. I was about to respond, but my busy office phone rang. I answered.

The words on the other end of the phone left me speechless. My eyeballs had enlarged, and I felt as though they might pop out of their sockets. I looked at Forbes and his lips read, *What?* No doubt my dramatic reaction had his attention. I ended the call.

I placed the phone back on the hook. "You will not believe the man in the water is Donald Lunzo Evans."

It was Forbes's turn for his bottom jawline to drop. "No fuckin' way!" he barked.

"I joked that shit into existence. Can you believe it, because I can't." I shook my head, still wowed. "Crazy as hell."

"My thoughts exactly. I'm sure some evidence might pop up. But it's time to bring Melissa Logan in for more questions about Sam. Maybe we should even notify her about the deceased being Lunzo."

I leaned back in my seat. "Maybe she has something she wants to get off her chest."

Forbes gave a half grunt then stood up. "More like blame."

"Whichever brings closure to Miss Moore," I reasoned. I still couldn't believe Lunzo was the man in the water. I wasn't surprised he was dead, working for Boss B; his enemies were more than a few. But the fact that I had called it had me tripping. Too bad I wasn't going to get the cuffs on him again. I had predicted my next charge was going to land him a life sentence. I guess karma had other plans in store for him.

Chapter 18

Tabitha

"Do you have the speech for the debate so I can go over it?" Chaise asked. She was my campaign manager. I had a debate coming up soon and it was crucial that the speech be a winner.

"Yes, I have it in my office for you," I confirmed. "I need you to shave down my tone in certain areas." I had to sound professional and to seem sincere.

"I have a few action words in line for that." She smiled. Chaise was full of wit. "Also, we have over fifty new volunteers as of yesterday. I'm adding it to the calendar for the day after tomorrow to set up the crews for the door-to-door appeals." Chaise threw a few more "dos" onto our to-do list, which was already about a million lines long. I was at the campaign office checking on a few things and preparing for the upcoming events.

"Yes, and we need to go through emails to be sure that everything is followed up on. Rhonda has been good at scrolling the spams, but the numbers have increased, so I want to add at least two more people." I gave her more tasks, which was normal when we talked. But Chaise was good at what she did. She graduated top of her class at UCLA in communication and journalism. I had confidence in her to get things done. She added the notes to her phone as I spoke. Rhonda was also present, taking notes and answering the phone. A few volunteers were in the room working on the design of some new promotional pieces.

"We have to keep in mind that Rhonda still has her duties as my assistant as mayor. She must not be overwhelmed," I reminded Chaise. She nodded her understanding.

King appeared through the door with two big catering bags I could see were from Panera Bread. "Someone said it was lunchtime," he announced, grinning at the same time.

"Awww, thanks, babe," I said appreciatively.

"Yes, food. I'm starved," Rhonda chimed in.

"Yes, and I have two more of these bad boys out in the car." King headed straight for the kitchen. Ben, one of the volunteers, offered to go out and grab the other two bags. I wrapped up my conversation with Chaise just as King returned from the kitchen.

"I hope you are hungry, sweetheart." He leaned down and kissed my lips.

I grabbed him by his hand and led him into my office so that we could be alone. I walked over to the edge of my desk and sighed. "Thanks so much for bringing the food. We are so busy working on this upcoming debate and other odds and ends."

King walked over to where I stood and pulled me into his arms and kissed me gently on the lips. He came up for air and then gazed into my eyes. He really was sentimental. "I just want you to know that I'm here for you and will be supporting you in every way. No matter what it is you need, no matter the time of day."

Again, he connected his lips with mine and kissed me

more passionately than before. He pulled me so tight, I could hear his heartbeat. Suddenly, I felt his hands grip my butt.

"Don't start that, you know how I get." I wiggled back from his grasp a bit.

He gently ushered me back into his embrace. "Come back over here for just a minute," King whispered to me with a wide grin.

I obeyed his command but said, "I can't let you drain me of my energy, sir. I need it for this debate." I kissed his lips quickly, then twisted out of his arms.

I had been standing for over an hour chatting with Chaise and Ronda. I craved to take a seat, so I walked around the edge of my desk and sat down in my posh office chair. "What's going on with you?" I asked him. I could read the stress on his face.

"Well, the body of one of our known drug dealers was found last night." He pushed his hands into his pants pockets, then began to pace over by the window. I had the blinds opened and he gazed out of them for a second, as if he had to think. "Normally, when dealers are found deceased, they have been shot or tortured. But this one is different." He shook his head in thought, still peering out of the window, then turned back to me.

"Well, murder can be like anything else, sometimes there's a strategy behind it, sometimes simplicity." I could put him up on the game all day long, but would he even get it?

King gazed at me and chuckled. "That sounds like mayor-slash-soon-to-be-governor talk." He seemed to always be humoring me. If he only knew.

I just laughed. "Speaking of the soon-to-be governor, I'll be working late, preparing for my upcoming debate."

"Okay," he replied. His cell phone rang and he answered.

His head bobbed up and down a few times and then said, "I'll be in soon." We kissed and he departed, just as suddenly as he had appeared.

As usual, I had a thousand things to fit into one working day. My debate was my top priority, and after King left I worked tirelessly with Chaise to perfect it. We had called it quits for the day and I raced out the door to meet up with Mikka. After burning up the interstate in my all-black Porsche, I pulled up to one of our warehouses, which was located in no-man's-land. Finding Mikka standing outside waiting on me had put me on alarm. I shut off the car as he stepped close to my car door and opened it.

"Mikka, this had better be G-fourteen classified. You know I have a debate coming up. And that means what? That all of my energy must be there," I chastised him.

He had called early that morning and told me he needed me to come down to see him later. We didn't discuss business over the phone in detail, so I agreed and ended the call. Originally, I had plans to go home after leaving the campaign headquarters for some much-needed relaxation. Instead, I'd come here, hence the reason I told King I would be working late and left it at that.

"I know, Ma. I wouldn't disturb you otherwise. Let's go inside." Mikka trotted off in front of me. He was walking kind of fast, so I had to dig those red bottoms into the ground with a bit more force.

Once inside, taking in the smell of the warehouse, I became fully aware of where I was. I hated the smell of metal. Soon I was going to make this location extinct. Mikka turned one corner abruptly and then stopped to face me. "I put the bait out and have filled your trap."

My cheeks flushed with a gust of anxiety. He opened the door, and I followed him into the room. The sight of him caused my breath to catch in my chest. My right hand instinctively went to my Tom Ford sunglasses. I had to see him with my own eyes and not through the lenses of Tom Ford's creation. Sitting tied to a chair, I saw him clear and in living color.

The Boss, I mouthed. My tone was clear of sarcasm but coated with a bit of shock. He was there, finally. I had dreamed about this many times. Who knew this would be the day I could actually have my cake and eat it too.

His head, which looked as if it had been swaying, lifted back onto his broad shoulders. At the sight of me, his eyes bulged and widened like saucers. His eyebrows sank with confusion. "Mayor," slid from his lips, as if he tasted the rise of bile in his mouth. Nothing could hide how surprised my presence had been to him. "Da Fuck." His eyes shifted from left to right, no doubt trying to make sense of what was happening. Mikka had done a good job.

"Son, you have stepped up. You've delivered our biggest competitor to me on a silver platter. Now he sits at our feet." In that moment I couldn't be prouder of Mikka. He had really stepped into his role as a leader of an empire. He was on the right path to earning the privilege to be first in line for the throne.

"Son." Boss B repeated the word as if he'd just tasted metal. He bit his bottom lip and gritted his teeth. I watched his gaze go from me to Mikka. I could feel the heat and hate rising from his body language and from his shallow breathing. And there was his sharply shaped Adam's apple, which seemed to bounce up and down in his throat.

"YO NIGGA, THIS YO MOMMA!" His words boomed. "Fuckin' weird shit y'all got goin' on up in here!" His eyes turned to slits and gunned both Mikka and me down. I smirked at his dramatic reaction.

His head sunk into his chest again. He shook it from

side to side, then grunted a sigh. Boss B looked at me. "So, you the bitch who's been on my back." He spat out the words at me as if they were venom. Mikka seemed to have glided across the room, his nine millimeter cracked across Boss's jaw so swiftly and loudly it actually made my own teeth grind. Blood splattered onto his, then oozed down the side of his mouth.

"Nigga, don't you ever disrespect my momma," Mikka huffed. The nine millimeter was in his right hand and his right fist was balled up, ready to strike again. I moved across the floor and stepped in between them.

"Mikka, let's allow our guest to speak his peace, even if he is a bit rude."

I looked at Boss B, still wearing a smirk on his face. His words were shit to me, I was cool with his tantrum. The rust smell of the room bothered me more than his weak attempt at word-bashing. Men threw around the word BITCH as if it was the end of women's humanity. How pussy of him.

"Agh, Agh, agh!" Boss B sat up and coughed up more small spits of blood. The blow of the nine millimeter had been capable of knocking out his teeth, but my observation was Boss B was doing the most with his dramatic performance. Then, suddenly, "Hah, hah, hah!" he roared out with laughter. His once-white front set of teeth was exposed and now were tinged red from the blood. "Nah, it's cool, ya boy hit like a bitch anyway."

"Oh yeah, nigga." Mikka cocked his gun and pointed it right between Boss B's eyes. I reached out and gently pushed his hand down back to his side.

"FUCK!" Boss B screamed out; his upper body yanked forward. "I been being fucked by a BITCH!" He shook his head with so much anguish, I was sure his neck had to hurt. "The mayor, at that. I just been slippin'." His words slid off his tongue as if he was disgusted with himself.

"You may not have been slippin', but you in my way. I'm trying to build here," I shared. My words were calm but straightforward.

"So, that's what this shit is about. Shi'dd you got your territory, I got mine. We both stackin' millions." I guessed this was his way of saying there was enough room for the both of us. "But now I know that it's you who out here tryin' to step on my Spain connect. Never could I have guessed you were female." He grunted, then dropped his shoulder. He smiled at me. "Listen, I'm a fair man . . . you let me go and I'll open that for you."

Now he had my full attention with his deal on the table for me. Surely he saw no reason I would refuse. I shook my head up and down to agree with him. "Really, so you'll help me?" I wanted to help him rationalize his offer. "From the looks of things, you not even in a position to help yourself. Take a look at yourself, Big Boss. You are sitting in death's chair." I mocked him. Mikka laughed out loud.

The shame in his eyes conveyed that I had gut-punched him. I could tell he was fighting to hold his tongue. His face was swelling by the second and he just looked plain stupid. "Look, we have expanded all the way to the Atlanta area. I am set up out there and have strong territories and police protection."

I was tired of being nice and ready to go. I sucked in a breath. "Boss B, let's be clear here. You can't do shit for me. You can't even keep your people in line right here in Maricopa County. Look at Lunzo." I sucked my teeth. "So bad for business . . . but to prove to you that I'm not all bad, I did you a HUGE . . . favor and helped you out with him."

"Fuck you mean, bitch?" he asked immediately with his nose twitching.

I smirked at him. I was really enjoying his agony, so

much so that I decided to give him more. Besides, he did ask. "Well, since you must know. We fed him to the fishes."

I was stunned at the sight of tears bursting through his eyelids and cascading down his swollen cheeks. His teeth were now clenched together so hard I could hear them rattle. "Do you know, that was my blood brother? You best kill me, you evil BITCH!" White drool formed at the corner of his tightly clenched lips. The bullet was slow but steady as it burst through the center of Boss B's forehead. On impact, it made a thud-like sound. His head split open like a watermelon, his brain splattered, and blood spilled over. Another one had bit the dust.

Chapter 19

Tabitha

I couldn't believe how the months had flown by since my bid for governor of the state of Arizona had been announced and my run as mayor had ended. I was glad that all the debates and campaigning were done and now I had my crown, which I was wearing beautifully. Truthfully speaking, I wasn't all that surprised. I always knew there would be no other victor over me. Tonight, as balloons and confetti filled the campaign hall of my celebratory party, it served as a vindication to myself and those in attendance of what I could accomplish. I stood on the podium as I was expected to do and proceeded to deliver my acceptance speech.

"Tonight, I really just want to thank everyone here who has been a part of this campaign. The job was well done. But as you all know . . . now the real work starts. Putting concrete policies in place to keep continuing to clean up this city is a huge concern. Along with creating more jobs that will fit the everyday working individual, I want to announce that we have a new outreach that will be coming to this city in the next couple of weeks. It will aid in the robust effort to put folks to work and clean these streets of dead bodies. More jobs and less drug traffic will be our anthem." The crowd exploded with a boisterous round of applause. I stood back and accepted the praise. This shit always pulled at their heartstrings; they were like puppets with strings attached to their backs and I was the puppet master. But I wasn't finished, I had more for them.

I lifted my right hand to quiet down the hand claps and shouted praises. "I will be working diligently in the first few weeks in my position to pass the bill for the raise of minimum wage in Arizona to the highest it has ever been. I promised this during my campaign, and I am steadfast in this goal." Again, shouts of praise erupted. Again, I raised my hands to quiet the pawns.

"But tonight, let's relax and have a drink." At the mention of a drink, every person in the room held their glass high in the air. They were already relaxed and tossing back the juice. My hand was still empty, and it was my turn. I stepped down from the podium and out into the crowd of people who mingled and congratulated me as I made my way through.

"Here you go, sweetheart." King moved in beside me with a glass of champagne.

I grinned as I held out my hand to retrieve the flute with the bubbly liquid inside. "Thank you. You knew exactly what I needed." I instantly moved the glass to my lips and sipped. I closed my eyes for a brief moment as the tingle of bubbles soothed my throat. "Oh, honey, this is just perfect." I could feel the liquid as it moved into my stomach.

"Anything for you. I'm so proud of you. I know I've said this a million times already, but congratulations on your win. When you're done with that glass of champagne, I will be sure to get you another one," he teased.

"That's so sweet of you, babe . . . tell ya what, why

don't you have the waiter just follow me around?" I joked. We both laughed.

"Governor King . . . has a nice ring to it." Chief Rogers approached us. His wife trailed in behind him. "Let me congratulate you on your win today. I know the campaign has been long."

"Yeah, it was a piece of cake," I waved it off in a play-ful manner. "I do this in my sleep, just ask King here." I snuggled up beside King and twisted my arm through his so that we were connected.

"Well, rest assured the First Precinct is at your service. We will work diligently to continue to crack down on crime and clean the streets. And I have no doubt with Detective King, one of the finest on the force, things will only get better." He jokingly pushed King's right shoulder.

"Thanks, Chief, but I can't take all the credit. We have a strong unit. I don't do it alone." King raised his free hand because the other was wrapped around a glass filled with champagne.

I reached out and grabbed his free hand and stood next to him. "You know, this husband of mine is modest . . . he's always humble. But Chief, with the help of your precinct and all the others' support, we will make our city one of the safest in the US."

"Governor, can I take a picture?" A female guest ap-proached, followed by three other people and interrupted us. My camera smile appeared like clockwork as more congratulations followed. Just like that, there would be no enjoying the night with relaxation and drinks. It would be nothing but lights, camera, action, as I had become quite used to. I was the main attraction of the evening. King, the chief, and his wife all faded into the background.

"Ahh," I snuggled into the luxurious feel of my Bentley, the seat hugging me as I shut my eyes. Jessie was our chauffeur for the night. King sat next to me. "It feels so good to be sitting here and finally be out of that place." My eyes opened. "I thought the night would never end. I swear, babe . . . if one more person had said *congratulations*, I was prepared to scream. I could barely get my champagne down without a damn *thank you*." My hand went to my forehead; I was becoming frustrated just reliving it.

King chuckled as I looked over at him. "They are just proud of you. Your speech was phenomenal. Hell, your presence was phenomenal. The people could not help themselves," he added.

I grunted in response. I wasn't buying the reason I was just tortured all night long. "Listen, I was trying to feel the buzz from my drink—a much needed one, may I add—with no interruption. Can't they understand that?"

"Ha, ha, ha." King laughed out loud. "You are something else, babe. Well, now it's my turn." He reached for my hand and sat up to look me squarely in the eyes. "Congratulations! I am so proud of you. And I can't wait to watch you do your thanggg." He sang it with a huge white toothy grin. "And as always, you have my support."

Tired, my head rolled to the left to lay eyes on him. "Hmph," I grunted. "Do I have your support enough for you to retire, Mr. King?" I wanted my sarcasm and shade to be clear. I was sick of his support speech. He would have to show me; fuck his words.

Chapter 20

Detective King

I was at my desk returning a few calls, about to look over some files, when I was interrupted. Apparently, Melissa Logan was at the front desk, demanding to see me. Initially, I was reluctant to see her since she had shown up with no appointment. And she also refused to tell the clerk why she had dropped in unannounced. However, she shared that it was urgent, and with reports of her being almost belligerent, coupled with the fact that I still needed to speak with her, I caved in.

"What's up, Melissa?" I sat down in front of her, and Forbes took the chair next to me. I had them take her to one of the interrogation rooms we used. Her eyes were swollen and red, probably from having cried a river. She appeared tired, fidgety, and anxious. I assumed her wild look was due to a lack of sleep.

She sucked in a breath before speaking. "Detectives, I am worried about my safety and for my child." She placed her hands on the table and fidgeted with them. Her nails looked as if she had been biting them. Clearly, she was nervous.

"Afraid for you and your daughter's safety?" I asked, confused.

Forbes followed up and shrugged his shoulders. "Afraid why?" The last time we'd heard from her, we were questioning her about a deceased person, but now she was the one afraid.

Her eyes darted from Forbes then back to me. Her jaw dropped. She stared at us like we had horns connected to our foreheads. She chuckled, but there was no smile present, only a frown that said she was frustrated. "Why do you fucking think!" she shouted at us. "They murdered Lunzo. You found him floating in a damn river." Tears flowed down her face. She sniffled, but the tears still came. "They may be after me. I'm afraid I am going to be next." Her chest moved fast with the deep breaths she kept taking.

I eyed Forbes for a brief second. It was our turn to play dumb, the way she had done about Sam's murder. "Who is *they*? Melissa . . . tell us who would kill Lunzo? Who is it that wanted him dead?"

Again, her eyes darted from Forbes to me. Both her hands went to her face, and she smeared her tears as she attempted to wipe them away. She dropped her head, then forcefully pushed it back up again. "Why do you keep asking me stupid-ass questions? I need your protection for me and my child."

Forbes sat up straight in his chair; it was time for him to play the concerned cop. "You come in here and ask for our protection, but we can't protect you if we don't know what it is we're protecting you from."

I opened the file sitting in front of me that I had intentionally brought in with me—Sam's file. Now was as good a time as any. I retrieved Sam's picture, which was conveniently placed on top. I used my pointer finger to carefully and strategically slide the picture in front of her.

"What about him? Your baby's . . . child's father? Could someone be looking for vengeance for that?" Her eyes shot from the picture straight to me. I could tell that at that moment she resented me and my question.

She gritted her teeth. "I have told you; I don't know nothing about that." Then she turned her eyes to Forbes as if looking for solace from him.

"Like Lunzo, he too was murdered, except he is your daughter's father. So it should matter to you." This time I gunned her down with a stare that read, *Help me understand.*

Melissa removed her hands from the table and rubbed both sides of her arms. She sniffled again. "It does matter." She adjusted herself in the chair. "I don't know nothing about what happened to Sam." She continued to stand on that lie.

I snorted. I was over her bullshit and wasn't ready to back down. "Okay . . . okay . . . maybe Lunzo knew. Maybe he shared." My tone was suggestive on purpose. "See, maybe Lunzo knew you were worried about Sam possibly trying to get custody. And just maybe he wanted to keep that from happening, you know, to kinda help you out?" I shrugged. Melissa looked at me. "Maybe it wasn't your fault. But perhaps he told you after."

Tears suddenly started to fill her eyes. One nearly escaped, but she quickly wiped it away. "I . . . I . . ." Her lips trembled as she stuttered. I watched as her emotions went from soft to hardened. "I told you, I don't know shit!" She forcibly pushed the picture back across the table. It slid off the table into my lap. "Now are you guys going to protect me or what? I'm a fuckin' US citizen, Detective King!" She mocked my name. But the tremble in her lips told me she was not as sure of herself as she tried to carry herself.

I retrieved the picture from my lap and placed in back

onto the first page of the file. "Well, like Detective Forbes told you . . . we have to know what and who we are protecting you from."

The chair suddenly flew back, and she was on her feet. "You know what, FUCK this. You guys are no better than the criminals walking the streets." Right after saying that, she raced toward the door.

"Melissa," I called her name. She paused and halfway turned to face us.

"Remember those streets you speak of. Your daughter has to grow up in them . . . without a father." I hoped my words stabbed some guilt into her.

Her eyes were fixed on me and full of contempt. She then shook her head, as if disappointed. "I'm outta here." She left the room in a huff.

I shut the cover on the file and sat back in my chair. "She knows something, if she was not directly involved. Which is highly probable."

"Yep, and soon she will break," Forbes predicted.

I sighed. My personal life was on my mind. Tabitha and her constant mention of me retiring was weighing heavy on the brain. No matter how involved I was at work, it still seemed to creep in. I could feel Forbes watching me.

"Man, are you going to tell me what's up? I know you. Something's been on your mind, and it's not this place."

I was expecting him to notice something sooner or later. I chuckled, then snatched at my tie to loosen it. Forbes was my guy, one hundred grand. Weren't just partners but friends, brothers. "You're right, but it does involve this place." Even though I tried to stall, it was time to vent. "And my wife, Tabitha."

Forbes raised his brow, suggesting he was surprised.

I exhaled. "She wants me to be there . . . no, she *needs* *me* to be there full-time to support her now that she is gov-

ernor. She is asking . . . well, almost demanding, that I retire."

"Are you sure that's what she is asking? What did she
say exactly?" Forbes asked. Clearly, he was caught a bit
off guard, the same way I was when Tabitha first hit me
with it.

"She said those words flat out. She was clear and adamant. Forbes . . . I never imagined I'd be saying this, especially when it comes to my personal life, but I'm at a
crossroads. It's a hard decision. My wife, who I absolutely
love and am rooting for all the way, or my career, which I
have built from the ground up and also love." I hunched
my shoulders in anguish. A feeling of uncertainty shot
through me. I really needed his advice. "What should I do?
Hell, what would you?"

Forbes rubbed his left hand across his head, chewed on
the dilemma for a few seconds, then released a heavy sigh.
"Man . . . listen, there ain't no easy answer to this. It's
deep, it's life-changing regardless of the decision that you
make. But . . ." He gave another heavy, deep-throated sigh.
"So, in a case like this, I think you need to follow your heart.
There's where you will be more content. Consider everything, leave nothing on the table."

Forbes's words really sunk in. I hadn't expected them
to be so profound. His advice was simple yet thought-
provoking. I was silent for a moment as I processed his
words. "Thanks, brother, I will consider all you've said." I
sighed out of sheer frustration. But it was also from the
small relief I felt in having sought out the advice of a
trusted friend. "Okay, enough of that Oprah stuff. In the
meantime, we must focus on the leads we've got on Boss
B's murder. All these years we've been tracking him for
drug trafficking. And now, boom, suddenly he's dead." I
slapped my hands together in a dramatic motion.

"Like who would have the balls to take him out?" I asked. I was so stumped by his murder that I thought I was being punked even though I had seen the body. "Just think about it. The biggest drug dealer in Arizona. A true force to be reckoned with." Forbes shook his head up and down, agreeing with me. "Again I ask, who would have the balls to touch him?"

Forbes had no answer. Instead, he just glared at me, then busted out, "Maybe it's connected with Lunzo."

It would have been easy to believe they both were connected. It reminded me of the Tupac and Biggie unsolved murders. It was way too easy to point the finger. Unfortunately, nothing was ever that easy to solve. "Nah, I think it's a rival for sure. My gut tells me so. A new drug corporation that is destroying our city. Yeah . . . whoever killed Boss B had to be as ruthless and as heartless as he was. I would bet my left arm on it." I was adamant, although willing to be proved wrong.

Chapter 21

Tabitha

Mateo had come through and secured the meeting with Rio Zarrio in Spain and I couldn't be more elated. I had only found out two days prior that the invitation was open for me to make the trip out there. That didn't bother me one bit; I had moved heaven and earth to reprioritize all my previous engagements in order to make this trip. With relentless determination, it all fell into place. The fact that Rio had even agreed to allow us into his presence was a major win. Rio was the king of Connects, like having the direct ear of the president. I was feeling like a real boss bitch, knowing that I at least had my foot in the door. I didn't feel that anything else could stop us from locking our spot at the top. I was still beaming with pride over Mikka for stepping up and landing us a one-on-one meeting with Rio. This proved to me even more that he was committed to helping to push this organization forward. I needed that confirmation from him more now that our empire was expanding to limitless production.

King walked up behind me and wrapped his arms around

my waist. "Ummm, I'm not ready for you to leave," he whispered in my ear, then kissed the nape of my neck.

I was packing my suitcase. I had told him I had to leave town on some political business. I then convinced him that I had told him about this trip weeks ago. Then I accused him of being so involved in his own career that he didn't pay me any attention. After that, he apologized to me for not being attentive enough and then ducked out of the conversation to avoid any further conflict. To keep him from prying any further had been my intention, and it worked like a charm.

"I'm going to miss you," he said while nibbling on my left ear.

I squirmed away from his grasp because it tickled me. "Aww, you a big boy. You'll be just fine." I grinned as I continued to load my things into the suitcase. "I'll be back before you know it. A week is not that long. Besides, you will be so busy on a case, time will just fly by. Now stop your whining," I teased him. I really wished he'd leave the room so I could pack, think, and plan.

Instead of him leaving like I secretly wanted, his arms were back around my waist and his breath hovered over my neck. I rolled my eyes because I was so annoyed. "I can assure you, there's nothing that will make me forget you're not going to be in this bed beside me for days." He squeezed me a little tighter.

I had to get rid of him. I turned around, gave him a big smile, and then kissed his lips. "Babe, I will text you every day and night before you go to bed so you won't feel lonely. Now I have to finish packing, Mikka will be here any moment to pick me up. We can't miss our flight." I conveniently left out that our private jet would be taking us to Miami, where I would use a fake ID to board a flight to Spain. Being a public servant in the area in which I was well known meant I had to take the necessary precautions. A flight to Spain might hardly go unnoticed.

We arrived in Spain late at night, totally exhausted. We headed to the private resort I had rented to rest up and get prepared for the meeting. We had been told to stand by but not given any specific information on when, how, or where the meeting would be held. So, I figured our best option was to rest up and be ready to make moves. The next morning, we woke up before the sunlight, got dressed, and waited.

The sun finally burst through the clouds, and then suddenly two SUVs pulled in. Rio Zarrio had sent for us. We rode in silence, and I was sure I could hear my own heart beating. I wasn't nervous about meeting Rio Zarrio, I was anxious about the outcome, that he'd turn us down flat. What would become of our empire if he refused us? What would happen to Mikka's future? I found myself holding my breath just thinking about it.

Mikka must have noticed I was turning blue from a lack of oxygen. "Tabitha," he called out, and that's when I finally sucked in a breath. It was then that I noticed the cool, calm composure Mikka had. Suddenly it hit me that my son was becoming a man. I realized that every day for months he had been showing me he was ready to take over the business.

It took thirty minutes, but we finally arrived at a ranch-like compound property. There were mountains in the background, and it was grassy, with horses running free. It was beautiful. The SUV came to a stop, and then we waited until the doors were opened for us. Muscle-bound bodyguard-type men dressed in cowboy boots and hats opened the doors. They escorted us inside through the house and then out a huge door that led to the backyard, where there was a massive pool with the bluest, indigo-colored water I'd ever seen.

A tall Spanish-looking man who was about my age, with dark brown, almost curly hair, medium lips, and a medium build was sitting at a table with a cigar in his mouth. I knew him to be Rio Zarrio. Two of his henchmen stood unbothered close by, but not in-ear hustling distance. Their intimidating presence was definitely to be felt. I approached, leaving Mikka a few steps behind. There was a protocol to follow in showing respect, and I wanted to be sure we abided by that. Rio abruptly stood up, revealing his true height. I knew he was tall, but standing in his presence I felt as if he was a towering giant. He was every inch of six foot five and as much as I hated to admit it, Rio was fine. I had to fight to keep from blushing in his presence.

"Welcome to my home." His tone was charming yet respectful. He greeted me like a true gentleman. I had not expected it. Again, I noticed his good looks. I had seen Rio years before from a far distance, but now that I was seeing him close up, I was mesmerized by his handsomeness.

"Thank you." I tried to sound steady and not shaky like I felt.

"Tabeetha . . ." He said my name in a choppy-sounding English, and I loved it. This time I couldn't hold in my smile.

"Rio Zarrio," I said his name in return.

"Please call me Rio. I insist," he answered with a disarming smile.

"Okay . . . Rio." I obeyed his command. Plus, I wanted to try it out on him. But I had to get back to the businesses at hand. I stepped to the side a bit to clear the view of Mikka. "This here is Mikka, my right hand . . . and, as you know, my son."

Rio gave me a nod that said he appreciated my honesty.

One thing I knew for sure, hiding such things from him was not a good idea. So, I never considered it, because I knew that he knew. He was Rio and he knew everything.

"Welcome, Mikka." Rio chopped up his name as well. Mikka spoke in return. He knew not to speak unless he was spoken to first. Like I said, showing respect to a powerful man like Rio was of the utmost importance. "So, I must welcome you both to Spain and into my casa. My casa is your casa."

"Thank you for having us and thank you for seeing us." Showing our appreciation for his willingness to take a meeting was important to convey.

"I'm familiar with Calvin, who worked diligently for my father, Diablo, when he was still in power." Rio held his not-yet-lit cigar close to his chest. "It is Mateo who reminds me of these things when he comes to me on your behalf. He says you are ready."

I knew it was time for me to state my intentions. Rio was a busy man who didn't need any kind of procrastination anywhere near him. "Yes, I intend to expand beyond Arizona, where I now hold full power in supply."

He smiled. "So I hear." This verified that he knew of Boss B's fate. He had heard after all. Spain may have seemed far away, but in essence, it was like Arizona was in Rio Zarrio's own backyard. He knew it all.

"I would like to branch out to Miami and beyond, but I will need you to supply me with a full drop with no cutback. I know the bite is big, but my crew can and will deliver." It was done. I had laid out my intention. I had practiced this over and over in my head long before the meeting was even set. Of course, how I would ask had been rearranged a dozen times. But there it was. I tightened on the inside to keep my organs still, which just minutes ago were shaking.

On the outside, I looked confident, assured, and not to

be fucked with. I kept my eyes on him, but there was no expression to be read on his face. Then, suddenly, he called out to one of his henchmen, who strolled over and leaned down within earshot of Rio, who muttered something. I nearly lost my breakfast. What the fuck was going on? Damn, was he trying to dismiss me? *Shit!* I screamed inside. My composure held on the outside. I was a boss, and I couldn't afford to get all twisted up. I would not fold, not even for Rio Zarrio. No matter the outcome, I was going to walk out with my head held high. Dignity meant everything to me.

Rio ended his secret conversation with his henchman, then he glared out at his compound. My eyes still remained locked on him. After several moments of torturous silence, he finally spoke. "Calvin. I remember his loyalty; he kept his word. This means everything." He laid his eyes on me again. For some reason that was a relief to me. "And I have eyes on you that say my bet is good. You . . . we do businesses. I watch you take over."

In that instant I stopped breathing. His words repeated in my head. *You . . . we do businesses.* It all felt surreal. Had he really agreed? His right hand went up and his cigar was back between his lips. Had it really been that easy? I couldn't speak.

"There's just one thing," he decided to add.

Again, I stopped breathing, and I could feel perspiration starting to seep from my pores. Was now the time that he'd remind me that my life and that of my son was on the line?

"I want to congratulate you, Governor, on your win," Rio declared.

I sighed. That was it. In his presence, I had somehow forgotten all about my political position. "Thank you," I managed to say.

He smiled. "Of course! I want you to settle into your new role as governor, but once you are all the way inside, hook me up with the upper crust, as all Americans say." I was confused and it must have shown. "Just the ones in the life."

I sucked in and swallowed hard. "No doubt," I assured him. But now I had something to say that was important, and maybe a deal-breaker. "Your request shouldn't be hard, but I really want to keep my political career and my criminal enterprise life separate. We do business, yes. But Mikka is my right hand and I give him the power to connect with you." I was clear and matter-of-fact. This part was crucial to our business relationship; there could be no misunderstandings.

"Now that I'm the governor of Arizona, I must retreat further into the shadows. I hope this is not a problem?" I stated with conviction. I had traveled a long way from Arizona to Spain to meet one of the top international drug lords. But I wanted to show him that I was one of the boldest bitches walking.

Chapter 22

Detective King

As much as I hated to admit it, Tabitha had been right. While she was absent, I would be busy with some case. However, that didn't stop me from missing her, especially at night when I climbed into our lonely massive bed. She was still away, and I found myself counting the minutes until she returned. But I was focused. I had LG crew members front and center for questioning on the murder of Lunzo. I was hoping some news on Boss B's and Sam's murders would surface.

"Man, y'all got me in here on some trumped-up charges. Stop fuckin' around and release me to the streets." TG was getting agitated. He had run the streets with LG tuff before he was murdered. I knew he had some knowledge of what had happened to his partner, and I thought maybe he was the avenger.

Today was my turn to play good cop; at least, that was the plan. I couldn't promise how long that might last. "Listen, I get it. LG was your boy. He was smoked out over what? Territory. We know business got to be han-

dled. Right . . ." I nodded at him. "Disrespect ain't toler-
ated, we get it. Lunzo had to go. He violated."

"Yep," Detective Forbes jumped in. He pointed at TG
and pretended to pull the trigger of a gun. "Pow," he hissed.

TG scowled. "Man, what the fuck that mean?" He
squinted his eyes into slits. "You tryin' to accuse me of silencing that nigga? Nah . . . fuck that." He shook his head
and denied it. "Yeah, I wouldn't have mind doing it. But
that nigga's blood ain't on my hands. Nobody in my crew
touched that nigga," he declared without flinching.

It was my turn to shake my head in denial to deny his
bullshit. "That's how you want it, TG? Denial?"

"That's how I fuckin' want it. Now, can I please go?"

I stood up and excused myself, and Forbes followed
close behind. We passed coworkers and other suspects or
victims being brought in. We headed to another interrogation room, where Skeet, another one of LG's homies was
being held. I twisted the doorknob and stepped into the
room first. I pulled out a seat and sat down. Forbes pulled
out a chair next to me.

"My main man Skeet, we meet again." Forbes broke
the ice, which was our strategy. Forbes had dealt with him
in the past, so he had an idea of who Forbes was.

Skeet gave us an emotionless glare that said, *Fuck the
both of you.*

"Rufus Pain, is it?" I opened the file in front of me and
appeared to look it over. As I expected, there was no answer. I looked up at him and introduced myself. "I'm
Detective King." Still no words came out of his smug
mouth. I grunted to clear my throat. "Look, I know you
are not here to talk. But I'm just trying to clear things up.
Get rid of some of the confusion." I dropped my head
again and pretended to read the file. I knew exactly what
was in it.

My eyes were back on Skeet. "You ever heard of Sam Moore?" I dropped the name to see his reaction. He stayed still, but the shift in his eyes told me he wasn't expecting that name to come up. Still no words, so I continued. "You know Sam . . . he has a baby by Lunzo's previous girlfriend, Michelle."

He screwed up his face. "What the fuck would I know about Lunzo bitches unless I fucked them?" He readjusted himself in his seat.

"True." I shook my head to agree with him. "Have you fucked them?" I asked. Every thought needed to be followed up on.

"Man, hell no, I ain't done that. I don't want that nigga's leftover pussy. Got me fuck'd up."

"Okay, okay, you can calm down. Now, I know y'all's crew rivals, but y'all know some of the same people. I just thought that since Michelle was good friends with your sister Dasia." His eyes bucked open at the mention of his sister.

He softened his hard stare. "Look, Detective, my sister is a college student; she clean in these dirty-ass streets. She ain't never had to be in these streets. I done seen to that. And I haven't allowed her to fuck wit' nobody from these streets either."

I knew that already, but I wanted to remind him I wasn't leading through the dark.

"So, any talk about my sister . . . pfft." He sucked his teeth. "You can dead that." He hunched up his shoulders and adjusted his weight in his seat. He was getting tired.

The time had come for me to really fuck with him. "Well, I just may need to speak to your sister about her friend Michelle and her deceased baby father."

"Look, man, leave my sister alone. You ain't got to bother her at all. You talkin' to me. That Sam nigga was a square. He wasn't from the streets, like us. He was smart, just like my sister, with her nose in those books. But he got mixed up with the wrong person, somebody running in a different type of circle. I think, and I ain't got facts, but he had a beef with Michelle. That nigga Lunzo probably killed that nigga. Shi'ddd, ask Michelle; her money-hungry ass know."

"What about Lunzo and Boss B? The crew that dominates? All the major players have been whipped out . . . what crew benefits? Come on, man, all we're asking is for you to give us two names. Plea out." I threw the dice. But I had the feeling Skeet was not the snitching kind.

"Yeah, time to save your own ass because the time is coming. I'm coming." Forbes gave him a sinister grin. He was the bad cop today, and I enjoyed watching my partner work.

Skeet huffed and stared Forbes down. "Mannn . . . fuck yo' threats," he sniffed and then shrugged. "And fuck both those dead-ass niggas. They was grimy as fuck!" he spat out. "And while I wish I could bring them back to life and kill them myself, I can't. So y'all can get rid of your fantasy that I'm going to name-drop just cause you say so. Nobody in our crew did that shit. Karma came for their sleazy asses."

We all sat in silence for about five minutes. Then I rose to my feet and exited the room with Forbes on my trail. This time we stepped into my office. I held my head back on my shoulders for a stretch, then sighed. "As much as I want to believe it's them—I mean, in the beginning I had no doubt at all that it was them." I rubbed my right brow, not believing what I was about to admit. "I believe him. This crew, not it." Forbes quickly agreed with me. We both knew what that meant. He and I had to regroup and start over from scratch.

I sat down in my chair, dialed the front desk, and ordered for TG and Skeet to be released back to the streets. "We will go back to the drawing board."

"Do you think the murders were isolated incidents? Different people for different reasons? Like maybe Boss B was killed by an enemy wanting to take his spot? And maybe Lunzo was murdered by a friend?" Forbes started throwing out theories at me. They weren't outlandish, but I knew neither was the case.

"No, I think it could be different henchmen for each job, but the order was given by the same authority," I concluded. But the question was, who?

Chapter 23

Detective King

Later that day

Although we had TG and Skeet in the office for hours interrogating them, I couldn't believe the day was not over. Forbes and I sat in my office for another two hours, racking our brains trying to pull some pieces of the puzzle together. Eventually, we decided to step away from the case for the day and start fresh the next. I was busy going over another case when I got the call that Chief Rogers had summoned me to his office.

"How is your caseload?" he asked once I was inside. He always followed up on our cases, but normally we got an email a day in advance. Today, I had been thrown in the fire without so much as a warning.

"They are going well. Remember that Moore case you gave me a while back?"

"Yeah, yeah, I remember. Any new leads?"

"I think it's connected to the Lunzo case. I just haven't been able to tie anything down yet. Got a few things to follow up on." I updated him, but I had the feeling that wasn't why he'd called me into his office. "So, you wanted to see me?"

"I did." He sighed. I could feel the bullshit coming. "You need to take a step back on some of these cases. Others feel they are not getting a fair crack at the big cases. And you know he who has plenty of medals has the advantage."

I couldn't believe what I was hearing. Like I said, I knew it was some bullshit coming by the uncertain gaze on his face when I entered the room. I counted to ten in my head. I had to remember this was the chief, and while we were friends, he was my superior. "This is my life's work, damn a medal." I took a breath. "Cleaning up the streets and getting justice for mothers like Miss Moore is my medal, which isn't something I covet for a souvenir."

"I understand how you feel, but I'm trying to run a department. I must delegate responsibility. Besides, I don't want to overwhelm you. You have twenty active cases. That's almost double what the other detectives have." I could have laughed at his sudden concern about my caseload. For years I had carried an excessive caseload that exceeded the others'. "I want to take Lunzo's case and hand it over to someone else."

What he said stunned me stupid. "Chief, that case is connected to Boss B. They shouldn't be separated. Besides that, I have been working with this crew for years, and I know them better than anyone else. Not to mention the crime they brought to the streets that still must be sifted through. And now they both are dead, both murdered." My tone was full of astonishment. This idea was ludicrous.

"King, it's not like the cases are leaving the department. You can still, on occasion, cross-check with the other detective to compare the information. You've seen this before. So, you know how it works."

His nonchalance had started to piss me off and I was growing unable to control it. To say I was confused was an understatement. I rubbed my forehead from frustration. "Chief, with all due respect, this is bullshit." And there it was. It had to be said; clearly, he was tripping. "Our streets are suffering right now with the increased gun power and fentanyl. Bodies are popping up daily. You need your best on the job, and we both know I'm it." He needed a reality check.

"King . . . I . . ." he stumbled over his words.

I stood up. The room was starting to close in on me. Either I was growing taller or the room was shrinking. Either way, I wanted out of it.

"Excuse me, Chief, but I have to go." I exited his office without waiting for his dismissal. I could not bear to hear another word from him. I needed to be out of this building to take in some fresh air and be alone with my thoughts.

"What's up?" Forbes met me in the hallway right as I was about to enter my office. I twisted the doorknob and went inside. "So, the chief has some new ideas, huh? Go ahead, fill me in."

"Chief has some new ideas," I repeated with sarcasm. "Yeah, try snatching my case load that I've worked my ass off over and throwing me into early retirement." I exited the hallway, leaving Forbes standing in the middle of the floor where he stood confused. I had no more to say.

Chapter 24

Tabitha

It had only been two days since we arrived back from Spain. We first stopped off in Miami. I wanted to lay eyes on the new territory. Mikka wanted to meet with the crew leaders and make some solid decisions now that we had the green light on the new supply. I was glad to be back in Arizona but not ready to get home yet. I had other business to attend to.

The candy-apple-red, fitted two-piece lingerie outfit I'd recently picked up for myself hugged every curve of my body as if it was painted on. "Damn, I'm sweet." I admired myself in the floor-length mirror. My makeup looked good, and everything on me was in place. *Ding-dong!* The ringing doorbell put an end to my personal love-fest. So, I had to stop admiring myself to get the door. I was at one of my unlisted private properties, expecting company.

"Chief." I smiled at him. His eyes ate me up with the longing of complete lust. He licked his lips as if he was about to have a juicy steak. He nearly jumped over the threshold, he moved so swiftly. He pulled me into his arms and squeezed me tight. *Damn, you feel so good*, he mouthed.

Chief Rogers had been a longtime partner in crime and lover to me, unbeknownst to anyone else. I met him through Calvin. They had grown up together in Baltimore, Maryland, and were best friends. This was a secret they'd made sure to keep private from everyone. The chief had been our guy in the shadows, who kept us posted on what was going on and warned us when needed. He also kept things at bay to protect our business, and that had not changed.

Our hands were all over each other and so were our mouths as we kissed each other with so much hunger and passion it spilled over like a boiling pot. In the midst of our kissing, we managed to make it to the den, where we began to rip each other's clothes off. Before long we were connected as one as we screamed out the pleasure we had waited for.

Satisfied, we lay in each other's arms afterward. "How were things while I was away?" I asked.

He chuckled. "You mean with your husband. That was simple. He's stubborn as hell. You really need to apply more pressure and convince him to retire. He's getting too close to finding shit out. I thought I'd give him a case that might touch him in a sentimental way. In trying to do something to redirect him, I pulled him off of Lunzo's case. But it ain't easy; the guy is relentless. Shit is just hard to do. I have to be sure to make it look legit and not so out of the ordinary. He ain't dumb, so I'm sure his reels are running. I told him I had to share the duties that others felt were overlooked because his strong hold on all the big cases."

"That sounds legit, favoritism in the workplace," I remarked.

"Yeah, he doesn't care about that. He knows what he brings to the force. King is my best detective . . . hell, if not the best one in Arizona. To be honest, if he doesn't retire any day now, he will probably be asked to run for chief again at another precinct. They offered it to him about seven years ago. Did you know that?"

"No, he's never told me that." I was surprised to hear that bit of news. King had kept that from me. All the boring shit he told me about the department, and he'd left that part out. "But don't worry, I'll handle it." I held up my head and kissed him to reassure him.

"How was Spain?" he asked.

"You won't believe it was like taking candy from a baby. Rio Zarrio jumped on board with no hesitation. And just like that, we are about to expand and explode. Miami is a go. Boss B has some territory in Atlanta that is now ours, plus some other plans. Expansion is a must." I slid out of the bed and walked across the room. The bar in the corner had a safe built in behind it, and in it was a briefcase. I punched in the code and it popped open.

"Here is a special thanks for keeping things shifted around on the force." I turned and winked at him. "Favor is always the best." Chief made his way over to me and pulled me into his arms.

"You will always have my favor."

I could feel him ready and at attention. The man was like a machine. I smiled. "You think you are slick. I feel that." I stepped back. He reached for me.

I laughed out loud. "OH NO!" I wagged my finger in his face as I jumped back a bit more. "You've had enough, mister. Remember, absence makes the heart grow fonder." I pointed at his hard-on. "Save that for Wifey when you get home and tell her she can thank me later." I continued to laugh as I headed off to the bathroom. I won't lie, it did look appetizing, but I had to go. I was no ordinary woman. I had time limits if I was going to run a tight ship.

"Come on, Tabbi," he called out.

I giggled as I turned on the shower and stepped inside. He knew me well enough to know even though I was laughing, I always meant what I said. And that was in everything I did.

Chapter 25

Tabitha

"Babe, I'm so glad you're back. I missed you so much while you were away." King gave me a half-hearted smile. "Yeah, work kept me busy, but it didn't replace you. I was disappointed that you didn't call as much as I thought you would," he whined, and I almost rolled my eyes. A crying-ass grown man was not my idea of sexy.

"Awww, my love . . . I was so busy, but I thought about you every second. You forgive me, don't you?" I gave him a seductive grin as I reached across the table and rubbed his hand. We were out on a dinner date at one of my favorite Italian spots. Actually, it was Calvin's favorite spot, but we ate here so often it had grown on me. I truly enjoyed the dishes they prepared, and what I liked most was they had private VIP rooms, which we always reserved. So, when King and I started coming here, I told him it was one of my favorite spots. Therefore, I wasn't surprised when I returned and he had made reservations for our date night.

"With plush lips like that, you're forgiven." He raised my hand to his lips and kissed it. "And you look so good tonight. That skirt says *hello* to every curve you were blessed with."

"Thanks, Mr. King. Now, refill my champagne glass," I ordered him sweetly.

"Always my pleasure." He reached for the glass, his eyes on mine. I played shyly and looked away. But really, I was sick of the affection; it was way too much. I wasn't in the mood. The guy could be too mushy.

"Thanks," I said, reaching for my now refilled champagne glass.

"So, how are you feeling about the transition in political power?"

I shrugged. To be honest, I hadn't even thought much about my new role. The truth is, I was just rolling with the punches. My mind was mostly occupied with the building of the family empire. To me, that was more of a challenge, and I had to make sure things were right for Mikka. Since I couldn't share that with the lead special narcotics detective, I said, "I'm not worried, if that's what you mean. My role as governor was intended for me, and I will be intentional in my role. I have the right people to back me up and we will be fearless in our goals. I'm anxious, though, but I think that's natural when doing anything new."

"What do you think your hardest fight will be? Where will you get the most pushback?"

I sipped my champagne and savored the taste. "That's easy. Getting higher wages for nine-to-five workers. Oh, and creating more jobs for the ordinary person. These obstacles are always the biggest pushbacks. Some think Republicans and Democrats both hang the fence when it comes to livable wages for the lower class. I have to agree they both hide their hands when it comes to this."

"Yeah, well, that doesn't surprise me. I can see money as an issue. No rich man wants to part with his riches no matter who's starving. To be honest, I thought you were more worried about getting help to stop these drugs from getting into our city." I had to contain my facial expression and resist the urge to call him a nigga. All he ever thought about was getting drugs off the street.

Again, I had to watch my mouth. I was so annoyed that I had to force a smile before saying, "Nah, I'm not worried. That's why I got you." He blushed.

"Yeah, I am a force to be reckoned with." King was feeling himself, but I had faked enough smiles, so instead I sipped my bubbly to busy my lips. His smile suddenly faded. "So, I have not-so-good news. While you were away, the chief took me off the Lunzo case. That is one of my most important cases; I really need to be on it. I have reason to believe it's a link to another one of my biggest cases. I just can't understand why the chief is snatching up my cases. He's saying to be fair; he has to delegate the work because other detectives are feeling like they are not getting the good cases and a bunch of other bullshit." For the first time since we sat down, he rested his back in the chair he was sitting on. He had a baffled look on his face.

"Babe, don't stress it. One thing is for sure: The department knows what you can do and have done. You have nothing to prove anymore. Let those other detectives earn their pensions. Besides, I need you. Maybe it's time you put down the badge. Come stand by me. I know I got the job, but as any politician will tell you, as long as I'm in this, I am in the political fight of my life. You know this isn't going to be it for me, right? Next up, senator. I must have you by my side." I stood up and walked seductively to him, and King looked up at me with hunger. Like I said, VIP was a fully private room. No eyes were watching.

I stood over him, reached out, and rubbed his face, then I straddled him. Chief had told me to step it up on my end, to get this crime-solving nigga off the streets. And I was on the job. "I need you to protect me from the wolves. All of those years you spent reading people, you are the man I need on this job. I can't do it without you. Will you do this for me?" I ground my ass into his lap, then nibbled on his ear. He moaned, then cupped my face and kissed me deeply. The nigga was caving like a bridge. I pushed him off seductively, then I sought out his other ear and nibbled on it. When it came to seducing him, his ears were his weakness. I could tell he was going crazy. He buried his head in my chest. "Will you do this for me? Will you sacrifice for me? Will you retire, Detective King?"

Chapter 26

Detective King

Traffic was rolling steadily after we passed the green light as Forbes and I headed back to the station. We had gotten the call that Brittany Miller aka Bossy, who happened to be Boss B's girlfriend, had been picked up on a drug possession charge. This was like an ace in the hole for us. She was really someone we needed to speak with. The fact that she was crazy enough to get picked up on a possession charge was a bonus for us. Someone had told us she had left town, but we knew it was a lie. We knew she'd surface sooner or later, and that day had come free of charge to the state.

"You think she gone talk?" Forbes pulled down the sun visor; on his side, the sun was beaming through.

"Sure, she'll give us the operation in exchange for that conversation we'll have with the prosecuting attorney. Besides, she has two kids in private school and she's now the breadwinner, which means she needs to be out on these streets."

Forbes nodded in agreement. "All true. And I'm sure you'll get it out of her. Sorry I can't be in there; I have to question the homicide suspect Burner." Bruce Burner was a case that Forbes was put on alone. He was being charged with murdering a friend.

I pulled into the station parking lot and put the car into Park. Inside, we headed in different directions. I stopped by the front desk and picked up a few notes on Brittany's arrest, then ducked into my office to grab a few files. I found Brittany aka Bossy sitting stiff, staring at the table in front of her.

I introduced myself. "Hi, I'm Detective Ronald King." She looked up at me but said nothing. "And you are Brittany Miller. Former lady of Boss B."

Judging by the shift in her body language, I could tell she didn't like how I had addressed her. "Good, guess you've done your homework. Now, Detective Ronald King . . . I know some shit too," she snarled at me. Now I have an idea of what this interview is going to be like. I waited. "I know you hunted Boss B and still you got nothing. Well, now he's dead." She shrugged her shoulders. "And that is dead to you and dead to me."

"That is true, but his dealings are not dead. You lived in the house with him and you are not dead."

"Yes, I did live with him. So what? Whatever that grown-ass nigga did had nothing to do with me, okay? I am a college graduate and I own two businesses. So, you have nothing to speak with me about when it comes to him." She was full of aggression. "Now, if you don't mind, I would like to be booked so I can bond out of here." She folded her arms across her chest. I took that to mean her speech was over.

I opened one of the files in front of me and read over it. Most times when I did this, I was just giving them time to think about what I was thinking. It really irritated them, not knowing exactly what the file had in it. Some might say I used it as a taunting tactic, and I might agree. "Actually, there will be no bond tonight," I announced without looking at her.

"No bond? Bullshit!" She got loud. Still, I did not look up at her.

I read off her charges. "Let me see, you are under arrest for possession of more than a kilo of cocaine and over ten thousand fentanyl pills found in a Bentley you were pulled over in today."

"So fucking what? Like I done already told those grimy-ass cops, that shit belong to Boss B, same as that damn Bentley. I just drove it today because my girls wanted to ride in their daddy's car to school. Check the registration; the car ain't mine," she insisted.

"That may or may not be true, but the fact is, you were in possession of it when you were pulled over and the department intends to charge you accordingly." I wanted to be matter-of-fact with her so that she understood. It appeared to me she understood well as I watched the weight of her shoulders drop, and tears form in her eyes.

She sniffed back the tears. "Look, I can't go to jail. I have two daughters out there who will be alone." She sniffed again and wiped at her tearstained face. "What is it you want to know?"

"Names. Who was his Connect? Who was he supplying?"

Her eyes bulged. "Detective, he ain't never told me the name of no one he did business with. Never told me anything like that. I can you tell where the stash houses are, and people who worked for him. He had some issues going on I think with his supply because he was acting really stressed out. He was expanding and made several trips out to Atlanta and Miami, but he needed a bigger supplier." She looked away. "Like I said, he was stressed out. He was beefing with someone who I got the impression he was afraid of. Someone notorious. Someone whose name started with an *M*. I know that because I overheard him mention it to Lunzo before, when he was upset. I didn't catch the full name. Never heard him mention it again. Like I said, he didn't talk about his business to me. And to be honest with you, I didn't care to know. I know the streets well because I had a brother in the game. But Boss B didn't require me to be a hustler. He was proud and respected my education. And I loved him for that . . ." She paused suddenly.

She had said a few things, but nothing I was satisfied with. There were no useful details in what she had said. I needed more, so I started to say, "So, you are telling me . . ."

"But . . ." She cut me off. "There is something else . . ."

Chapter 27

Detective King

I had nearly snatched Forbes's door off the hinges when Brittany finally dropped some important news on me. He and I both raced to the chief's office. It was an urgent situation and we had to get him to hear us out. I didn't anticipate it being easy; the man had just snatched an important case right out of my hands and given it to the least active detective with the least medals. I didn't know what to expect from him. I had known the chief for most of my career, and not once had I doubted his leadership until this moment. I was working on persuading myself that it was for the best. So far, I was failing miserably to accept it.

"You need an arrest warrant for Melissa Logan?" he asked as if he hadn't just heard me.

"Yes, we need to bring her in, in connection with the murder of Sam Moore. I just received some feasible information that might be credible. I already had reason to believe she had a motive."

Without any more questions or hesitation, he signed the order. That was the chief I was used to. Forbes and I rushed out to the last known address we had for Melissa.

"King, I'm still in shock that Bossy gave up that information to you. Hell, I was worried about what she wouldn't say. But I never would have guessed this one."

"Tell me about it." I could only shake my head as what she told me ran through my mind. *There is something else . . . Melissa Logan used to be my friend, but we don't talk much anymore. She told me that you all suspected she murdered Sam, her child's father. Well, I guess she was struggling with this on her conscience when it first happened and she had to tell someone, so she chose me. According to her, Sam came over to her house to take the baby because he found out she was still messing with Lunzo. They argued, he hit her at the door, then he pushed his way inside to get the baby. She said she went to get the gun to scare him off. But when he saw the gun, he tried to take it. While struggling, they fought over it, and the gun went off and shot him. She said that's when she called Lunzo over to help her get rid of the body.*

I couldn't believe it either. Now we just needed the actual truth from Melissa's mouth. It sounded like she murdered Sam in self-defense. If only she had reported it instead of tampering with evidence. I released a heavy sigh. "I just don't get it."

Forbes nodded his head in agreement. "Man, dumbass decisions people make to get away with murder," he groaned. "But back to you, I still can't believe you're going to actually retire."

I had already made up my mind and shared it with Detective Forbes before anyone else. I still couldn't believe my decision. "I can't believe it either." I kept my eyes on the road. "But no rush, right? It's not like I'm retiring tomorrow. We are too close to finding out who Boss B is in competition with and probably responsible for his murder. But first, let's go handle this." I sped up a little more. I was ready to get it over and done with.

The task force, along with Forbes and me, pulled up at the same time. The task force was our backup in case Melissa tried to forcibly resist, and because her charge would be murder, which usually classifies as a danger to others. Forbes and I climbed out of our unmarked squad SUV. Right away I noticed Miss Moore as she pulled in. I wasn't sure why she was there, but I needed to warn her to stay back. I noticed who must have been Melissa's daughter and her granddaughter sitting in the backseat.

She rolled down her window right away. "What's going on, Detective King?" she asked. Her eyes roamed the scene.

"Miss Moore, we are here on business. You might want to take your granddaughter and leave."

"Leave? Well, what is going on? Somebody hurt?" She instantly got anxious and started to get out of the car. She shut the car door to keep the child out of earshot. "Is this about my son's murder? Is this about Sam?"

"Miss Moore, I can't discuss this now, but I need you to stay back. Get back in your car." The task force was in place and ready to move. I turned and walked away. Forbes was already in position by the car, so I joined him with my gun in hand.

The lead task force officer banged on the door. "MELISSA LOGAN, THIS IS ARIZONA POLICE DEPARTMENT PLEASE OPEN UP!" he yelled, but there was no answer. He repeated it three more times along with the banging but received no response. I knew the next course of action would be to kick down her door, and we all move in with our guns drawn on everything inside. I was about to give the order.

"DETECTIVE KING!" Miss Moore screamed my name. "I have a key." That part got my attention and I turned to face her. "I've been calling her all day and she has not answered, but I have a key. I normally go in and wait if she is not home."

"One second; don't make a move until I say so," I called out. Then I spoke with the team and informed them that she had a key and I wanted to use that course of action instead of breaking down the door. I walked Miss Moore up to the door. I stood behind her with my gun drawn in the air, ready for when the door opened.

"MELISSA LOGAN, THIS IS DETECTIVE KING, ALONG WITH APD. I NEED YOU TO COME OUT WITH YOUR HANDS IN THE AIR!" I announced as I moved inside the unit with all reinforcements, who scattered about the house. I approached the kitchen with the lead task officer ahead of me. And there we found Melissa Logan lying on the kitchen floor in a pool of blood, dead as a doornail.

Chapter 28

Tabitha

Even though I was the governor of Arizona, I still had to fulfill a few leftover engagements I had agreed to carry out as mayor. Today, I was attending a ribbon-cutting ceremony for a housing development that had been built for low-income people. The development had encountered a few issues that had pushed the project back, but finally it was ready. I was elated about the project. This sorely needed housing project was special to the city and even more special to me. Literally.

"Governor King." The CEO of Arizona Housing Authority, Daniel McNair, approached me as I made my way up the concrete sidewalk to where the people had gathered. Charles and Mikka were behind me, enforcing their security detail along with two other guards I had taken on since becoming the governor. I stayed back, watching things from a distance.

"Daniel, how are you?" I spoke as we shook hands.

"Just glad you could be here today. I know you have a lot on your plate now that you're the governor of our fine state."

"I wouldn't miss it."

The board members with whom I was familiar stepped in and spoke. "Well, we are ready to get started if you are." Daniel informed me.

"Sure, let's do it." I was ready to get this over with so I could get on with the rest of my day. Daniel said his spiel to the crowd. I got up there and delivered a heartfelt speech. Shortly after that, we were cutting the ribbon. My plan to sneak out of there was derailed when I saw Daniel approaching me with a stranger in tow.

"Governor, I'd like you to meet the new president of the board, Lane Lovett."

"Governor King, it is so nice to meet you. I know you carry a good reputation. And I can assure you the board here has also had nothing but good things to say about you."

"They better," I teased. "No, really, it is nice to meet you as well, Mr. Lovett, and welcome. You have become a part of something great, joining the agencies board."

"Thank you. I'm so glad to be a part of this and look forward to the work ahead. My fellow board members say you have been a huge support of the agency," Mr. Lovett assured me.

"It is my duty to always be supportive of my people and be the best servant leader for them I can be." I started giving him my usual I-give-a-fuck speech. I didn't know if Mr. Lovett was married or not because he didn't have a ring on. But he could barely contain the grin he was wearing while gazing down my throat, making it clear he was delighted by me. And not in a professional way. I was saved as the media from a few local outlets yelled out for me to pose for a picture. *Governor, Governor, Governor.*

Mikka stepped to the side just a bit to make sure he wasn't in any of the pictures, but he remained very close. I posed for about ten pictures and then quickly tried to shoo people out of the way and say my goodbyes at the same time. Then I gave Charles and Mikka the nod that said I was done talking and taking pictures. That meant *get these motherfuckers off me and whisk me away to the car.* Charles and the other two guards approached to get close as Mikka moved ahead to collect his car. He was my driver for the day. Once he had me secured in the vehicle, everyone else was dismissed and we took off.

We had business to discuss, and Jessie was unavailable, so it was just us. "Ma, that Lane dude was smiling at you like a lovesick puppy. Dude looked like he was ready to risk it all. And his grin was ridiculous." He laughed.

"Well, I guess that means he will swallow all my shit and Daniel can get everything he asks for when it comes to increasing these budgets to get more housing developments, as I keep urging. Shit, more developments mean more territory for us." I looked over at my son, who was wearing a sneer that let me know he understood perfectly well.

"'I see Dollar Signs,'" Mikka sang out, then chuckled. "You are wild, Ma."

I grinned at his silliness. "It felt good to be cutting that ribbon in our new territory today. And it's ready just in time since part of our shipment arrives in four days from Spain. I want that shit unloaded, distributed, and gone in no longer than five days."

"I'm already on it. Trey is at the warehouse right now, making sure everything is a go. I already approved one, two, and four. We had to double back to three because we still had some shit to move around. But I'm headed over there soon to meet with him when I drop you off."

"What about warehouse six? It's in the supreme district. I want to be sure it's secured top-notch before we store."

"I already made sure it's secured, and the space will be confirmed by noon tomorrow. I will meet with Locco in two days. And I fly out to Miami on Monday for the shipment that lands from Rio."

"And don't forget to meet up with Mike Petrelli," I reminded him. Mike Petrelli was the main Miami detective we had on our payroll to help keep our noses clean. When me and Mikka stopped over when we returned from Spain, I had upped his percentage in preparation for our expansion. He would now have a heavier load to watch out for, and he was critical in watching our back.

"I'm already on it."

"Hey, Ms. Perez," I spoke to our housekeeper. Ms. Perez had been with me since Calvin, and she was cool. Her mother had worked for Calvin for years, cleaning his first car lot and first small house. When he expanded his car business, and we bought this bigger house, she had referred her daughter, Lola Perez. Ms. Perez had retired early at the age of fifty from her factory job because of a back injury and she could no longer lift heavy things.

"Hi, Tabitha, how are you? I haven't seen you in over a week."

I sighed. "Whew, I know. I've been extra busy. How are you doing, though?"

"I'm good. Getting those great-grandkids this weekend, so I will be busy. But I love having them. They keep me young; at least that's what I've been told." She laughed.

"Aww, it has been so long since you brought them out. Kiss them sweet faces for me and I'm going to hit you with an extra bonus this week so you can show them a good time. No cooking. My orders." I smiled. Just like Calvin was generous with her mother, I did the same. I paid her sixty thousand dollars a year and that didn't include bonuses. For me, it was a tax write-off from Calvin's car lots, which I still owned and operated.

"You are so good to me. Thank you. Mr. King is out back by the pool," she informed me. My feet were killing me standing in heels all day. I made my way to the laundry room, where I hopped out of my high heels and slid into a pair of Gucci slides I kept stored in there. Outside, I noticed King sitting around the lounge table with a bottle of Hennessy resting on the table.

"Day was that bad, huh?" I referred to the bottle of Hennessy, meaning he was in the need of something strong and would get straight to the point. That brown liquid was always the answer.

Whatever was on his mind had him so deep in thought that he didn't even notice me walking up. My voice had startled him. But he smiled at me despite his tribulations. "Now that I have laid eyes on you, it's all better." He stood up, stepped around the table, and pressed his lips against mine.

I grunted, "Mmm . . ." I pretended to be savoring the taste of his sweetness. "How sweet that is."

"And there is more where they came from," he said as he pulled out a chair for me to sit on. He then made his way back around to his side of the table.

He dropped down in his chair. "Wine or a shot?"

"I'll take both, but let's start with a hard shot."

"That sounds about right to me." We both busted out laughing. He poured my shot, and the sound of it filling the glass was soothing to my ears.

"So, what's with the Hennessy on a weekday?" I pried. I reached for my shot with eagerness to swallow it. I wanted to feel that brown liquid nurse me back to sanity.

"Babe . . ." He shook his head, then roared with a groan. "First off, my last couple of days have been crazy as hell. I've been trying to solve the case of a murdered father only to find out it was at the hands of the baby momma, who herself is now a murder victim. Therefore, leaving a motherless, fatherless child."

I lifted the shot glass to my mouth and emptied it. It burned, but it felt wonderful. "Damn, that is crazy. As if Arizona doesn't have enough problems already. How unfortunate."

"Well, thankfully she has a grandmother who is more than willing to raise her. Regardless of the fact that it was her son that her mother murdered."

"Okay, just pour me another shot. Because that whole story is just too deep, I need to be drunk to process it."

"Indeed," King agreed. "Enough about my toxic day, how was your day, babe?"

"It was okay actually; the new terr . . ." I nearly bit my tongue off, trying to stop myself from saying the words *new territory*. What the fuck was I tripping? I needed to slow down on the Hennessy shots; they had my tongue loose and my brain relaxed. "Ahh . . ." I raised my glass in the air. "This Hennessy has a girl tongue-tied." I played it off as if I meant to say something else. "But as I was saying, I cut the ribbon on a new housing development for low-income families. You know, it seems there's just never enough housing. But AHA is revitalizing and growing to help with this need for more communities."

"And with you as governor, the sky is the limit, a blessing for all those in need." King smiled. And I wanted to laugh. "I'm so lucky to be married to a woman with a selfless heart, always thinking of the best interests of others. I bow to your servitude for others."

He was such a poor, dumb guy. I downed another shot, thinking to myself, *servitude*. What a funny guy.

Chapter 29

Detective King

It felt like I had just closed my eyes when no sooner was I awakened by my ringing on-call phone, which meant homicide. It was three minutes after three a.m. when I glanced at the time. I loved my job, I truly did, but the one thing I loathed about it was being woken up from a deep sleep. After twenty years I still wasn't used to it. But it was one of the hazards of the job, so there was no use in dwelling on it. When I got that call it was something serious. Someone had been murdered and the evidence was fresh, so when I hit that scene I needed to be wide awake, refreshed, and ready to solve the case.

I arrived on the scene. All I had been briefed on over the phone was that a husband had been shot and killed. His wife was able to get out of the home safely with the baby. One look at the body lying on the ground and I knew the victim whose blood was still fresh in his body. Van Buren was another small-time dealer in the area, but he was known for robbing other crews of their stash.

"What do we have here?" Forbes was now standing next to me.

"Take a good look, it's Van Buren," I disclosed, nodding my head toward the blood-riddled body.

"Van Buren the stickup kid?" Forbes's eyes bulged as he looked down at the body. He shook his head. "Damn, sure is him. King, this shit is wild." He slid his hands into his pockets then sighed. I could feel where he was coming from; bodies were popping up everywhere.

"AGHH, AGHH, AGHH!"

Forbes's and my head snapped around to the gut-wrenching screaming coming from behind us.

"PLEASE, LET ME SEE HIM. HE'S MY HUSBAND. PLEASE!"

Two uniformed cops were trying to hold up the woman who insisted she was Van Buren's wife. She was hysterical as she tried to break her way free to see the body. I insisted they let her go. The body was lying out in clear view, the coroner was out, and we were still checking him over for evidence.

"Mrs. Van Buren, first let me give you my condolences. My name is Detective King, and this is my partner, Detective Forbes. We will be the lead detectives on this case," I informed her. Next, I asked her straight out if she had seen anything out of the ordinary. I knew this moment was difficult for her, but the first forty-eight hours in a murder investigation are critical. And if she had been an eyewitness, we needed to know now.

Her face was as white as if the blood was draining from it. She was shaking, but she started talking. "Detective, I don't know who they were," she claimed right away. Honestly, that part didn't surprise me. A lot of the time victims were afraid to reveal who their captor was. "But I do know what they were after." Her voice trembled. She glanced over at Van Buren on the ground, grunted, and started to cry again. But she huffed back her cries and went on. "Van had several kilos he was hiding and supposed to take out of town in a few days. I don't know this for a fact . . ."

She sniffled and wiped at her face. "But I think he stole them." She shook her head. I could tell this bit of information angered her and she was embarrassed. "I told him no. I begged him to stop doing that shit. I was afraid because of it and threatened to leave, but he claimed it would be okay. That who he stole it from had plenty and wouldn't come looking for it . . . but I didn't believe him." She cried some more. "Detective, what if they try to find me and the baby?" She was shaking, huffing, and crying.

"Listen, don't worry," I told her. I motioned to the two officers who had tried to hold her up earlier. "What's your full name?" I asked.

"Maria . . . Maria Van Buren."

"Well Mrs. Maria Van Buren, we are going to take you down to the station for an official statement. Then we'll see what we can do."

Back at the station, we took Mrs. Van Buren's statement and were about to wrap up our meeting when she handed over a key and declared, It was where the kilos were stored. Right away we made the decision. We knew for certain that whoever Van Buren had stolen the drugs from, they were looking for them. What better way to taunt them than with a live viewing of their goods in the hands of the DA? And my speech was clear. *These seized narcotics that are believed to have been part of a heist will be in the hands of the DA. Anyone who wishes to claim them may do so. The war on drugs in our city is inevitable and we will not stop until they are off our streets. The day of conviction is here."*

"What a day! This drink is much needed. Bottoms up!" Forbes took a huge gulp of the glass filled to the brim with Budweiser. After a taping with one of our local news stations, we decided to go grab some food and cold brews. I left home at three o'clock in the morning, and time had flown by, what with going to the scene, then back to the station to question our witness, and finally seizing the drugs. It was almost dinner time and we were exhausted and hungry.

I also had a cold Budweiser in front me, but I was nursing the glass mug instead of drinking it. I had so much on my mind with these cases, it was crazy. And here I was talking retirement. I ran my hand across my frustrated face. "These bodies are popping up everywhere. I got to get this shit off our streets before I retire. And this isn't your typical Boss B crew shit we got going on here. See, they are struggling for product right now. They gotta be." I shook my head trying to figure out whose product this really was. Who had enough juice in the streets? Had they gotten rid of Boss B? Was this product theirs?

I snorted out loud because I was so annoyed with trying to figure it out. I had to relax. "Enough of this work shit. I need to drink my beer and get in your business." I chuckled.

"Aww, damn . . . this ain't good. Let me get another drink." Forbes laughed.

"Any excuse to knock them back, huh? I get it. Now, how's the dating going? You been energized and extra calm and shit," I teased him.

Forbes shook his head in agreement and let out a laugh. "All right, you got me. Man, I ain't going to lie. She's great, smart, successful, fine, and full of energy." He grinned hard and all his teeth were exposed.

"All good, then, I knew it."

His grin disappeared. Forbes dropped his head and looked at his beer but didn't pick it up. "I'm really starting to like her, but . . . but I'm apprehensive, though. This life we lead is hard on a relationship. It broke up my last marriage. You know . . . you were there." He looked off at nothing, then back at me. "I'm just saying I can't go through that again."

I could see the pain in my partner's eyes from just reflecting on it. I felt bad for him. There were no words to describe the hurt of loss, even a breakup. "I understand the pain that you are feeling. I know all too well . . . the loss of Joyce. But even being alone on purpose forever will not guarantee you happiness. There's no trade-off for safety." I hated to be the one breaking the harsh reality to him. But now was the time to be honest.

He nodded, agreeing that he understood, but the depth of his apprehension was on every angle of his face. He lifted his glass back to his mouth and finished it off with aggressive thirst. The empty glass made a thud as he sat it on the table. "Well, I'm not sure about my future life, but what I am sure about is that gangster-style press conference you did tonight. That got some dealer somewhere reeling, knowing their product was stolen and is now in the hands of the DA and the feds. Whewww. Man, they must be pissed."

"Nah, more like they fucked," I remarked matter-of-factly.

Chapter 30

Tabitha

To say I was livid would not even begin to describe how I felt. I had nearly run out of my office to Mikka's house on foot when I saw the evening news. My husband had not warned me that he was going on television for his fifteen minutes of fame. But fuck it, that wasn't even the problem. The fact that he was on the news, flashing what didn't belong to him, as if it was Bob Barker of *The Price is Right* game show. I was frantically pacing the floor at Mikka's so long and hard that I'd surely ground a hole where I marched. Mikka and Trey were just as pissed, but they watched me like a pair of hawks.

"Tell me again how much money is tied up in those kilos my own dear husband is laying claim to on the news?" I had my back to Mikka and Trey, holding my bottom lip with my teeth.

"It's worth a million five, flat." Mikka's tone was uneven.

"A MILLION FIVE!" I boomed. "THE FUCK, MIKKA!"

Mikka huffed, "That nigga Van Buren is known for scouting crews, then robbing their stash for his own lil corner that he runs. Two days ago he hit one of our spots that had just been re-upped from the old stash. That nigga was planning to hit another when we found out it was him. Me and Trey set out to headhunt him ourselves. The nigga, like Omar from that show *The Wire*, he lay in wait."

I couldn't believe he was quoting TV characters to me. I sneered, "Well, this ain't no damn TV show, right? This real life . . . and because of that fuckin' peon, we about to be put under a microscope. King got that shit in his hands now. That nigga's like a hound. He can probably sniff whose stash it is. We don't need no heat. NONE, MIKKA!" I barked at him.

"I know. Trey and I got this under control. Now we need to know who gave up that product to the cops. The nigga would not give up the product, which was not a surprise. He knew his fate no matter what. So, you know he was dealt with accordingly."

"And you're not done. While I hate to lay bodies in the street at this time, a message has to be sent. Not only for his small crew, but for anyone who might dare be a follower with misjudgment. I want the bodies of two of his main crew leads. The message must be loud and clear. I want any territory that he thought was his to be null and void! And anyone who tries to override that is a dead body."

Mikka locked eyes with me; he understood. "Done," he replied. His body language said he was ready to get started. I was eager to get out of his way so that he could. Without saying another word, I slid on my Chanel sunglasses, even though it was dark outside, and left. I had to get back to the office even though it was late. There were a few documents I still needed to read over and sign before the next day.

Chapter 31

Detective King

For the first time in my career I was starting to feel like if I read one case, I was reading them all. Homicide and drugs were rampant on our streets. It seemed as though for every dealer I nabbed, their absence bred five more. So many grieving parents for one stupid, unexplained reason or another, which mostly led back to a life of crime or narcotics. I had to somehow make a difference. There was a king cobra out there and I had to chop its neck off.

I had been sitting at my desk going over and comparing murder cases for the past five hours. Homicides alone had increased over the past several weeks. Between making arrests on drug offenses and being called out to investigate a new murder, I had been going nonstop. And today I was about to close out the file on Sam Moore. This one hit me differently, though. Sam was a young man actually trying to make his mark in life the legal way. I opened the file in Excel and hit the first key, then stalled.

I sighed as I swiveled around in my chair and gazed out my office window for a view of the city. The sun was beaming, and it looked so beautiful. I longed to be out in it, and besides that, my growling stomach was telling me it was time to eat. I shut down my computer and decided to head out for lunch, something I didn't do often enough. I was a block away from the precinct when I decided what I would eat.

I pulled up to a famous taco truck. I got out of my un-marked squad car and ordered four steak tacos. I climbed back in my car and loosened up my tie. I picked up my first taco, pulled back the wrapper, and took my first bite. "Mmmmph . . ." I shook my head with approval as I sa-vored the taste before swallowing. Mouth open, I went in for my next bite, then paused.

Across the street, I recognized Mikka as he climbed out of his all-white, two-door Porche. I wasn't surprised to see him on this side of town. But I quickly became confused as I witnessed him shaking hands with Locco, a known dealer who was making moves on a big scale. True, Locco was not as major as Boss B had been. But from what I had been able to gather having been watching him for the past twelve months, he had the potential to be. I watched as they disappeared into a local rib joint.

I asked myself, were Locco and Mikka meeting up a chance encounter? No way. Clearly, the way they shook hands seemed intentional. My mind was now reeling with more questions. I was instantly intrigued. What would the two have to talk about? The dealer and one of the security guys for the governor. My cell phone rang, drawing me back to reality. Forbes's name was on the screen.

"What's up, Forbes?" I answered.

"What's up, King?"

"The chief has called a meeting with all the detectives."

Now that was the last thing I was expecting to hear, a damn meeting. "Shit," I exclaimed. "Can't a brother enjoy his tacos?" I glanced down at the juicy taco in my hand.

"What taco . . . man, King. I know you didn't go to our favorite taco spot without telling me," Forbes whined on the other end. We were totally hooked on those tacos. I would've given him the same speech if he had them without telling me.

"In my defense, you were just at the gym this morning. I'm saving you." I laughed.

"Yeah, okay, payback is gonna be a mutha. Get back to the station before I make sure you get a fine," he joked. We both chuckled. The call ended.

My eyes fell on the rib joint across the way. I wasn't certain about what I had witnessed. Maybe I was overreacting. What I did know was, my steak tacos were getting cold and I was not having that. I bit into my taco again, then casually slid the rest in my mouth and chewed. Then I pulled out another one. *Shit, I got to get back to the station*, I complained to myself. Just that quick, I had forgotten the effect those delicious tacos had on me. Instead of finishing number two, I wrapped it up carefully and slid it back into the bag. I looked out of the rearview mirror, then checked my side mirror before pulling out.

Chapter 32

Tabitha

"IS THAT BITCH DEAD?"

I focused my eyes on both Mikka and Trey. I had met up with them to see if they had taken care of business. Maria Van Buren had a date with consequences. Who did she think she was? Did she really think she could hand over my product to the cops and I would never know? Did she think she could cross me and still keep on walking and breathing in this city? Had the cops not shared with her the consequences of her crazy-ass actions? Had her man's death not taught her anything? All these questions raced through my mind, but the only answer I could come up with was the woman must have been crazy because she basically signed her death warrant the moment she made the decision to cross me.

"Yes, Trey took care of that shit."

"Just like you said, and the body is out so she can be found," Trey assured me.

I knew he would follow my instructions to the letter. He was loyal, just like his father Rocko had been.

"Shi'dd, the crime scene probably crawling with cops right now," he said.

My arms were folded across my chest as I thought of the lost kilos. My product gone, all because of one weak female. "I can't believe that bitch just gave up my product like it was a donation to the poor. I swear, if I didn't have that event at the clinic today, I would've cut that bitch's throat myself. FUCK!" I screamed. I was so angry, I could feel the heat rising off of me. The very thought of my product being in the hands of anyone except me was too much for my sanity.

I was seething with anger. "Detective King thinks he's so fucking smart. Thinks he can one-up me. Wait until he sees that whore's throat cut wide open. I hope the message is loud and clear that his actions killed that bitch. Hmph," I huffed. "Taunting me with my own supply. Yeah, we will see," I half laughed. "Yeah, I'm going to get the last laugh. Always."

I reveled in my victory as I thought of how fucked up King would feel when he realized what his actions had resulted in. "Mikka, police traffic is heavy on the East for the next two days. I need all stores closed over there."

"How are we supposed to shift clientele without overflow? Mikka asked.

"You won't; they are going to have to figure that shit out on their own. I ain't worried about that. I want you to re-up the West with extra product. And I want all payouts done tonight in that area. Trey, don't forget to have your ass on time tomorrow night in Miami. Handle that business and get right back," I ordered him.

"No doubt," he pledged. "Early in the morning I gotta run down and put money on Lamont's books for the month, then I'm out."

"Lamont Bell with his weak ass?" My eyebrows raised

with question marks. I was surprised to hear him talk of Lamont. "You still put money on his books?"

Trey hunched his shoulders in submission. "It's my mom's. Ya know how dat shit be. It's her brother's son. She ain't forgetting him." Trey was convinced.

Lamont had hype back in the day. He was a number one shooter and feared on the streets, but his fault was bigger. He became weak for the little hoes around town that always had him trickin'. That shit got him caught up. When your head isn't in the game, that is always the first step in your downfall. Ever since Dale's murder, I stayed mindful of that. It was the number one lesson I tried to keep Mikka focused on. Now I had to work on Trey, but that would have to be another day.

"Just handle my shit." I rolled my eyes. I really wasn't in the mood. "I'm calling it a night. I need to be home with my husband when he gets word that his snitch got her payback. It'll be something to see." I looked at my watch to check the time. "It's so late. It will probably make the morning news, though," I predicted. It brought me inner joy, just imagining the look on King's face. I nonchalantly but swiftly flew out of the door to get home. I wanted to be home to see his face. Either way, I had a show to watch. I was looking forward to seeing his pitiful face whittled with guilt when he heard the news for himself. It was going to smack him hard.

Chapter 33

Detective King

I can't say I was surprised, but I definitely felt responsible standing over the body of Maria Van Buren. I'd rushed out to the crime scene when I got the call. Once again we were hovering over a body, searching for evidence. "This shit is connected to the drugs. Somebody's mad." I bent down to get a closer look at her bullet-riddled body. The coroner hadn't showed up yet.

"Maybe . . ." Forbes said. He didn't sound convinced, though. "Or maybe she was withholding info that somebody needed. We can't be sure that whoever killed Van Buren knew his wife knew anything about what he was doing. I mean, the product was stored in another location and not at their house."

I chewed over his assumption. "Yeah, well," I hummed. I wasn't too sure that I believed that one. But it was never good to throw out any possibilities up front.

"Detectives," Chief Rogers greeted us. He didn't always show up at the crime scenes, but sometimes he went out of his way. Lately, he had been dropping in on more of them. With so many bodies dropping like flies, guess he thought he'd patronize us.

"Chief," we both acknowledged at the same time.

He stood over the head of Maria's body, gazing down at her while chewing on a toothpick. "I'm getting word that this was about a robbery. Somebody thinks Van Buren left some money behind."

Another theory. After studying the dead body for several minutes, I stood up. "No, this was an execution. Killing her was the reason for the visit. This is a message." The more I examined the bullets that were pumped into her, the more convinced I was.

Chief Rogers bent down to examine the body more closely. "Why is her shirt removed, and her pants pulled down?"

"Staged," I said flat out. I too had questioned that upon arrival. The exact bullet holes told the story. This was a professional and it was very personal.

"I see what you mean." The chief got back to his feet just as the coroner showed up. Forbes had stepped over and was helping keep back the crowd that had started to gather.

"Look, hurry up so she can get covered up. Clean up this scene and clear these people out of here. The news outlets are crawling all over the place because of the story a week ago. I don't want them connecting these two stories." Suddenly, he seemed agitated. The coroner had the crime lab go ahead and snap pictures of the body. I jumped in behind the chief as he walked away.

"Chief?" I called out to him.

He stopped walking and turned to face me.

"This is no coincidence. Even you know that."

"King, I don't know that. And you can't know it for sure. Yes, I agree with you that it appears to be execution style. But you have a woman with no shirt on and her pants pulled down. The word already out is this was a robbery gone bad. It's not looking like a hit over that drug interview. Now get this half-naked woman off the streets and clear the scene. Then report back to the station."

Before I could respond, he stormed off. I stood stupefied for a brief second before walking back over to the corner.

Forbes was next to me again. "There are no bullet casings in the area," he pointed out. "Not one."

"Why don't you share that with the chief? No casings. Professional hit. This fucking bullshit," I snarled, then walked away. I was done for the night. Forbes could make sure the scene was cleared. I needed to clear my head.

I walked inside the house and breathed a deep sigh of relief. I was glad to be home, out of the streets and not on the job. I headed straight for the bar and poured me a drink. I took a shot of Crown, then poured another one for the road. I stepped out into the hallway and headed for the stairs.

"Baby, I thought I heard you come in," Tabitha said. "I hope you're hungry." She was smiling at me. She stepped in close and kissed me on the lips.

"You cooked?" I asked.

"Nah, I just picked up some Chinese," she replied.

I was glad she hadn't cooked. I would hate to tell her I wasn't hungry after she'd gone through all that trouble. She worked hard as it was, so when she took the time to cook, I liked to show my appreciation.

"Okay, I don't really have an appetite just yet. So I'ma go take a shower and unwind first." I lifted my glass to her, thinking this would give her an idea about how I was feeling.

I stepped out of the hot, steamy shower and held my head back. The hot water had steamed off some of my growing frustration. Standing at the sink, I ran my hand across the foggy mirror and gazed at myself. I could see the exhaustion in my eyes. Maria Van Buren ran through my mind. How could the chief not see the two cases were connected? I was baffled.

A text came through.

Wife: *Babe, come on down for dinner.*

Me: *Be down in a sec.*

We sat around the island in the kitchen. I mostly stared at my food while sipping on some wine.

"You haven't said much. How was your day?" Tabitha asked. "Are you still not hungry?" She eyed my plate as she forked some orange chicken into her mouth.

"Nah, I don't have an appetite yet. This day has been crazy. You know, we did the interview on the news about the drugs that we had in our possession from a victim. Well, we think her husband robbed a dealer of those drugs. We came in possession of those drugs because of her. Now she's dead . . ." I dropped my head. I almost felt ashamed to say it out loud to my own wife. "I think she's dead because of me. Me getting on the news taunting whoever those drugs belonged to."

"Come on, King, babe, you can't blame yourself for that. She made a choice to be involved. To help you all out, to do what she thought was right. Besides, how would anyone know she told? Her name was never mentioned on the news, was it?"

"Of course not. But I'm sure the dealer probably expected that someone close to Van Buren knew where the drugs were. Who else would be that close to him beside his wife?"

Tabitha glared at me, then shrugged. "Maybe . . . but not necessarily. Sometimes things are not so black-and-white. You must not blame yourself, babe. Solve the case first. Catch the killers." She picked up her wineglass and drank from it. I appreciated her positive speech, but I wasn't so sure.

"Hmph, well the chief thinks it's a robbery, so he'll probably try to pass it off to someone else or limit my time on the case. He's really been tripping lately."

"Babe, I'm not sure if you realize it, but you have a lot on your plate and the chief knows it. I genuinely believe he has your best interest at heart. Trust his leadership."

Not once since I had been on the force had I ever counted my workload as unpleasant work. I viewed my job as who I am. So in retrospect I never felt overwhelmed or like I had a full plate. For me, it was never enough. Maybe from the outside looking in, perhaps I could see Tabitha's point of view on the chief's prospective. I sipped my wine with a little more understanding. I put down my glass for the first time since I had sat at the table, picked up a fork, and tasted my orange chicken.

"Babe, this is good." I chewed. I left out the fact that it was ice cold.

"Anything for you, Detective King." She grinned.

Chapter 34

Detective King

With the help of my wife, I had been able to release my guilt just a little after arriving home from the horrible scene where Maria Van Buren was murdered. I still couldn't shake the guilt I felt completely, but I knew it was my conscience playing around in my head. I woke up with the need for coffee and made the kitchen my destination. My cell phone rang just as I reached into the refrigerator to grab the half-and-half creamer. I shut the door and skipped back over to the counter. Gia was lit up on the screen. At the sight of her name, my lips couldn't help but form a smile. "Hello," I answered.

"Hey, how are you?" she asked.

Not prepared to tell her how I really felt, I sighed. It would've been so much better if she had just said *hey*, but I hated to lie to her. Gia didn't like lies, not even white ones. She preferred honesty at all times.

I reached into the cabinet and retrieved a coffee mug. "This morning that might be a tricky question. But now that I hear your voice, it's all good." I set my glasslike coffee mug on the espresso machine.

"Wait, what's going on?"

I knew that would be her follow-up question. "The force, but it's all good." I tried my best to sound nonchalant. "I'm so glad you called, though." I made another attempt at changing the subject. I continued to try to put a distance between her question and my answer. "I've been so busy I haven't had time to call you."

"I figured as much, and I've been busy too. But I was thinking about maybe flying out there soon. It's been a minute and I really need a break."

There was another reason for me to smile. We lived so far apart, I was always glad when she came to town. "That would mean so much to me. It will do me good to see you."

"It has been a minute. Tell you what, I'll let you know so you can plan to get away," Gia said.

"Good, make it soon." I really longed to see her, especially since I was feeling so detached.

Tabitha caught me off guard as she rounded the corner wearing a smile. I hadn't expected her to be down so quickly. Normally, I would already be sitting down and halfway through my coffee before she came down. "We will talk later." I wasted no time ending my call with Gia.

I picked up my glass mug.

"Was that Forbes?" she quizzed.

"Yeah, I gotta run soon after having this one cup," I lied.

"Babe, you need to invite him over soon, and his new friend."

"Yeah, I'll do that."

Tabitha had taken Forbes in since she and I had started dating. She treated him the same as Joyce had. I opened my briefcase, which was sitting on the table in front of me, and pulled out a file. I sipped my coffee just as Mikka popped into my mind. I had to admit the curiosity of his being in the company of Locco had puzzled me in some way. I gazed over at Tabitha as she opened the refrigerator and fished out the Italian sweet cream she used in her coffee. I watched her closely.

"Babe, Mikka has some really nice things," I started to say. I almost hesitated, but I went on. "He drives a Porsche and has a Mercedes G Wagon. And he lives in a house that I'm sure cost close to a million dollars." I dropped facts, not questions. I wasn't sure what I was getting at, but I said it anyway. I quickly decided not to mention Locco.

Tabitha carefully poured the creamer into her coffee. She stirred it slowly and carefully. "Umm-hmm," she replied, her tone nonchalant. She continued to stir her coffee, never looking up at me. From her body language, she appeared clueless about what I had said.

"How does he afford the lifestyle he has? I know he is the head of your security. But . . . I'm sure, or maybe I'm assuming, the income he earns from that can't pay for all that." This time my tone screamed sarcasm. Maybe now she would give me some eye contact.

Finally she looked over at me, but everything about her read nonchalance. She gave me a light shrug. "Okay, so you're asking me how he can afford these things?" This time I felt her tone held a bit of sarcasm. Her coffee mug went slowly to her juicy lips. "Ummm . . . now that's good," she replied, then grabbed a bagel from the box Lola had brought in. She strutted over to the table to join me. I waited patiently.

"So . . ." she finally began. "I do pay Mikka well. One, he is very good when it comes to protecting me. Two, I want him to continue. The house he lives in his uncle paid for when Mikka was not yet seventeen. And as quiet as it is kept, his uncle Calvin left him quite a bit of money when he died. Calvin made a promise to his sister on her deathbed that he would take care of Mikka as if he were his own. To put it mildly, Mikka is wealthy. What are you really asking, babe? And why the curiosity?" She eyed me and continued to sip her coffee.

I was surprised at the information she had just shared. Her question kind of stalled me, though. I hadn't expected her to ask me why I had asked. I had tried to keep my tone casual, conversational like, which is really what I was doing. Tabitha knew nothing of Locco. She might have thought it was strange if I tried to explain I had seen Mikka with a known drug dealer. Besides that, she had answered my question about Mikka's finances and now it all made sense. I should have figured his uncle would leave him an inheritance since he had raised him. "No reason; I've just always wondered how he lived the way he did. Thought I'd ask you."

"Sure." She gave a light chuckle, then again sipped her coffee. "It sounds quite nosy."

"It does, huh." I laughed. The alarm on my phone startled me, I had almost forgotten I'd set it. I sometimes did that, so I didn't let the time pass by. I shut off the annoying alarm ringtone. "Dang, I gotta run. Let's go to dinner tonight. I'll make reservations at your favorite steakhouse."

She smacked her lips and twisted them in a pout. "Babe, that sounds so good. But not tonight. I have a meeting to discuss some new policies."

I straightened my tie, then lowered my lips to meet hers. "Guess I'm eating alone then." My lips gently smacked against hers. I stood up straight and looked at my watch, I bid her goodbye, then I rushed out the door, promising to call her later.

Chapter 35

Tabitha

Since King had opened his mouth and asked me about Mikka and his finances, this morning I was feeling puzzled. I wasn't sure if he was fishing or just being plain nosy, as detectives are known to be. Either way, I didn't like it. I didn't like conversations where I was being asked to justify something. Had he been anybody else, I would've put him in his place and quick. He almost wasn't safe, but I had other agendas, so I played along—nosy-ass cop.

"What's up, Ma?" Mikka greeted me at the door. We had met up at one of the spots to discuss business.

"Hey." I brushed past him and took off my sunglasses at the same time.

"You good?" he asked.

He knew me well and could sense when something was on my mind. I sat my deep-red, small-chain Saint Laurent purse on the table. I turned to face him. "King asked me about your lifestyle situation this morning."

Mikka's face took on the same puzzled look that I had earlier. "Me?" He pointed at himself. "Why that nigga askin' about me?"

I hunched my shoulders. "I don't know . . . it was strange." I replayed King's questions in my head. "Asking how you can afford this and that. He said he was just curious."

"Hmph, that nigga weird. But he is a cop and they be nosy as shit like that. Niggas always got their mind on where it don't belong." He shook his head.

I had thought the same thing, but I was still a bit perplexed. "I have no idea why he would ask these questions . . . but I do know I don't like it. I told his simple ass your *uncle Calvin*," I made quotation marks gesture with both hands, "left you well off. That seemed to satisfy his curiosity . . . I mean, he is aware that Calvin was rich, so . . ."

"I don't know, retirement might not be so good for him. He'll have too much time on his hands, which means he will be all up in our business. Maybe he should just be dealt with."

"Lay him to rest, huh?" I probed further, wanting to know exactly what Mikka meant. "Well, that might possibly be a good idea," I said. Then I backtracked by saying, "Nah . . ." I quickly tossed out the idea. Killing a cop, especially one I was married to, was no small matter. At least it shouldn't be the first option, and for good reason. "He is a cop, after all. And even when he retires, he will be an ex-cop."

Mikka frowned as he appeared to consider my words. The table held bottles of Hennessy, Crown Apple, Jack Daniel's, and Patrón. He walked over, picked up the Jack Daniel's, and filled a shot glass. He downed it, then grunted. "I guess you're right." He set the glass back down on the table.

I picked up the Patrón and poured me a shot. I figured I could use a drink as well. As a matter of fact, I needed about three of them, and I was planning on having them.

"Hey, do you think King ever wonders if we look alike?" Mikka asked with a silly grin on his handsome face.

I wasn't surprised he'd asked that question. It was a valid one. Mikka looked a lot like Dale, but you could definitely see me in him. I saw it all the time. "Hmph, I sometimes wonder if everyone who comes in contact with us thinks that. No one has ever come out and said it to me."

I glanced at Mikka, and we both burst out into laughter at the thought. People looking at us thinking, *damn they favor each other, but he's Calvin's nephew.* People really were dumb. They were so green, allowing themselves to be deceived that way.

"On a more positive note, business is good despite the few mishaps we've had. Profits are on the rise, and I foresee it only getting better," Mikka said.

"Sounds good," I responded.

"But let me put this out there. We need to acquire territory out in Nevada; the demand is strong out there. Their supplies are weak at best. Nobody out there can push the weight and have the manpower that we possess. I have some connections out there and I want to go down and scope something out."

Listening to him, I could only smile. I could close my eyes and easily see Dale speaking to me about his ambition and dreams. However, Mikka had a different aura of know-how. He had been groomed by me and Calvin for a long time. Dale was good at what he did, but he was working on a different level and still trying to elevate himself. Had he lived a little longer, he would've been king of Detroit streets before turning thirty. But his son was on the mark, and I had his back and front. Mikka had made me so proud. He'd shown tremendous growth in the empire.

My cell phone clock started to sing; it was time for me to move on. "That means this meeting is over. I got a quick meeting with the chief, then a PR one."

"Well, Governor, I won't hold you up then," he teased.

"Boy, shut up." I laughed as I reached for my Saint Laurent bag, then rushed out of the door. I had to be on time to meet the chief because I didn't have an extra minute to stay over.

As usual, the chief could barely keep his hands off me. I had only been in his presence for five minutes and I'd already had to break his embrace several times. He grabbed me by the waist yet again and tried to slide in with a kiss. I ducked it and dipped from his arms again. "Chief, get a grip. This isn't about that today," I reminded him.

"Come on, Tabbi, it's like that?" He was relentless and he reached for my arm once more.

"Damn right!" I was adamant. "Now, where is my damn product? I need my shit like yesterday. I thought you had King's ass under control. Instead, his ass is out here running amuck at my expense, literally. But I draw the line when you start fucking with my money." I was getting more upset by the minute, and he knew it.

"Well, I think your message is loud and clear, T . . ." He paused. "That woman had a brand-new baby. Now it has no parents at all."

I couldn't believe his ass of all people was trying to be sentimental. This unfortunately for him was not the time, mainly because I was losing money and possibly customers. "Nigga, are you growing a conscience?" I growled at him. "'Cause if so, now ain't the time."

He gave me a weak smile, but I wasn't buying it. "You know better than that. And I got King under control."

"Really, because I can't tell with his whole PR campaign courtesy of one of the biggest news stations in town." My face was lit up with anger.

The chief tried to come closer, but the steam rising off from me stopped him in his tracks. "Listen, calm down. You know I always got you. And to prove it, I have secured you product from the evidence room." My eyebrows went up with excitement.

"Well, I stopped it short of making it through all the protocol of evidence. It's untraceable and out of sight. King or no one can touch it."

"When will it be in my possession? When will it be available to make me a dollar?" That's what I really wanted to know; I could give two fucks about his Inspector Gadget smarts. The scowl on my face and my arms folded across my chest said just that.

"I just spoke with Mikka before I got out of the car. He is going to meet me in the morning to pick it up." He slowly started to take baby steps toward me. His grin held most of his face like I was a delicious snack, and his hands were outstretched as he reached for me. "Now, can I have my treat?"

I rolled my eyes at him and laughed as he eased his arms around my waist. "Damn, girl, I crave you." His head was in the nape of my neck and he nibbled at my shoulder.

My head fell back from my shoulders and I giggled. "You should," I teased him. "King will be pissed when he can't find that evidence." My giggle turned into a laugh. I could picture King's shocked face as he tore at theories and pointed fingers at everybody but the chief as he made accusations.

"I'm sure he will be. But don't worry your fine self with that small shit. I got his ass under control." His tone was now more of a brag than the weak, unsure voice he had at first. He was trying to impress me, but it would take much more than that.

I suddenly pushed him off of me. "You better," I warned him without the blink of an eye.

Chapter 36

Detective King

I really wasn't in the mood to be out partying and mingling with crowds. But tonight the department was having a celebration for the closing of some of our cold cases. I was happy to know that Sam Moore's case was among the ten-plus cases that were being closed.

Closing cold cases was never a small thing. Since most of them were more than a decade old, when we closed one it meant that a family finally had closure. It really put it into perspective for me as to why I did what I did. Nothing pleased me more than being able to tell a grieving family whose loved one was murdered that we caught the perpetrator. So as much as I would have enjoyed being home and going over a file, this was precisely where I needed to be tonight. I was so glad to have my beautiful wife by my side. With her being the governor, her schedule was always so booked, I almost had to request appointments to see her. So, this meant a lot to me, her making sure she could be here and that she supported me as much as I supported her.

"Babe, you look so handsome tonight, like a juicy steak that I will bite into later." She bit her lip seductively as she playfully flirted with me.

"And I assure you, a brother can't wait." I smiled. Forbes was coming toward us.

"That must be her." Tabitha held her lips tight and allowed the words to slip through the crack of her clenched teeth as she attempted to whisper.

Forbes was on top of us before I could respond. "King, Mrs. King," he joked. We grinned. "This is my friend, Dawn Griggs."

"Hi," Dawn spoke up before Tabitha and I could. She seemed slightly nervous. I attributed that to the fact that she was meeting the governor of Arizona. Even when Tabitha was mayor, we would encounter people who treated her like she was celebrity. I just stood by and watched her work.

"Hi, Dawn. It's good to meet you." Tabitha held out her hand for a shake.

"Ditto," I followed. "So, you are real," I joked. "I was beginning to think my guy here dreamed you up." I playfully slapped Forbes on the back as he stood next to me.

"Ha ha," Forbes mocked.

"You know his imagination sometimes runs wild," I continued to tease.

"Babe, stop it." We all laughed at my humor. Dawn seemed to relax in that moment. "My husband is a comedian, or so he thinks." Tabitha intertwined her right arm around my left arm as she squeezed in close to me.

"Yeah, never mind this guy. He's a rookie," Forbes joked. We all continued to laugh. Dawn seemed to get comfortable in those moments.

"So, Dawn, are you from here?" Tabitha asked.

"Actually no, I was born and raised in Chicago," she replied.

"Oh, you are a long way from home." Tabitha seemed surprised that she wasn't from Arizona.

"Yeah, that I am, definitely." Her head bobbed in an agreeing motion. "But I did my residency here. And I fell in love with the weather . . . well, granted it gets extremely sweltering here sometimes. But it beats the freezing cold and snow eight months out of the year. So, I stayed," she ranted.

"Sounds like a legit reason to stay. So, you are a doctor, then?" Tabitha smiled.

"I'm a physicians assistant, actually," Dawn clarified.

"Okay, that's impressive. Forbes, I guess your days of paying the doctor to treat you are over," Tabitha teased. We chuckled some more.

Dawn jumped back in. "I actually followed your campaign for governor."

"Okay, okay, and what was the people's opinion?"

Dawn smiled. "I only heard good things, I promise." She held up her hands in an "I swear" gesture. "And you definitely got my vote."

"Hey, hey, I told you, no sucking up to the governor," Forbes teased.

Dawn playfully smacked him on the shoulder. "See, we got us another comedian here." She eyed Tabitha and they burst into laughter.

"Did we miss something?" I looked over my shoulder to find the chief and his wife, Leslie, standing behind us.

"Nah, you are just in time. We were trying to establish whether Forbes is a comedian or not. What do you think?" I asked.

"Forbes, funny . . . nahhh," the chief replied.

"Ha, ha . . . high hatters." Forbes waved at us. We all laughed together.

"Who is this beautiful young lady I've never seen before?" the chief asked.

Forbes, still laughing, tried to clear his face. "Dawn, this is Chief Rogers and his lovely wife, Leslie. And this beautiful woman . . ." he wrapped his arm around Dawn, "is my friend, Dawn Griggs."

Dawn outstretched her hand again for another round of greetings. "Nice to meet you both.

"Very nice to meet you as well, Dawn," Leslie added.

"Looks like we might be attending a wedding in about a year." Tabitha poked around for hints.

"That or the ER," Forbes joked.

Dawn nudged his shoulder. "He does not get enough." She laughed.

"So, Governor . . ." Leslie stepped close to Tabitha. "What's the verdict on the tax rise this year?"

Tabitha smiled, but I knew my wife was not in the mood to talk politics. I can't say that I blamed her. She was in governor mode mostly twenty hours a day. Before leaving the house, she had made it clear that tonight she wanted to give her mind a rest. But she was a trooper and pretended not to be bothered that her free time had been ruined by Leslie's question.

"Leslie, nice try." She tried to appear only to be teasing. Not only did I know she didn't want to be bothered with governor work-related questions, Tabitha didn't wish to be baited about decisions that weren't written in stone yet. I watched to see how she would play it. "Let's just say it's up in the air." She gave a grin that I knew was fake but looked so natural. I laughed inside because she had sidestepped that well.

"Sorry for my wife's curiosity, but you know she had to try." I knew the chief was trying to lighten the mood. "I'm going to take her now . . . let's go, sweetheart," he encouraged her playfully.

Leslie was still standing in the same spot, her gaze directly on Tabitha. For a minute I thought something might be wrong. She leaned into Tabitha and appeared to be trying to sniff her scent slightly. "What type of perfume is that?" she finally asked.

"It's a delightful smell, huh?" Tabitha asked. "It's called Royal Princess Oud by Creed. It's simply the best."

"Smells expensive. But I swear, it smells so familiar, like I've encountered it in my laundry." Dawn, Forbes, the chief, and I looked on as we listened.

Tabitha smiled and giggled. "It is a déjà vu aroma, so captivating," she said.

The chief reached for Leslie's left hand. Even though his face held a huge grin, I thought I caught a hint of uneasiness. "Governor, will you please excuse my wife? She always thinks she has smelled something or seen someone before. Come on, sweetheart, let's go visiting so you can sniff out other familiar smells." We all laughed.

"Whatever." Leslie gave a small grin.

Again, for some reason things felt a little off. I wondered if the chief was embarrassed that Leslie had asked Tabitha about politics that at this point were still confidential. He had joked about it when she asked, but maybe he was just hiding the way he really felt.

I turned to Tabitha as they sauntered away. Her perfume massaged my nostrils. "Babe, I told you that perfume entices people. It's aromatherapy for everyone in the room."

"Hmm, looks like it." Tabitha licked her lips, and I wanted to snatch her and run home to bed.

Chapter 37

Detective King

A week had passed since the party, and I was still feeling good about some of the cold cases that were now officially closed. I still had some murder cases that weren't cold yet and needed my attention, so I was all in. My core focus, which I was going after with ferocity, was the crackdown on the drugs that were taking over my city. Boss B was dead, but I knew he wasn't the one I was after. But he could lead me to who my real intended mark was. If I could figure out who was behind his murder, I'd know with certainty who was bringing the drugs into the city. I was more than certain it was all connected. I was also sure that the drugs we confiscated from Van Buren was connected to the supplier. So far, we had not heard anything about that either. I for one was glad those drugs were locked up and secure and not on the streets.

There was a light tap on my office door. Forbes stuck his head in. "Got a minute?" He held up a file, which meant he had some new information on one of the cases that we were working.

"I always got time for my favorite partner."

"Your only partner." Forbes stepped in and took a seat. "I just got the fingerprints back on the Rodney case." He opened the file and pushed the papers over to me. "His prints are all over that damn gun."

"Hmph, I am not shocked. That asshole is a ball of sloppy, same as I'm sure the trunk of his car is going to light up with blood. You put in for a warrant for his arrest?"

"Yep, being drawn up as we speak. When would you like to go out on arrest?" Forbes asked.

Confused by his question, my eyebrows went up. That was an odd question coming from him.

"I was hoping we could go out in the morning. I have a dinner date with Dawn," he explained.

The mention of a date with Dawn and it all suddenly made sense to me. I could only smile. "I see, obligations call. So, this thing is getting serious?" I quizzed with enthusiasm. I sat back in my chair and studied my partner and friend.

Forbes bounced his head back on his shoulders and grunted. "Aww, here you go with that. Why you think that?"

He was not about to downplay this. I sure wasn't going to allow it. "Brother, who are you trying to fool? You, the guy who can't wait to jump outta bed at four a.m. to arrive on a crime scene, are willing to push off an arrest for a murder until the morning. Oh yeah, buddy, this is serious." I used my dramatic tone to drive my point home.

Forbes could only stretch his cheeks back into a huge grin and he followed it up with a chuckle. "Okay, you got me." His hands flew up in the air. "Damn, can't get nothing past your Inspector Gadget ass." We both laughed.

"Damn right. I stay suspicious all the time," I declared.

His face dropped and I could see the seriousness outlined on his forehead. "This time, I want to do things right. And by that, I mean I don't want to scare her off just yet with the demands of this job."

"Aye, trust me, I get it. And you know you've got my understanding." A knock on my office door interrupted us.

"Come in," I called out.

"Detective King, I have the pictures you requested from surveillance." A uniformed officer stepped up and handed them to me.

"Thanks so much," I responded. The officer exited the room. I wasted no time pulling the lid back on the file. "These are pictures of the surveillance of the possible dealer Boss B was beefing with." I was anxious and my heart had started a rapid beat.

"Shidd, let me take a look." Forbes pushed closer to the edge of his seat. I pushed the file over to him before I went any further so he could see first. Right away he started to flip through the photos. "Hah." Forbes chuckled.

"What's so funny?" I asked.

"Man, it looks like we got pictures of some asshole's head for the most part."

"Hell no." I reached for the file, and Forbes slid it back over. I flipped through the pictures and paused as my eyes pinged in on the back of an unrecognizable head, just as Forbes had said. Yet the back of the head was eerily familiar to me. I tried to appear normal and compose myself in front of Forbes as my stomach did flips and I started to feel sick.

The back of that head was in my opinion identical to Mikka's. There was no way I could tell a now babbling Forbes that. I could not hear one word that was coming out of his mouth as he continued to talk. My mind wandered back to the interrogation of Boss B's girlfriend—Bossy. According to her, Boss B was beefing with someone whose name started with an M.

"So, we will meet in the morning and head out with that arrest warrant on Rodney. If you're good with that?" Forbes's words finally came through to me.

I cleared my throat at some point; in my shock, uneasiness, and urge to run to the bathroom and throw up, my voice had failed. "Ummm . . . yeah, yeah. That's cool. Around nine-ish will be good," I agreed as I loosened my tie.

"Yeah, nine o'clock in the morning works. Aye, you good? You look a little frazzled."

"Oh no, man. I'm good. I drank too much coffee this morning; it's kicking in. Think I'ma go out for some fresh air."

"Okay, cool. I have to run over to ballistics to check on a weapon for the Chancey case. I'll have them send you the results later since you will still be here."

"Good, that works. Enjoy your date. Tell Dawn me and Tabitha sends her our best."

Forbes laughed as he stood up. "Oh, I see you got jokes. Later, King."

I gave him a fake chuckle in return.

I nearly tripped over myself getting out of the building. I sat in my car for almost thirty minutes. With the file in my hand, I stared at the picture with the back of the head about twenty times. Each time, I could clearly see Mikka's head. Tabitha and I had dated two years before we married. While Mikka and I weren't particularly close, I had been in the same room with him hundreds of times. I knew how he looked. Not that I was watching him for any speculation, but I was a detective and I paid attention to everyone in detail most times.

I didn't know much about Mikka personally besides the fact he was Tabitha's nephew by marriage. She always said she had pretty much helped raised him since she'd been with her then husband Calvin. When Calvin died, Mikka remained in her life, and they were very close. He had worked for Tabitha as her lead security when she was mayor and transitioned into that same position when she became the governor. Mikka was quiet and didn't talk much, but the conversations we had were always cool. He was always respectful, and he didn't appear to have any problems with me. We just had never built that much of a relationship. Since Calvin was his blood uncle, I got the feeling he wasn't cool with Tabitha marrying again. But Tabitha assured me that wasn't true. Lately, she had been encouraging us to hang out a little more, so we could build a stronger relationship.

Mikka had recently invited me to drop by anytime for a drink if he was home. Today, I would take him up on that offer. I wasn't sure why, but I needed to be in his home so I could look around and, most importantly, get a better closeup of the back of his head. Without hesitation, I drove until I reached his house. I didn't know if he was going to be there, but I took a chance. He lived in a gated community, but he had made sure I could get in when I stopped by, so that was no issue. I pulled up to his house, got out, and rang the doorbell. I fought to keep my nerves in check. I had to appear normal.

"King, what's up, man?" He didn't seem surprised or shocked that I was at his door. His greeting was normal. I expected him to raise an eyebrow or something. I had been to his home several times with Tabitha and a few times without her. Normally it was on some errand she sent me on that included Mikka. But never had I just dropped by without him knowing. But he had left that invitation open. I decided to remind him of that right away.

"Hey, Mikka. I didn't know if you'd be home or not, but I was out this way working on a case. I skipped lunch, so I thought about stopping by for that drink."

"For sure, for sure. Come on in." He stepped aside and I went in. I heard the door shut behind me.

"Come on, let's go in the den. So, what case you out here on?"

"I had to speak with a wife whose rich husband was murdered in a home invasion robbery."

"Oh, that's fucked up. These niggas out here tryna get it. Either that or she set his ass up." He looked at me and laughed.

"Believe me, both scenarios sound plausible. Her grieving doesn't appear to be sincere. I just had to break the news to her that we would like her to take a lie detector test. Let's see how that plays out. If she shows up with her lawyer or alone to take it. Hell, she may not even show up at all."

"Damn . . . that shit gets real."

"No doubt, no doubt," I agreed. I wondered what my next move was going to be.

"Well, you can have a seat and I'll get that shot. Will that be Hennessy, Patrón, or Don Julio?" Mikka named all the liquor he had on hand.

"Whew . . ." I scratched my head as if I was undecided. "That Don Julio sounds so inviting, but I am still on the clock. That Hennessy might make me equally too comfortable. Let's do the Patrón."

Mikka laughed. "Aye, all your assumptions are spot-on." He had a bar area in his house, but we were in the den, so he stepped out. While he was away, I walked around the room and gazed over the pictures, which were few. I looked at some of the things inside. Tabitha had explained to me his financial situation, so I understood how he could afford the things he had. Nothing appeared out of place or suspicious. I took a seat on the couch. The television was playing the movie *Taken*.

"Here's that drink." He placed a shot glass in my hand.

"Thanks, man. So, listen, I know I stopped by because I was in the area, and to get this drink. But I also wanted to invite you to a basketball game. You know your aunt wants us to bond more, and I totally agree."

"Aye, that's cool, man," Mikka said agreeably.

"Well, before I got the tickets, I thought I'd check your schedule. I know you're always busy doing security for your aunt. And I'm sure you have a life outside of that." I wanted to ask what other shit he was into besides security, but that could've made the conversation go left. We were not on that type of terms yet. I had to play it cool.

"Aye, it's cool. Just let me know what games are coming up and the dates. Then we can go from there."

"Sounds good. I look forward to that game. I also look forward to this drink." I tried to release some humor. I lifted the shot glass to my lips and swallowed it all. I was thankful the shot immediately calmed my rattled nerves. "Can I trouble you to use your bathroom?"

"Sure, you know where the one is close by here."

I nodded my head. His house was huge for only one person. He had like four bathrooms in this house. I used the bathroom and then made my way back into the den. The reason I had really asked to use the bathroom was because of the way his head was facing. If I left the room and returned, I would be able to get a glance of the back of his head.

I didn't have time to stare as I entered the room, but I did get a quick full glance. In person, I wasn't sure. "Thanks for the use of the bathroom," I said, making small talk.

"You good. Would you like another shot?"

"Nah, I better not. One is enough. I have to get back to the office, but I'm glad I got a chance to stop by."

"Aigh't cool and let me know about those tickets."

On the way back to the station, I replayed the view of the back of his head over and over again. I thought about him as the guy I had met. Once I was back in the station's parking lot, I picked up the file and glared at the picture some more. Beside the picture I thought of Mikka, the guy I had met and been around for over three years now. Who was he really? If the back of this head belongs to a drug lord, how could I not know that? There was just no way. Maybe this head didn't belong to him. Maybe it was a coincidence that they were similar. I was so anxious to solve this case, my imagination started to run wild. I had to solve this case, but not with these crazy thoughts that Mikka might be a drug lord. But who was it? Would I ever know? I was retiring soon; at least my wife expected me to. Who was this?

"Shit!" I yelled and then forcibly threw the file over my head into the back seat. I could hear the contents as they scattered, and just as they did an idea came to mind. This could be the big break I needed. The seized drugs from Van Buren were bound to have traceable fingerprints. And I would find out who they belonged to.

Chapter 38

Tabitha

"So, how'd it go?" I sat down and got right to it. I had taken a break to meet up with Mikka and Trey. They both went out to Miami and Atlanta to do some collecting and scope the movement on the new product from Rio Zarrio.

"It was all good. We collected, held a few meetings, and scoped the territories. People are buying the shit like it's going out of style. Honestly, as much as Rio fronted us with, I think we could do with more. We are definitely ready and in need for the next shipment. This is only the beginning," Mikka said.

I thought about what he said. I never doubted that we could sell the product he'd given us. The need was always there, and it would only continue to grow. That was a conversation that we'd have with Rio.

"Speaking of shipments, it's time for the next one to come in. It's on the way to Arizona, but the news is Rio Zarrio is coming to town with it."

Mikka had thrown me a fast curveball and I couldn't have been more surprised. My mouth nearly dropped open. "What? Why?" jumped from my lips.

"I'm not sure about that." Mikka shrugged his shoulders at the same time. "But he wants to meet with you."

"Shit." I wasn't ready for this curveball that had hurtled my way. I simply didn't have the time. "I'm just too busy. I barely get to wipe my ass, let alone have enough time to sit down with him to talk. Can't you do it?" I shot Mikka a damsel-in-distress look, but my tone was more demanding.

"He wants us all there. But he wants to meet with you personally. His instructions were clear."

Fully irritated, I sighed loudly. "Fuck it," I said, so tight-lipped that it came out more like a whisper. "I'll switch shit around to accommodate him. Is he choosing the location?"

"Of course," Mikka smirked.

"Right . . . well, everything is in order. His portion will be ten million. Is it all gathered and banded?"

"Yep. Took care of that yesterday. But what are we going to do with the product we got back from Van Buren's fuck-ass robbery? Did you ever thank the chief?"

I looked away as I thought of the thank-you I'd given him. I had paid him well not only with money but with my body. That was his thanks, but I couldn't tell Mikka that. "I haven't had time to do that. I'm the governor. Remember, I ain't got time for the preliminaries." My tone was full of sarcasm on purpose. "Anyway, he knows." I sighed. "But as for the product, I want it to be delivered to Atlanta for sale. I know product is moving swiftly down there. But let's turn it up in the A. Trey, I want you and Lil Rod to take it down, and get it distributed with the crews."

"Got it. Are you still thinking about promoting him? Lil Rod? 'Cause he ready."

I trusted Trey's word, but I was trying more and more to leave these things in Mikka's hands. I looked at him for the answer.

"I see his hustle and his loyalty. I say leave him out in Atlanta to see the product all gone. Let him do the reporting. Then we'll revisit this," Mikka suggested.

Trey nodded his head in agreement. "No doubt, that sounds like a plan."

"If that is all, I gotta go. All is well that ends in profit. Mikka, make sure Rio is on my schedule. I have so much shit to do daily, I don't want it to slip. We can't afford that. Trey, make sure you get Lil Rod set up in the A; lodging, whatever he needs. Then get back here for the meeting."

Trey nodded with assurance. I exited as swiftly as I had arrived, on to the next thing.

Chapter 39

Detective King

"Detective King, I haven't seen you down here in a long while," Officer Angelo said as I approached. And he was right; I had refrained from visiting the evidence room as much as possible. In my opinion it wasn't a pleasant place to be; so many old things—bloody things. The kind of things a person wouldn't be pleased to see on a daily basis and the knowing of what they meant. What bothered me the most was when I'd see things like old tricycles from the eighties that you knew belonged to a still missing or murdered child, and even to this day the cases remained unsolved. But today I had no choice. I was on a mission to lay eyes on the drugs seized from the Van Buren case. I would be putting paperwork in requesting any fingerprints or DNA that was available. In order to accomplish that, I had to get into the evidence room, which was in the cage like vault in the very back.

"Yeah, I know. But I'm back." I gave a slight laugh.

"Well, the process hasn't changed since ten years ago when you were last in here," he joked. "Just need your signature right here." He pointed toward the signature line in a booklet lying counterclockwise on the desk. "If you don't have the evidence ID number, I can get that for you."

"I already have it," I informed him as I set the pen down. I thanked him and headed on inside. The evidence room was kept clean, like any other in the department, but to me it always carried a smell of old moldy boxes. The dust was still thick in the air; maybe it was all in my head, but that's what I always got when I stepped inside.

I shook my head as I made my way down one of the many long aisles that would lead me to the cage. I tried my best not to look at the evidence stacked on shelves or set out in boxes on the floor. Somewhere amongst all this time I had evidence that was stored from my murder cases. Boss B, LG, Van Buren, and various others all had clothes down here that was still being held as evidence. Inside the cage, I searched identity number after identity number ongoing for about half an hour and still I had not come across the one I was looking for. Assuming I had the wrong one, I pulled out my phone and looked at the ID number I had taken a picture of.

Sure enough, it was the one I had memorized. It just wasn't there. Perplexed, I trekked back to my office, sat down at my computer, and typed in the identity number, checking to see if it had been moved to another facility. That did happen on occasion, and sometimes it took them a few days to update it in the system. In taking a closer look, there was no trail of the evidence product. Confused and frustrated I sank back into my chair. "This can't be," I mouthed out loud.

I picked up my phone and dialed Forbes, but he didn't answer. The chief; I had to see him. Maybe he could shed some light on what was going on. I knocked on his office door and he yelled out for me to come in.

"King, my favorite detective. You good?" he said in a cheerful manner.

"I'm all right. Listen, Chief . . . I was just down in the evidence room. I wanted to see the product from the Van Buren seize. And . . . well, it's not there." I didn't know how else to say it.

The chief's face turned to confusion, and he pushed his chair closer to his desk. "Are you sure?" he asked me.

"Quite sure." I had written the identity number on a piece of paper and put it on his desk in front of him.

He immediately picked it up, glared at it, then put it back down, turning to the right of him where his computer was sitting. I knew what he was about to do: attempt to locate it by the number.

"It's not in there. I've already looked." I'm not sure why, but that gesture annoyed me. He should have known I would check the computer before coming to him with it.

He stopped and faced me again. Suddenly his eyebrows went up, as if he remembered something important. "Ah, a few weeks ago we had some items sent over to the overstock warehouse that were never officially tagged. They've had some trouble with things that were not supposed to be in the destroyed pile being destroyed. This was likely one of them."

I wasn't sure if I heard him right, but his words seemed surreal as they played back in my head. "What the fuck! DESTROYED!" My voice boomed. "Chief, do you know how much evidence that was?"

"I'm aware, but King, sometimes these things happen." His tone was too calm for me. Was he trying to maintain professional decorum when this thing was a catastrophe?

"BULLSHIT!" I yelled. I could not control or hide my anger. I paced back and forth, my hand massaging my forehead. I had an instant headache and my head felt like it was going to explode. "I . . . I just can't believe a woman . . . a mother lost her life turning that over to us. And you're just sitting there like some bad meat was thrown out by accident."

"King, I need you to calm down." The chief was still relaxed but his tone was stern. "Remember, I'm your superior," he reminded me, as if I'd forgotten. I stopped pacing and gazed at him. He just didn't get it.

"I hate to bring this up at a time like this. But you've been quite aggressive lately. You really should take it easy." Was he slick trying to threaten me? "I know this work is your passion."

"Hmph." I shoved my hands inside my pockets and shook my head. That was all he had to say, this was my passion? More bullshit! I was over this conversation that didn't seem to be going anywhere. "If you'll excuse me, Chief," I said.

"You're excused, Detective," he said. I exited as fast as I had appeared.

Out in the hallway I ran into Forbes. "I was on my way to your office," he said once I was within earshot.

I kept my eyes focused on my destination, but I said, "Never mind that, I'm leaving for the day." I opened my office door. "I just came out of the chief's office, and he informed me that the product seized from the Van Buren case was accidentally destroyed." Sarcasm and anger outlined my tone with no doubt.

"Destroyed," Forbes repeated, his tone puzzled and dumbfounded.

"Lock my door when you leave," I said as I exited. I had nothing further to say on the matter. If I did, I might explode, and it wouldn't be good.

Before I knew it, I was entering Tabitha's office. When she saw me, she immediately got a surprised look on her face. She wasn't used to me dropping in on her unannounced, especially this time of the day. Normally I was at work.

"Is something wrong?" she asked right away.

I looked at my beautiful, successful wife and did the only thing I could do. I gave her the usual happy-to-see-her smile whenever I was in her presence. This moment was not about me, it was about her. I wasn't here to cry on her shoulder about my problems. What she needed was my full support and I wanted her to know I was ready to commit. "You know, I've been thinking about when you said I needed to put a time on my retirement. And you are right, it's time for me to support you. I am going to finish up what I'm working on. Give me six months to a year and I'm done."

She stood up and walked around her desk to meet me. "And you'll be all mine?"

"All yours." I pulled her into me, and we kissed. The office phone started to ring. She turned around and lifted it to her ear.

"Thanks," she said, then hung up. "Babe, as much as I would love to stay here in your arms and gaze into those sexy eyes of yours, I have to get going. I have a really busy day."

"I'll go if you lay those juicy lips on me one more time." We kissed again, long and hard.

"All right, babe . . . I'll see you later," she assured me.

"I love the way you kick me out with a smile. But I'll see you later, Governor," I teased.

"Sure thing, but I'll be in late, so you can have dinner without me." She winked at me as I exited the door.

I was still reeling inside about the missing evidence and the way things had gone with the chief. But seeing Tabitha had made me feel much better. And I had meant everything I said to her. In less than a year, I would walk away from my career, my passion, and what I thought was my life.

Chapter 40

Tabitha

Just as Mikka had said, Rio Zarrio had chosen the location. It took us about forty-five minutes to arrive, but we finally made it there. I thought we'd meet in a hotel or an unknown warehouse out in the boonies. Instead, we pulled up to a beautiful mansion with a view of nothing but mountains. There were three guards standing outside as I climbed out of the car. Jessie got out to open my door. Mikka and Trey both climbed out and went to the back of the car, where all of the money was.

One of the guards started to lead me inside while the other pushed out the dolly Mikka had requested prior to the meeting to put the money bags on. The inside of the mansion was ridiculously exquisite, with Italian-style floors that were beautiful. Instead of meeting with Rio, I wanted to sit on the floor to talk about who designed them. As luck would have it, I wasn't standing in the same space as Rio. He grinned in his usual suave way. "Tabeetha." As much as I didn't want to be in this meeting, I loved his accent, so I returned the smile. "Just as beautiful as the last time I saw you."

"Thanks, Rio." I had to fight the annoyance that kept creeping back up. I had told him that I had to keep a low profile. However, at the moment that was hardly the case.

"You like my new purchase." He threw his hands in the air, referring to the house.

I looked around as if I was admiring the place. "Very exquisite."

"Glad I can impress the governor." He chuckled out loud.

I gave a half smile. I was fresh out of fake smiles. "Speaking of me being the governor, remember our last visit, when we discussed me keeping a low profile?"

"Low profile?" he repeated, then laughed. "I get it. You're wondering why you are here? Don't you want to see Rio?" For the first time he didn't smile, and that sent a chill down my spine. Had I said something wrong? Had I not smiled long and hard enough? Had he read through my fakeness? Shit, that money better not be short. Was I being paranoid?

"Of course I want to see you. It's always a pleasure." I reached down deep and dug out a grin and edged it with a bit of mild seduction. "And I can't wait to give you this. If I may?" I asked for permission for Trey and Mikka to approach with the bags. They each held two big totes and one of his guards held two. There were six bags in total.

He gave the signal for the go-ahead. As they moved forward toward the big space between us to drop the bags, I was proud to say, "Here is your return." I hoped this smoothed over whatever mistake I must have made.

I breathed a sigh of relief at the return of Rio's smile. "I'm not surprised you are a woman of your word. Calvin was the same. That is why I do business with you. Rio likes two things: his return and to be updated."

I just glared at him. Suddenly I was a ball of confusion. What the fuck was he getting at? I knew it meant something, but I had no idea what. The blank expression on my face was clear and I could tell he recognized it.

"I hear your husband did a live campaign for the city with seized product." And there it was. Damn, he was tripping off that. Rio thought I was trying to hide shit from him. My loyalty was in question, and that was why I had to be here.

"That?" I opened my mouth to explain. "Oh, I can assure you that was all me. Only my product was involved. I wasn't trying to hide it or anything."

And there was that damn smile again. Now *I* had become annoyed. Now *I* was pissed. I wished he'd knock that shit off. "In future, remember, Rio likes to know all."

"Not a problem. We go on?" I asked. Fuck what he was preaching, I needed to know if we were still in business. We weren't dead yet, so he wasn't that pissed.

"Of course, of course," he assured me. Then he turned his attention to Mikka. "Mikka, I hear nothing but good things. You are the future. See before you go, I doubled the product this time." He winked at me.

And just like that, our wish for double the product had been granted without us even asking. That was on my list of requests since I had practically been dragged against my will out to the meeting. But I guess a good Connect knows what the client needs before they ask.

"You're the best," I made it a point to say. I knew he would appreciate my gratitude. All men were like boys. They fed off women's gratitude and need for them. Deep down they were all insecure assholes. Ugh.

Chapter 41

Detective King

Two Weeks Later

The past two weeks had flown by, but I kept busy with a goal in mind: Get the dealer who had flooded my city with drugs and crime. Even the seized drugs being destroyed would not stop that. It was vital evidence but not the end of the show. It did dampen my mood in ways, but I had been able to hide it from Tabitha. I didn't see the need to bother her with department troubles. Today nothing could bring me down. I was the happiest I had been in a long time. Although it had been nearly two months since Gia said she'd come to town, she finally had. Gia was here and today I would get to see her.

Gia brought me all the joy a daughter could bring to a father. While our relationship was a bit estranged, we were both working hard to fix that. Our relationship was touchy for years after we found each other. Outside of myself and Gia's mother, who was now deceased, no one knew she was my daughter and I, her father. Gia was my greatest secret, but not by choice. I had not always known about her. Gia's mother, Renee, had been my high school girlfriend who got hooked on drugs while we were in school. I could remember hearing the rumors and defending her against all of them. Our senior year she had started to hang with a different crowd, and that changed her. We started to argue more and eventually drifted apart. After we'd broken up, she found out she was pregnant and decided not to tell me.

Soon after, she moved to Philadelphia, where she had family. Years later, after she'd unexpectedly died, I found out about Gia, who was by then an adult. To my surprise and almost complete horror, I found out that my daughter—my one and only child—was a drug queenpin in Philadelphia. I could remember literally losing my breath when I found that part out. It was then, at that moment, that I knew I had to keep her a secret. As close as Joyce and I were, I never even told her. However, not once had I ever considered not meeting and getting to know her. Since we'd known each other, I had tried but failed to convince her to get out of the life. But even I knew it was much more complicated than that.

"Ronald King." Gia approached the table with a grin. My heart leaped out of my chest at the sight of my daughter. She looked just like her mother, with caramel-colored skin, a thin nose, and big deep eyes. She was tall, just like me, and could give Tyra Banks a run for her money. One would never take her for a queenpin. I stood up and hugged her tightly. I didn't care who was watching. We were at the Olive & Ivy Restaurant, known for its delicious cuisine. I chose an outside table, so we could feel the breeze and look at the scenery.

"I swear, this is so embarrassing." She chuckled.

"Girl, how many times I got to tell you, I don't care what these people think. I'm yo' papa," I teased. She hated it when I said *papa*.

"Oh please stop this torture or else I'm going to have to crawl under this table." She laughed some more and then we both sat down.

"I'm so glad you finally made it. I thought you had changed your mind. It was months ago that you said you'd be coming," I whined. I said I wasn't going to bring it up, but it was hard not to. We really had to do better at seeing each other more often.

"I know . . . ahhh." She sighed and removed her sunglasses. "I've been so busy. I had to make a run out of the country on some business . . ." She paused and chewed her lip for a minute and then looked off into the distance. She never shared her work with me, and for good reason. "Well, and you know, I had to hold off. But I told you I was coming and look . . . I'm here in the flesh." She turned her gaze back to me.

"And you are. Forgive me, I don't mean to complain . . . it's just that we don't need to let so much time pass before we see . . ." I paused for a minute because I was getting choked up and emotional. Seeing her just made me realize how much I missed my daughter. How I wished things were different. "I just miss you is all . . . but as you say, you're here now." I grinned.

The waitress approached. "What can I get started for you?"

Gia wasted no time. "Let's do a bottle of your Dom Perignon." My daughter had expensive taste. She stayed true to it.

"I'll take another water." I had already had one glass but another sounded refreshing to me.

Gia smiled. "Water . . . ah, come on. Bring two wineglasses." She winked at the waitress.

"Sure." The young waitress smiled as she walked away.

"Gia, I have to go back to the office after."

"Ahhh . . . come on. You don't see me that often. Have

a drink with me. Besides, I didn't get to drink with you at that wedding of yours." She guilted me all while smiling.

"Oh, okay, I see how you do." I chuckled.

"So, how is the new wife doing, the mayor . . . wait my bad, the governor?" I knew she was teasing me.

"Yes, governor now." I laughed out loud at her humor, then nodded my head. The waitress arrived with the Dom and my water. She placed the wineglasses on the table. She popped open the bottle and filled both glasses. We both ordered smoked salmon, and then she left. "Tabitha and I are fine. Married life is good; we're just both so busy, sometimes our schedules clash."

"That sounds about right. That you guys can expect a governor and a detective to share the expectancy of late nights and early mornings." She picked up her wineglass and sipped. I loved her logic; it was perfect.

It was time I shared with her face-to-face my newest life-changing decision. I sipped my wine before speaking. I sucked in the taste as it hit the roof of my mouth. "I've decided to retire from the force."

Gia's eyebrows rose and a question mark took over. "You're leaving your job? When? Why? Is it because of your marriage, the clash?" She used quotation mark gestures with her fingers.

"Yes and no. Tabitha is governor now, and we both know she'll probably be in politics longer than I will still be on the work force. So, we . . . I decided," I rephrased. I wasn't sure yet how Gia felt about Tabitha. I didn't want her to dislike my wife, so the last thing I wanted her to think was that I was being pushed to give up my passion. Gia didn't exactly approve of me being a cop, but the one thing she had learned about me quickly was the hunger I had for what I do. And she respected that. "I've decided to get behind her to support her one hundred percent on her political climb."

Again, Gia picked up her wineglass and sipped slowly. Then she carefully placed her glass back onto the table. She sucked in her bottom lip and nodded her head that she understood. I wasn't sure if that was a good sign or not.

"Are you two planning on starting a family of your own? You're both still fairly young, early forties and all." She gave me a sly grin.

"Once again, you got jokes." I chuckled. "But no, I can say for sure we won't be starting a family. We both are content with each other. Besides, she's devoted to her nephew, her previous husband Calvin's sister's son, Mikka. She treats him like a son in every sense of the word."

Gia nodded her head. "Yeah, I remember you saying that a few times." The waitress approached with our food.

The mention of Mikka had started my mind wondering about him once again. "I sometimes think something's up with him," I blurted out, and regretted the words as soon as they left my mouth. I had not meant to say that to Gia, who was tasting her salmon. She gazed up at me and swallowed.

"What do you mean, *something's up*?" She was now interested.

At first, I bit down on my words. I actually hated saying them, but I had to be honest. I also was secure in talking to my daughter. "You know, I mentioned before that he does security for Tabitha." The conversation I had with Tabitha that day briefly ran through my mind. I rubbed my face as it played out clearly to me. "But I think he might be into something other than just security." I decided to leave the picture of the back of his head, or at least what I thought was it, out of it for now. I wanted to get a little bit more proof before I started singing that tune again. Down deep I still prayed it was not him.

Gia's eyes just grazed over mine, as if she hadn't heard what I said. Like she was trying to be sure about what I had just said. Then she burst out laughing, as if she had picked up my hint. "Heck no. At least I hope not, or else your pretty wife's career would be done . . . over, finished." She made a throat-cut gesture, then laughed some more. "You are wild. But check this out, though: If he's into something like that, as close as you say the two of them are . . . maybe she knows." She giggled.

This time my eyes traced her face, and they bulged out of the sockets as I considered what she said. Slowly, my lips spread into a smile. Gia was joking again. "Tabitha? Never . . . as governor, she is trying to stop the war on drug trafficking. Surely she wouldn't condone her own step-nephew being a part of the problem." I forked up some salmon into my mouth and savored the taste. I watched as the grin Gia had been wearing suddenly faded and her face turned hard and serious. Something was clearly wrong. "Wait, you were kidding, right?" I asked. Her face was still stonelike. "You don't actually think? You can't believe that?" To think anything else was preposterous.

"Why not? No one is perfect." She leaned forward, almost closing the space between us. "Even you created a drug queenpin . . . that you have no choice but to hide." The scowl on her face and the tone of her voice were clear signs the conversation had gone sour. I hated it. Her words had stung me like a thousand bees.

I had to clear my throat to speak. I was made so emotional by what she'd said. "That's not fair . . . I love you, Gia!" I was now sitting on the edge of my seat. "And it kills a bit of me every day, not being able to be in your life, especially as you grew up. All that I missed. Precious moments." Tears stung at my eyes. I often thought and blamed Renee for being selfish for not telling me about her. I would have been a good father to her. But I tried to push it aside because it only made it hurt more.

The anger on her face only seemed to harden at my words. Gia suddenly rose to her feet, her gaze never leaving mine. "Yeah, it's fine, Mr. King!" Her calling me by my last name with *Mr.* in front of it was the telltale sign that she was upset with me. And there it was, once again, our visit had ended with an argument. That was another thing I had learned about her: When she was upset, she would run away.

Chapter 42

Tabitha

"Do you want to set a limit on the questions you will answer? Because once you open the floor you will probably be bombarded, mostly by the press," my assistant Rhonda said.

I was in my office meeting with her and Chaise, who had been my campaign manager but was also the CEO of the public relations firm I used. I had a press release coming up about the state minimum wage. This would be the talk at the local level. Then I'd be speaking with local officials before heading off to DC. There, I would visit the White House and speak with congressional representatives.

"I don't want to limit the questions. I don't think that's a good idea. Most of the time people think we are trying to hide something, you know, in the small print. So, I say let them ask all the questions they want. What can be answered will be. What can't, won't be. But at least they will see that we are being open, and nothing is hidden behind the curtains."

"Noted," Rhonda wrote down on her pad.

"Remember, we have the script for any question that is up in the air. And if we follow the script, it won't seem vague," Chaise added. I nodded my head in agreement.

"Up next is your meeting with local officials to discuss the gun laws. That is going to be a three-day meeting."

I rolled my eyes at the thought of having to endure such a long meeting. I sighed with frustration. "Three days." I lounged back in my chair. The mere thought of it gave me a splitting headache. "This will be like the battle before war." Rhonda and Chaise laughed. "Must we do a full three days? We can't break it down to one day?" I knew it was an impossible ask, but I did it anyway.

Rhonda shook her head with a fake pout on her mouth. "We had to spread it out to make it bearable. One of those days will be the luncheon with the families who have lost family members to gun violence. I recommend we do that on the second day because we all know this will be an emotional day. This way on the last day, when we get ready to wrap up the closing, everyone can end on a positive note."

"I think that's a wonderful idea. Set it up for six months from today," I said.

"For the next two months your schedule is booked for full twelve-to-sixteen-hour days. You may be able to squeeze two days off during that time."

"I figured that, but . . ." I sighed. "We will have to make it work. You two just keep your schedules open."

"I'll do that. Because the last thing we need is you giving a press conference and cursing someone out because you're at a loss for words," Chaise joked.

"Right." I chuckled.

"Well, I don't have a man right now, so I'm on board. You, Governor, might end in divorce." We all burst into laughter. Rhonda was always considering men. The girl was man crazy.

"Nah, that's why King's retiring. He's going on the payroll. Rhonda, note that."

"I got it," She tapped her pen on her pad, like she was noting it.

"Now, about the formal event coming up in a few days. Is everything ready? All the catering services paid for? Valet picked? And everyone working screened? I don't want any hiccups." I was always clear on these types of things, even when I was mayor. Being in a crowded room where I let my guard down, I liked to feel safe. So, all staff were vetted with a full background screening.

"Yes, everything is handled all the way down to the staff being screened," Rhonda assured me.

"All right then, ladies, that's it for me. I have to head out." I dismissed them and wasted no time in grabbing my purse. Charles and another officer who worked security for me part-time walked me out to my car. I had driven in today since I had no outings to attend. Unbeknownst to them, I had personal business to tend to.

"Finally you show up." I walked into the house, where the chief and I conducted most of our meetings. He had arrived before me and appeared to be grouchy.

"Yep, I'm here." I was not playing into his mood. I walked right past him and over toward the bar. I set down my Gucci bag.

"You have been inaccessible these days. I haven't been able to talk to you about anything." He was really getting under my skin. I guess he tracked me down here so he could bitch and moan. But I was about to match his energy.

"What do you expect? Huh? I'm the damn governor, not some regular JUMPOFF!" I boomed. "I've been busy," I blurted out, facing him now.

"See, I knew you would change when you became the governor. You have no time for me already."

The more I stared at him, the more pathetic he looked, like a whiny-ass kid who's been told he can't go out to play. "Chief, don't nag. It's weak." I shook my head at him with pure disgust. He dropped his head like I had chastised him. "Now, what was so important that you had to talk today no matter what; 911, remember."

"I've been trying to reach you to see how things at home are." He paused and waited, as if he expected me to reveal something.

But I was confused. "Home? Why do you ask? Things are fine." I shrugged. But I instantly saw the surprised look on his face.

"So, King's good?" he asked, and this time my suspicions were raised.

"Yeah, he good. What's up?" I was over the games already; if he had something to say, I wished he'd just spill it. This back-and-forth guessing game was getting on my nerves even more than his damn whining.

"Well, ever since he found out about the product . . ."

Now that got my attention. "What does he know about the product?"

"You know his trolling ways, always investigating. Leave it to him to go looking for the shit. He came to me, of course. I told him it had been destroyed and the nigga flipped on me."

The thought of him saying King, the always subdued and in control one, had flipped out tickled my funny bone for some reason. I laughed out loud. "Flipped on you? King?" I asked. I had to be sure.

"Yes, that Goody-Two-shoes-ass nigga. You mean he hasn't mentioned anything? I know he talks about his cases with you."

"He does. But he hasn't mentioned that. Was it a couple weeks ago?"

"Round about two."

I couldn't help myself but to laugh again. "That must be the day he came to my office talking about retiring for sure. He even put a time on it, which is something he has never done before. Y'all must have pissed him off royally." I chuckled some more.

"Clearly," the chief agreed. "I guess you and me will get ours, then. Get him out of the office and the city is yours when it comes to trafficking drugs."

"Yep, sounds like a plan." I was ready for the day King finally left precinct and his position. Now I had another issue to bake with the chief. "So, what's this shit your wife asking about my perfume?" I hadn't had the time, but this was at the top of my list to dig into his ass about. "That shit was real suspect and outed in front of company."

"Tabitha, that was weeks ago. That's how much of a ghost you've been in my life."

I rolled my eyes. Here he was, whining about that shit again. "Chief, focus, please." I cut that shit right off. "Now, what's really up?"

"Listen, like I said before, Leslie's always talkin' about she smells something or seen something before. That's the shit she does. There's no way she can connect your scent to me. I ain't that damn stupid, babe."

"Fool, are you sure? Don't fuck up my life being careless." He had no idea how much I meant that. Because the consequences would be on him if Leslie were to stop breathing. And that was a fact.

He started to walk into my space. "Babe, I got you, always. Now come here." He reached for me.

I guess he was over being in his feelings and now he wanted to play. But I stepped backward quickly. "Down, boy, not happening today. I have to go."

"Come on, babe, pleasssee." He begged like Keith Sweat. But it was not working today. It was actually annoying me. I rolled my eyes.

"Chief, don't beg." I gave him a look that screamed *pathetic*. He dropped his lips into a pout. The man was really getting to me today.

I snatched my Gucci bag off the bar and stepped past him again. I turned to face him. "I'll schedule something so we can spend some time together. And from now on, bring an extra outfit whenever you meet me for anything. And the shit you do have on around me, leave it with me so I can burn it." Without another word, I made my exit.

If the chief didn't watch it, I would make other arrangements for him. I had been fucking him for years, and to be honest, I enjoyed it. He was good at what he did. And his help in the department was a plus. But this whining and treating me like I was a trick wasn't going to be happening. I was the biggest drug dealer in Arizona and the fucking governor. He'd do better to remember that shit—badge or not.

Chapter 43

Tabitha

I sat down on the chaise in my bedroom and breathed a sigh of relief and relaxation. I was home after an eight-hour day instead of the twelve-hour one we had planned. I was supposed to have a meeting at a local official's office about the five-year plan they were working on. However, as luck would have it, their main water line broke at the last minute and they didn't have time to plan it anywhere else. They didn't have to tell me twice. I nearly tripped over myself running out the door. I immediately turned off my work phone. I told Rhonda I had a splitting headache and stomach pains. That meant I was ill and do not call me unless there is blood involved. If anything arose in any other case, she could call Chaise and she could be my spokesperson for the situation.

My plans were to shower, eat dinner, have a full bottle of champagne, watch a movie, and fall asleep wherever I landed. I didn't want to be bothered by anyone, and that included King; hell, especially him.

I heard a light tap at my bedroom door and knew it could only be Miss Perez. "Come in," I urged.

"I just wanted to hang up Mr. King's suit that was delivered from his tailor," she said.

The formal event for the city council was in a couple of days. We were both gearing up for it. I had my private fashion consultant coming in with some designer dresses for me to pick from.

"I'll hang up the suit," I offered. I stood up and took the suit out of her hands.

"Thanks. I'll be leaving for the day soon," she announced before leaving the room. "I whipped up some chicken breasts with herbs, asparagus, and mashed potatoes. Make sure you eat." That was just like her, to cook without even being asked to. It really wasn't her job, but she'd cook for King and me whenever she felt like it, especially if she didn't see the chef around. I really only called him when I had special meals I wanted prepared.

"You spoil me." I smiled at her sincerely. "I'm just so tired, I hadn't even thought of food yet." I yawned. "I'm going to shower first, then I'll be sure to grab a bite before climbing into bed. Which I can't wait to do because I'm so bushed."

"You work too much. Don't you worry, I'll lock up before I leave. Do you need me to grab anything for you?" Miss Perez was always going above and beyond the call of duty, and that's why I made sure to show her my appreciation.

"No, you've done enough. Thank you and I'll see you tomorrow," I said. I walked over to King's closet. Inside, I noticed that his safe, which he always kept locked, was slightly ajar. I paused for a moment, but then I decided to ignore it. I took a few more steps and hung up the suit. Here I was, the drug dealer my detective husband was after, except as far as I knew, he didn't have a clue. But did he? Why hadn't he mentioned to me that the product was missing? This was something very important to him. He shared most things about his cases with me. Why not this mishap? Was he trying to set me up? I knew the saying, *A bullshitter will never let a bullshitter know they are bullshitting them*, or something like that. Was he bullshitting me? If he hid that from me, what else could he be hiding? Fuck it, I was about to find out.

When I looked inside the safe, to my complete shock there was a file on Boss B. I couldn't believe he'd actually brought home the file I would be most interested in. I thumbed through it like it was classified documents from the White House. I tried to soak up every word.

Then I came across an interview with Boss B's girlfriend, Bossy. *Fed-ass bitch*, I mouthed quietly. I should have known she'd be talking to the cops. I shoulda permanently shut that hussy up. I'm not sure why I had let her live so long after him. My eyes continued to scan the interview meticulously. She seemed not to know much, but she did tell them Boss B was beefing with someone who had the initial *M*. I reread that part five or six times. The letter *M*; who else could she be referring to but Mikka?

"Shit," I said out loud. I turned the page and my heart nearly stopped when I saw the picture. It was the back of someone's head. I had given birth to the boy and I knew him frontward and backward, inside and out. It was Mikka. Did King know? Had he connected the letter *M* to the head? A note on the file said: *Drop unknown suspect pictures off to Detective King*. My legs were a bit wobbly from the shock, but I made it back to my room to retrieve my cell phone.

I called Mikka twice but he didn't answer. I would curse him out about that later. I remembered him telling me that he'd be home. I practically ran out of my house, jumped into my Porche, and had to fight the instinct to do the mad dash. But I was the governor, and the last thing I needed was media attention for speeding. I'd be accused of driving while intoxicated before even being tested.

I rang Mikka's doorbell four times before he pulled the door open. His facial expression was one of disbelief and shock.

"Don't look so surprised. I am your mother," I reminded him in case he suddenly had memory loss.

"No, it's cool. You just normally call first. I mean, you have a key, so you always invited." He shrugged his shoulders.

Something was suspicious. I could read him like a book. Clearly, he was anxious for me to leave. I could see it in his extra-surprised demeanor. I stepped past him, then paused and turned to face him. "You have some girl in here?"

"Yeah, upstairs. But she knows to stay put." He seemed sure of himself. I wasn't so sure. But if she did come down, that would be the last time she did anything.

"Hmph, is your bar open for business?" I instructed him to lead the way and he did. He stepped out of the way so I could enter first. He then shut the big double doors behind us. I walked over to the bar, fished out the bottle of Hennessy, and poured myself a shot. I wasted no time downing it.

"Aggh!" The brown liquor burned my chest, but it was an instant relief. I poured another and put the bottle down. I had the urge to drink from the bottle, but it wasn't ladylike, and I didn't want to be a sloppy drunk. I had to be sober when I handled business.

"That bad?" Mikka questioned. He didn't know the half of it, but he was about to be informed.

"Today . . . well, not even an hour ago, I was home. I went into King's closet to hang up a suit Miss Perez picked up from his tailor. Inside the closet I noticed his safe was open." I waved my hand casually. "I looked inside and found a file that had the name *Boss B* on it. In that file, there's a transcribed interview that King had with that bitch Bossy."

Boss B's girlfriend, Mikka mouthed.

"Yep, well, that fed-ass bitch didn't know much, or at least she didn't tell them everything. She claimed not to know anything about Boss B's business. What she did tell him was that Boss B was beefing with someone whose name starts with an *M*." Mikka considered what I said.

"You think she knows it was me? I mean, she wouldn't know me from nowhere. Unless she was told the full name?" He was grasping at straws, trying to come up with an answer that might satisfy his curiosity.

"I honestly just don't know, but inside that same file I found a picture of the back side of a head. I recognized that head to be yours." This time Mikka's eyes bulged.

"Me." He pointed at his chest. "King got a picture of me? The fuck!"

I could only shake my head. This was so fucked up.

"What you think that nigga knows?" Mikka asked.

"That's what I'm trying to figure out. Could be that he knows absolutely nothing. Could be he got us pegged down to our family roots." I hunched my shoulders and rolled my neck.

"SHIT!" Mikka boomed, and the look on his face revealed that King had put something together. "Some weeks back, King dropped by here for an unexpected visit."

"What?" My head nearly jumped off my body. I think my blood pressure rocketed sky high in that moment. "Why didn't you tell me about this until now?" If dumbfounded was a person, it would look exactly like me.

Mikka's eyes told me he was at a loss for words. He seemed totally lost. He rubbed his face in his hands.

"MIKKA!" I screamed his name. He needed to say something. I was upset with my son, and that was something that didn't happen often.

"I . . . I don't know. I didn't think much of it. He was talking about how he was out this way on a case and wanted to stop by and have that drink I told him to drop in for. And some shit about you saying we needed to bond, which I knew you had. He claimed to be getting us some tickets to see a game. I've been busy with all this other shit. It just slipped my mind."

All I heard was pitiful-ass excuses for what I considered to be a major fuck-up, and I would not take it lightly. "Mikka, use your head and THINK!" I stepped in front of him and tapped his head with my forefinger. "Why would he do that? Huh? Did I not tell your ass not long ago that this same nigga was asking about your lifestyle? HUH?" I yelled. I huffed because I was so full of frustration. "Really, Mikka, if you want to take over this business fully you can't let weak-ass shit like this slip by you. What the actual FUCK!" My voice boomed out again.

"I'm sorry, I promise I didn't know. But you're right." He knew I was disappointed in him big-time.

I shook my head as it all ran through my mind. "Chief just told me recently that this nigga knows the product is missing. Chief told him it was destroyed. That must be the reason he's now officially saying he is going to retire. But the worst part is the nigga never mentioned to me that the product has gone missing. He comes home and tells me all about the disappointing shit at the department. But that he kept to himself. I'm still trying to sort out what that shit might mean." I paced.

"It's settled, then. You know what has to happen next," Mikka declared. And he was right.

"You know who else we must call." I put the shot glass to my lips and welcomed the liquor down my throat. This day was always en route to take a detour. It just happened a little earlier than expected.

Chapter 44

Detective King

It had only been two days since I met with Gia and I still felt uneasy about the way things transpired between us. So much so that I had been sitting at my desk most of the day, staring at the computer screen but not reading or scrolling for information. I had gotten up a few times for coffee and a bathroom break, but that was it. Forbes had been out all day following up on leads for separate cases he was working on. For that I was glad. I needed the time to think and sort things out in my mind. My conscience was truly bothered knowing the pain she felt growing up without me. Her being cheated of the love and guidance only a father can truly give. I would never stop trying to make up for that. That was why when she had hurriedly left the table I went after her. I knew apologizing to her would be hit or miss. She had a strong mind and was stubborn. However, to my surprise she had accepted my apology, hugged me, and told me that she wasn't angry.

Before she climbed into the SUV rental, I told her I was going to arrange a trip to Orlando, Florida, for her and I. According to her, she loved amusement parks with fast rides. So, a father and daughter trip to Disney World really appealed to her. While I told her I hated fast rides or heights, to make her happy I was willing to ride anything she chose. She vowed to hold me to that.

A smile spread across my face as I thought about what she'd said: *You should let me pay. I'm the millionaire.* She loved to remind me that she had more money than I could dream of. As I always did when she offered to pay for anything, I flat-out refused. I told her I would let her know the dates once I had them, but it would be soon.

I moved my mouse to wake up my computer. I typed in Boss B's case number and instantly my mind wandered to my safe back home. I clenched my jaw tight and thought hard. Had I left my safe door open? This morning I had woken up with my mind all jumbled up with thoughts of Gia and wishing things were different. I had opened the safe and shuffled around a few things looking for a document that I needed. I played it over in my mind so I could retrace the steps in my head. "Ah, yes, I would have closed it. I'm just being paranoid. Get it together, King." I gave myself a pep talk as I calmed myself. I had never left my safe open before, even when Joyce and I were married.

I looked over at my buzzing cell phone. Tabitha's name lit up. "Hey, hey, sexy," I greeted her flirtatiously.

"Hey, handsome?" She flirted back with her seductive tone.

"To what do I owe the pleasure—and it is a pleasure to hear your sweet voice." The sound of her voice woke up every bone in my body.

She gave me a girlish giggle. "You will be utterly shocked, but I have the rest of the night off and it's still daylight outside."

She was right, I was utterly shocked. One or both of us normally got home when it was already dark outside. We barely had dinner together unless we scheduled it. Once we were in bed for the night, it was a fifty-fifty chance I would get called out on a homicide.

"Oh, well, now that is a shock. What do you have planned to fill the rest of your day? I know you hate being idle. Are you going home to start planting a garden?" I teased her.

"A garden. Umm, I can call someone over to do that." She laughed. "Now stop playing with me. What I had in mind was we could spend some time at the cottage. I'm here already actually. I wanted to prepare a home-cooked meal for my man with my own hands. No chef in sight."

"Is that so, Governor?" I loved calling her that and she enjoyed it too. We had a nice role-play that we did in bed. "You gone get in the kitchen and put it down from scratch for your man?

"Ummm . . . hmm. You think you can handle me and that case at the same time?" She continued to flirt, and I loved it. It didn't take much more than a mere touch for her to turn me on. A touch and added words almost drove me crazy. I was beyond attracted to my wife.

"Yeah, I think I can fill that order." This unexpected news was giving me life already. I was glad she finally had some free time. I had no problem cutting my hours short at the department. I had spent most of the day in a trance anyway. The thought of my wife's cooking, which she was good at, and her soft body wrapped in my arms was enough for me. I hit the Shutdown button on my keyboard, stood up, slid back into my Calvin Klein suit jacket, and exited with a renewed sense of purpose.

The cottage was a little over an hour away, so I left the station and made that my destination. We both kept a wardrobe there, and Tabitha always made sure it was stocked with any maintenance things we might need. Traffic was flowing good, the sun was still shining, and suddenly I had a change of heart. It was time I did something I had never done with Joyce. It was now a must that I tell Tabitha about Gia, once and for all. I could no longer go on hiding my daughter from the second-most-important person in my life—my wife. If she loved me, she would accept and love my daughter. Either way, it was time. No more hiding my daughter, no matter what. The drive was lengthy, so I practiced a few ways I would say it. As I eased my car into the driveway, I came to the conclusion that the best way to say it was to just blurt it out from the heart. Right then, my cell phone rang, and the name *Forbes* lit up on my car Bluetooth.

"What's up, Forbes?" I greeted him.

"King, where you at, man? You out on a lead and left me? If so, you might want to come back." He talked a mile a minute, not giving me time to answer his questions.

"That serious, huh? What's up?" I inquired.

"We have an unexpected visitor who has info about Boss B's death—an informant." The word *informant* always got the blood flowing, for better or for worse.

"Ah, for real? Listen, I can't get back until the morning. Like I said, I'm out on important business." I couldn't tell him I was about to rendezvous with my wife or else he might try to convince me to ditch her and come back. I sure in hell wasn't about to leave what Tabitha had in store for me. I was as giddy as a kid in a candy store. Both our schedules were crazy, and we had a date for some Mr. and Mrs. Nasty Time. I was not about to break it.

"It's cool, don't worry about it. I'll go in and sit down with him and get all the information he has. Tomorrow, I'll share it with you."

"Now that sounds like a plan. I'll talk with you then." I was trying to end the call. Like I said, I was overexcited to get to Tabitha.

"Wait, before you hang up, I have something else to

share with you . . . Dang, I forgot." He sighed. I could hear a smack in the background that must have been his hand hitting the desk.

"Don't worry, you'll remember as soon as you hang up. Add it to the list for the conversation tomorrow."

"Shit, I guess you're right . . . Oh snap. I got it." Excitement was back in his voice. "The informant already gave up a lead that is worth looking into. Remember the lead on the letter *M* for the person Boss B was beefing with, but that was said to be a mistake? According to the informer, the initial does not start with the letter *M*. Not only that, the leader is likely a female, but he is not sure of her name."

I had heard some shocking and crazy shit, but this would beat it all. My eyes bulged out their sockets. "No fucking way. I wouldn't have missed a detail like that."

"Listen, I was thinking the same thing. And I honestly ain't all that sure about this informant. Not that I believe he's lying, but . . ." I didn't like the apprehensive tone Forbes had taken on.

"What do you know about him?" Informants could be questionable from time to time. Their reputations sometimes made the difference on what type of witness they made. As much as I hated to admit it, most were after self-benefits.

"His name is Lamont Bell. He's been sentenced to forty-five years for murder, and he's trying to get his sentence cut. Says his cousin is close to the biggest crime boss in Arizona, but he won't give me anything else until we negotiate."

"Hah." I chuckled. "Biggest crime boss in Arizona. He's full of shit and a waste of our time. Get his lying ass back to lockup."

"Partner, as usual you are right. Hell, what was I thinking?" We both laughed out loud.

I ended the call and climbed out of the car. I almost laughed again, thinking of the information the informant would have given us, leading us on a wild-goose chase. Female queenpins were very common, but Arizona had never had one yet. Men dominated in the drug game in this state. Lamont would have to pull another Get Out of Jail Free card because that one had crashed and burned before he could get it out of the gate.

I slid my cell phone into my pants pocket and prepared to use my key to unlock the door, where I would find my devoted, beautiful, loving and sexy wife waiting for me.

Chapter 45

Tabitha

In anticipation of King's arrival, I had been watching the front driveway like a hawk. At first I allowed him to attempt to open the front door, then I pulled it open on cue. I was dressed in an all-black, two-piece lingerie set that fit me like a glove. "Welcome, Ronald King, I am completely at your service," I announced, wearing the brightest grin a girl could find on such short notice.

The lustful smirk on his face said, *so far, so good*. "You look scrumptious, babe." He pulled me into his arms and kissed me, tongue and all.

"Now, now." I eased back and tapped him lightly on his chest. "You can't taste all of me in one lick." I ran my tongue seductively across my lips.

He smiled. "Okay, I see." His eyes continue to eat me up. I shut the door, then grabbed him by the hand to lead him into the den.

"I have a nice dinner prepared for us, and . . ."

"Hey, hey," he cut me off. I could feel the resistance in his walk. "Can we stop for a minute?" I stopped and turned toward him. His facial expression had flipped from lust to seriousness. "Listen, I know you got this night planned for us and I'm more than excited. But I have something I would like to share with you."

I didn't know what his confession was about to be, but that shit was not in the plan. And to be honest, it didn't matter.

I gently placed my finger over his lips. "Not now. Share later." I gave him a reassuring smile. "Right now dinner is ready and we should eat it while it's hot. Besides, I have a long evening planned and we, darling, have an exciting night awaiting us." I winked at him.

Lust was twinkling in his eyes again. This shit was too easy. I couldn't make it up. "I'm at your command." He offered me his hand again. I slid my hand over his and led the way into the dining room.

The table was already set with dishes and silverware. It looked really grand. Candles were on the table, but they were not yet lit.

"This looks nice, babe." He referred to the elegantly decorated table. I had pulled out the crystal to grab his attention on purpose. Diversion was the goal.

"Thanks, and it's going to look even better once dinner occupies it. The food is ready in the kitchen, it just needs to be brought in. So . . . I was thinking since I cooked it, you can serve it."

His face formed a grin. "Oh okay, so you gonna put me to work?"

I leaned in and kissed him. "Of course," I said. "And don't worry, the night is filled with more work for you to do." I ran my hand down the front of his crotch. Then I stepped away with my eyes still on him.

His eyes scanned my entire body with admiration. "You are just so beautiful." His tone was light and meant to be enticing, but I needed him to do as he was instructed. He read my expression, "Okay, the food is in the kitchen . . . I can handle that, since I know my reward is coming."

I snickered, "More than you can imagine." I bit my lip temptingly.

He skipped off wearing a grin. I slowly followed behind him, careful not to give my presence away. I had my phone in my hand with the camera on with full view of the kitchen. But I was standing right at the edge of the kitchen within earshot. King entered the kitchen, his skip immediately turning to a hard stop. His eyes fell on the area where the six-seat kitchen table was normally located. The space was vacant of the table, and in its place was a chair sitting on a huge plastic tarp.

He attempted to turn, but a gun went to the back of his skull. "What's up, ole Curious George–ass nigga." I could see a hint of familiarity on his face as he placed Mikka's voice right away. I had the camera zoomed in on him so big, I could literally push it up his nostrils if I wished it.

I watched King's Adam's apple as it moved up and down with his nervous swallow. "What's going on?" he asked.

Mikka shook his head in disappointment. "You and the damn questions. Tell ya what, I got a demand. Sit yo' ass in that seat." He gestured to the empty chair that sat lonesome in the middle of the tarp.

King's body tensed up. I could see his chest rise and fall in a now rapid motion. "Why you want me to sit there?" I could tell he was being careful not to make a sudden move because of the steel to the back of his skull. "And why do you have a gun to my head? TABITHA!" He screamed my name.

"Yeah, call her name. Maybe she'll come. TABITHA!" Mikka yelled. I knew he was teasing King. "You happy? Now go sit yo' ass in that seat," he ordered once again. "I

won't say it again. AND PUT YOUR HANDS UP!"
Mikka boomed.

"All right, all right." King seemed reluctant and nervous. He took slow but deliberate steps, but he made it to the chair. Obviously, he was surveying the room as any skilled detective would. But it was useless because this was not his scene; it belonged to me.

"Now turn around slowly, sit, and make no sudden moves. And don't test me."

It was time for me to appear, so I slowly stepped from behind the corner I had been holding up. King's face went from shocked, and nervous to dumbfounded as I too now stood holding a gun pointed directly at him. Now that I had him covered, Mikka lowered his gun, placed it in the back of his pants, and reached for the rope.

I looked King square in the eyes as Mikka tied him up. He looked mortified. "Shocked, right?" His eyes left mine and roamed the room. I knew he was sizing up the situation at hand. He blinked, and I thought I read reason on his face.

"Babe . . . Tabitha, is this some type of joke? Because if it is, it ain't funny, hah, hah." His mouth made a laughing sound, but his eyes said different. He knew this was no joke.

Mikka let out a chuckle. "Yeah, Mom, is this a joke?"

King's mouth fell wide open and he twisted his body hard and looked at Mikka. He was clearly stunned. King turned back to face me, and I saw anger this time, "What the fuck does he mean, *mom*? He means *aunt*, right?" His facial expression and tone were classic.

"Well, the boy is smart; he would know his own momma." I laughed. "At least, I hope he would."

Confusion outlined King's face. His eyes roamed the room, looking at nothing in particular. I could see they were full of confusion. Mikka started to walk toward me and he cast his eyes on him. Mikka stood next to me. He gazed at us both, his eyes grew wide, and I knew he saw it now.

Well, I'll be damned, he mouthed. "I can't believe I never recognized it before. I must have been blind not to see it." His eyes ran left to right under the lids; clearly, he was baffled.

"Do you have any more questions?" I asked him. The least I could do was be fair and answer his questions. I mean, why not?

"Do I have any questions? Hmph. Besides the fact that this shit is crazy. And I guess kind of weird. Why am I tied to a chair? Clearly, Mikka being your son can't be the reason."

I chuckled. "That could kinda be some of it." I waved my gun around, then added, "But there might be a little more to it." The guy really didn't have a clue. I would have to spell it out for him.

"Look, the faster you explain, the faster I can understand why you, my wife, are fucking keeping secrets and shit from your husband."

My head snapped to the side in shock. He had never come at me like that. I guessed the gloves were off and he was no longer trying to control his anger.

"Whoa, my nigga." Mikka stepped toward him, but I moved to the side of him and interfered. "Watch the words and your tone. Respect my mom," Mikka's body language, words, and tone demanded.

King huffed and put his attention toward me, blatantly disregarding Mikka. "Tabitha, get to the point, please."

"Man, this nigga . . ." Mikka tried to bypass me to get to King, but I stood in front of him. King was pissing him off and he was going off script.

"Mikka," I said to get his attention. He stood down; he never challenged me, he respected me. I sighed. "Well, Husband . . . I tried to explain to you some time ago, but you didn't listen. Mikka was not your business, but you are always a detective first. Constantly snooping." I strolled over to the kitchen island and picked up the pictures of Mikka that I had retrieved from the safe.

I watched his eyeballs almost bulge to the edge of their sockets. At that moment I had no doubt that he knew for sure that it was Mikka. What was he going to do with them? "Yeah, you left your safe open."

"WHY WERE YOU GOING THROUGH MY THINGS!" he shouted. He had some nerve getting pissed when he was out here betraying me and my son.

I shook my head from side to side and kept my composure. "You do remember that you moved into my house. Right? You are not either part owner nor is your name on the deed. At least as far as I can recall. Meaning anything in it is my business." I was calm and matter-of-fact.

His facial expression went from confusion, anger, and back to nervousness again. It was now clear to him why he was tied to a chair and guns were in his face. "Look, those pictures ain't of no consequence. We don't even know who is in that picture. See, no face is showing. No face, no person." He shrugged.

I laughed out long and hard. Was he really going to try to play the stupid card on me? "King, don't play me dumb. Please don't toy with my intelligence, especially where my son is concerned, and especially when you got two damn guns pointed at your head." My tone was a threat—intentionally.

"Hey, we all have secrets; this one will be ours. I never told anyone that was Mikka in the picture. I was never certain of it myself. Besides, you are my wife, and that makes Mikka my son as well. So, I say no worries, we will keep this secret in the family." He tried to come off nonchalantly to assure us of his loyalty to us, but I wasn't stupid.

I waved off his bullshit because that was exactly what it was. "Pffftt." I sucked my teeth. "I wish it were that simple. But we have a business to run, and with Boss B finally out of the way, we are on the right track and headed to the top. That means we can't have anyone . . . especially a cop . . . well . . . besides Chief Rogers knowing who we are." I shrugged my shoulders. There, it was out.

King's mouth popped open wide and his chest thrust forward, as if he had been sucker punched in the gut. "Oh no, not the chief?" The disappointment in his tone and the edge on his face said he was both disgusted and confused. And I loved it. I couldn't wait to gloat.

"Yes, the chief, your boss and my man. Wait no . . . my side piece," I boasted and smirked at the same time. Chief Rogers stepped out so that he was now visible. He had been in the back of the house the whole time, waiting to make his debut. He had been surprised when I'd called only a few hours after our meeting, which I was sure he considered hadn't gone so well. Since he hadn't been able to lay a hand on me, either way he was elated when I invited him to our private party. According to him, he was on his way back to the station to pull a late shift, but this was one U-turn he was more than willing to make.

King's eyes turned dark as he scowled at the chief. "You motherfucking snake. I always knew you were a shady bastard," King said.

"Whoa, King, now calm down. I don't get the feeling—especially from where you are sitting—that you're in a position to be tossing around insults." Chief reached into his holster and pulled out his piece. He lifted it upward and rubbed it in a threatening matter.

"OH FUCK YOU AND YOUR GUN!" King stared Chief Rogers down. "When I think back, you sometimes gave me a strange feeling when I was around you. I just knew something was up with you. It was this grueling feeling in my gut, but I pushed it aside."

"Dude, I told you that you ask too many questions. But yes, you have solved another case; it was me."

"I'll be damned," King mouthed. His eyes then left the chief and went to the floor. He gazed at Mikka. "Mikka, did you have anything to do with Van Buren being murdered."

"Another jackpot," was Mikka's answer.

"Wait, Tabitha, you just mentioned Boss B." His attention again turned toward Mikka. "Mikka, did you murder Boss B?"

Mikka sucked his teeth. "Shit, oh how I wish I could take the credit for that one."

"It's okay, Son. I'll handle this one," I intervened. I eyed King long and hard. "See, I have that snake's blood on my hands. It's simple. He violated me with disrespect one too many times. There are rules to this shit, and only one person, and I do mean one, can be the fuck on top."

The look on King's face was not complete horror. He glared at me with his eyes full of tears. I watched as he tried to suck them back in, but they fell rapidly down his cheeks. "So, it's you I've been chasing all this time. My own wife, newly elected to the governor's seat—a murderess and queenpin?" The guy looked as though he was about to be sick as the words and the true meaning of them left his mouth.

I thought he should be proud, but who was I kidding? The nigga was a fuck boy. I smirked at him. He was a clown to me, and I was enjoying his misery. I wasn't done, though. I went on, "Yeah, and let's add a few more things. Lunzo, Maria Van Buren, all those bodies were on my word. Cases solved."

King shook his head. "What a piece of work you are. So, this is how you raised your son, to be a murderer and a drug dealer. I saw him with Locco, and I received a tip that

Boss B was beefing with somebody whose name started with an *M*. I should have known. And you, Chief Rogers, you scoundrel. Taking me off cases, trying to slow my trail. I got to admit it, y'all played me."

"Hey, me and your wife here tried to get you to retire. Maybe you would have stayed out of that chair a little bit longer," the chief taunted him. Mikka laughed too.

"Well, King, now you know all. You are always asking questions, and now you have answers. And guess what, you can retire in peace because all of your cases have been solved. You don't need to wait another six months." I chuckled. "But there is just one more thing you must know. This I owe to you. It was I who murdered your prim and proper wife."

If I had splashed a paint of blood in his eyes, they would not have been more bloodshot red than now. "YOU FUCKING EVIL BITCH!" He growled so hard, the veins in his neck stood out. His breathing became pants and his teeth were clenched tightly together. He said, "You will pay for his . . . she will see to it . . ." A bullet landed in his chest, and another in the center of his head. The sound of his brain splattering out of the back of his head made it official. Detective Ronald King was no longer. The mission that we had started over four years ago had been completed.

"Mikka," I yelled at him, "you couldn't wait another fucking minute. He was about to say something important." I stomped my right foot with agitation.

"Aggh!" Mikka grunted. "That nigga ain't have shit relevant to say. His mouth is better off shut," he barked.

I glared at King's bloody shirt with a bullet hole straight through his chest, and his brain splattered on the tarp, "Or maybe not . . . but I guess we'll never know," I concluded.

Mikka put his gun in the back of his pants. "I'll go now and get the car to the chop shop."

"Me and the chief will have the body wrapped up by the time you get back. I'm so glad all the blood and guts landed on the tarp. No splatter." I was so thankful for that. We always used a tarp when a murder was done inside. The goal was for an easy cleanup and no evidence of blood.

"So, we good here, Mikka?" the chief added. "Just hurry back for this body."

"Bet. I'm out." Mikka fled the kitchen and rushed out the front door.

Let's get started, I mouthed to the chief. We had to do our part with the body so it would be ready for Trey and Mikka. One thing I was sure of, and I learned this best with Calvin, teamwork made the dream work.

Chapter 46

Tabitha

After Mikka and Trey made it back to the cabin to retrieve King's body, we ran down the plan one more time to be sure it was airtight. Chief Rogers left before me because he had to get back to sign off on a request to a judge for the warrant some idiot detective needed. Not that he needed an alibi, but this could potentially be one for him if it came to that in the future. My plan was to just send him to hell if he ever needed an alibi, so for his own sake he should hope that he never did. My alibi was simple; after a day at the office and a string of meetings with my PR manager and assistant, I went home exhausted, preparing for a hot shower, and dinner, and bed. Miss Perez would vouch for me too. Then I would just add that I called King, and he said he wanted to cook dinner for us at the cottage. But I had to wait on the call from him before heading out there. That call never came.

Now morning had come, and I was home as planned. It was time for the next part of the plan to be put into place. King going missing would not go unnoticed, even though he really didn't have any immediate family. He was married to the governor of Arizona, and he was a lead narcotic homicide detective, one of the best in the state. His sudden disappearance would be a big deal. My role was to be the concerned wife. Not the grieving wife, because I had no idea that my husband was dead. He just didn't come home the night before.

I scrolled through my cell phone until I found the name that would be the first pawn in the next step of my game. "Forbes, good morning?" I said in my normal tone of voice. "This is Tabitha, King's wife," I added.

"Tabitha, yeah." He immediately sounded puzzled. Forbes and I knew each other well, but I had never picked up the phone to call him. "Good morning to you as well. Is everything okay?"

"I was hoping to ask you the same thing. Are you at the office? Is King with you?" I hurled questions at him.

"Umm, no, actually, I'm home and King is not with me."

"He didn't come home last night . . . and . . . I, well, I thought he might be out with you on a call or something."

"No, I haven't seen him since earlier yesterday, before I left the department. But I did speak with him later that evening . . ." He paused. "He was on his way somewhere . . . somewhere important, like it was business. You know he has been working hard on his open cases, following up leads. Some he didn't even share with me."

Now it was time for me to become the really scared wife. Every part had its place. "Ahh, ahh," I cried softly and sniffed. "Forbes, something is wrong. I spoke with him last night and told me he wanted to cook for me out at the cottage later in the evening. He told me he had something to do first but that once he arrived, he'd call me so I could head out there. That call never came. I fell asleep. I woke up around two o'clock in the morning and he still wasn't here. I figured something must have come up. This morning when I woke up, he still was not home.

I've tried calling several times, but he's not answering. His phone is just going to voicemail. This is not like him, Forbes." I sniffed some more. I didn't want to grunt and scream yet.

I could almost hear Forbes thinking on the other end. Surely he was in detective mode, probably picking apart every little word I said to get some type of scenario and cause. "Listen, honestly, everything is probably fine. The guy is a workaholic. His phone has probably died, and he never has a charger on him. He's always at the office begging for mine. I've told him a thousand times to buy an extra charger to keep in his office, but he never listens." He released a light chuckle. "I'm going to make some calls and get back with you."

"Oh, would you? Thank you so much, Forbes. I knew I could count on you."

"Absolutely, and no need for thanks. You and King are like family. And I don't want you to worry."

I hung up the phone satisfied, with a huge grin that filled my entire face. I looked at the time on my phone. I needed to take a shower and whip out my sad and distraught look for Miss Perez; she would be in soon. Then wait on Forbes and his news, because next up would be the stage play of my life: *The Grieving Wife*.

Chapter 47

Tabitha

"No! No! No!" I screamed at the top of my lungs as my body went limp. I would have hit the floor if Detective Forbes and Mikka hadn't caught me. I knew it would hurt if I actually landed on the floor, but I was all in when it came to carrying out my part. Aunt Margie had rushed out of the back. Just like when Dale and Calvin had been murdered, she was there for me. She had arrived the day after I reported King missing to the police. I had called her and told her my husband was missing, and she was beside herself with grief for me.

Mikka had picked her up from the airport and brought her to the house. She had come through the door and wrapped me in her arms and prayed for King's safe return. And she said with a voice full of optimism, "Tabbi, he's going to be fine. He'll be back at the police station. His friends and coworkers are going to get him back to you. Somebody he's arrested or someone's family member or friend who has a beef with him are just trying to scare him, just like you said the detectives told you. And you have a whole city praying for you. So don't you worry, he will be back. And until he gets back, I will be here for you and Mikka. I'm going to take care of you, okay?"

Now here she was again, with her arms around me. Down deep inside, she knew her optimism had gone bust, but I was breathing a sigh of relief. The shit was over. It had been over a week and finally they had found King's body in an abandoned house as we had staged. I was so angry that it had taken them so long to find him. I had hoped they would have found him in a day or so, but I'd miscalculated that he was one of the best detectives in his department and the rest of them were incompetent fucks. I joked with Mikka a few days earlier when Aunt Margie was out of earshot that if it took them any longer to find him, I wouldn't be able to squeeze out a tear when I was told. As soon as I opened the door I could see the weary look on Forbes's solemn face, and I knew what he was about to tell me.

"I'm so sorry, Tabitha. But I promise we are going to find the person who did this." He tried to assist Mikka in helping me stand so that I could make it to the den to sit down, but Aunt Margie had booted him out of the way.

"What do you think happened? Who would do something like this?" I asked through hiccups and big-winded huffs as I cried. I was tired of fake crying; it gave me a headache to do it. Outwardly, I could produce a flood of tears and sincere emotions, but I simply did not want to do it. I had planned to have him buried by now.

"We have no idea as to who, specifically. We assume it could be a suspect from a case, maybe somebody he put away. Or it just may be random violence; it's hard to say. We really don't like to work off assumptions; it never has a good outcome on a case. But we will find out. The chief has everybody on it. We even have other departments from the other cities in Arizona who have volunteered working on it. The first forty-eight hours are critical. We have lost some time because we are just finding his body now, but we will turn every stone. He was my partner and I take this personally, so don't you worry."

I wanted to tell him I wasn't worried, and that he would never find out who killed his partner. We had covered our tracks well, like we did in all the murders we committed. So far, there hadn't been a body that could be traced back to us. Now I was going to enjoy watching him and the entire state of Arizona, especially the Maripoca County Police department, run around chasing down leads for their beloved Detective Ronald King. I could now stand up and take a vow of mission accomplished. Long ago, when I'd first been elected mayor, Calvin and I had a plan. I would be a politician and he'd be kingpin. We would run more drugs in this city than it had ever seen before.

With Chief Rogers in our pockets, we had firsthand knowledge that we would have one problem: the renowned lead narcotic Detective Ronald King. At the time, he was becoming known for being the beast of the streets when it came to taking down drug traffickers. So, we hatched a plan: snatch his happiness, slow down his reign, and hopefully get him to walk away from the force. Our secret weapon for this would be to take out the love of his life. The chief had told us how much he adored his wife, Joyce. So I murdered her.

But we had judged him wrong. King did mourn his wife, and instead of it slowing him down and driving him away from the force, it fueled his hunger to clean up the streets of drug-related crime. We were stumped with ideas. Then Calvin died not long after that, and suddenly I had a plan. I would marry Detective King and manipulate him into giving up his career to support me in my ambitions and, last but not least, murder him. Now I would run the city, and hell, maybe even the whole damn state as governor, and be the head of the biggest drug organization this state had ever seen. I was Detective King's wife.

Chapter 48

GIA

I cried nonstop for a full week when I found out about my father's murder. I simply was not prepared to accept that he was gone. All the time I had missed growing up without him, not knowing who he was. Then he'd found me, and I pushed him away because of his absence and blamed him for the decisions my mother made. Her decision not to tell me about him until she was sick and about to die. She told me she didn't want to leave this earth and leave me alone. I was shocked, surprised, angry, and confused. So, when she passed, I chose not to find him. I assumed he had a family of his own and wouldn't accept a stranger saying, Hey, here I am, your daughter, who's been hidden for sixteen years. Mom was estranged from the two or three cousins she had left in the city, which meant I had no one. So I found myself a full-time job in the mall, stayed in school, determined to finish my senior year, and tried to pay the rent. I was working and barely making ends meet when I met and started to date Cash.

Cash was a huge dealer in the streets. He was making mad plays and getting all kinds of money, not to mention he was cute as shit. It started out normal, with me going on rides with Cash when he'd make drops and collect money. Then Cash got picked up on an old murder charge and needed a good lawyer. He had some money saved, but he needed more. To help my man, I agreed to make a few runs, and before long it became like second nature to me. I had the money Cash needed in no time. Before long, he was back out on the streets and soon, dead. He was shot by a guy who was jealous of him because of his come up. With Cash gone, I was sick with grief. But the one thing I decided I didn't want to do was work a nine-to-five. I had graduated high school but was not ready to do college. Instead, I regrouped and started to plan my life in the drug game. I didn't want to drop off or pick up anything. I wanted employees. I wanted to level up in ways Cash never had. Luckily, I had been introduced to a Connect that would make it happen. Literally overnight, I started and built an empire, all the while keeping a low profile. But anybody who was somebody knew that I was the queenpin of Philly.

Then my detective father located me, and my life was never the same. I loved the guy from the first time I met him, but I refused to show it. He told me right away that he was a detective and admitted that he knew I was in the life. Even then, he didn't know how deep it was until I finally told him. It was for that reason and that reason only I would have to be kept a secret. I was angry and resented him for it. Whenever the mood struck me, I lashed out at him, but he never let that push him away. The bottom line was he loved me unconditionally, and I loved him. Now, I would never have the chance to show it.

Nothing made sense to me. I mean, who could kill a detective? I was aware that between drug busts and accused killers he had arrested, most might have ideas of doing him harm. But who would have the balls to really go through with it? Those were burning questions that I didn't have any answers to or could get because I was a secret.

What hurt the worst was not being able to attend his funeral. I didn't even know about his murder until a few weeks after he was buried. I was out in Arizona for a meeting about opening a nightclub. While sitting around in my hotel room watching the news, I saw what I would never forget. The governor, Tabitha Knight King, dressed in her finest with a pair of dark black Saint Laurent sunglasses plastered over her eyes.

"I stand here today in honor of my late husband, Detective Ronald King." She sniffled, then tipped her sunglasses back snugly on her nose. "Not only was King a public servant, he was also endeared to the community. He gave every waking moment to thoughts of making this city safe for you all." She sniffled again. "It is with a heavy and completely broken heart I say thanks to you all for the support and love that has been bestowed upon me. To the city to which he devoted his life, I thank you for all you have done to . . . to . . ." She started to choke up and cry so hard she couldn't finish. I sat in shock and replayed what she had said over and over again in my head.

Lost from hurt and pain, I was left with a hole in my heart. I didn't know what to do or who to turn to. So, I packed up my bags and headed back to Philly. I couldn't shake that public outcry that Tabitha had done on the news. I had to know more. I touched back down in Philly and called up the best private detective it had to offer—Walt Nash. He told me to give him two to four weeks, and today was the day.

I pulled up to Walt's office and made my way inside. His assistant led me to his office. I sat down in a chair seated right across from him. My heart was beating fast. What was he going to reveal?

"Gia, how are you?"